Hidden Intent

BOOKS BY TEYLA BRANTON

Unbounded Series
The Change
The Cure
The Escape
The Reckoning
The Takeover

Unbounded Novellas
Ava's Revenge
Mortal Brother
Lethal Engagement
Set Ablaze

Colony Six Series
Insight (prequel)
Sketches
Visions
Travels

Imprints Series
First Touch (prequel)
Touch of Rain
On The Hunt
Upstaged
Under Fire
Blinded
Street Smart
Hidden Intent

Other
Times Nine

UNDER THE NAME RACHEL BRANTON

Lily's House Series
House Without Lies
Tell Me No Lies
Hearts Never Lie
Your Eyes Don't Lie
Broken Lies
No Secrets or Lies
Cowboys Can't Lie

Noble Hearts
Royal Quest
Royal Dance

Finding Home Series
Take Me Home
All That I Love
Then I Found You

Other
How Far

Picture Books
I Don't Want To Eat
   Bugs
I Don't Want to Have
   Hot Toes

Hidden Intent

TEYLA BRANTON

WHITE
STAR
PRESS

This is a work of fiction, and the views expressed herein are the sole responsibility of the author. Likewise, certain characters, places, and incidents are the product of the author's imagination, and any resemblance to actual persons, living or dead, or actual events or locales, is entirely coincidental.

Hidden Intent (Imprints Book 7)

Published by White Star Press
P.O. Box 353
American Fork, Utah 84003

Printed in the United States of America
ISBN: 978-1-948982-16-0
Year of first printing: 2020

For my faithful readers who always inspire me to write.

Chapter 1

$\mathcal{I}$ was in my rusty red Toyota, heading toward my new client Luna Medina's house, when Paige's call came in.

I hit the speaker button on my phone, secured in the dash holder. "Hey, Paige," I said. "Good to hear from you. What's up?"

Paige Duncan was a homicide detective with the Portland Police Bureau, and also my fiancé's partner. She often called me in to consult, which was a fancy word for asking me to read scenes or emotions her perps might have imprinted on objects near the victims. It was a dubious honor, but today I was happy she'd called, even if it involved me in another murder case. I had a wedding to plan in less than three weeks, and I'd need both her and my sister's help if it was going to be anything other than a trip to city hall.

"You have to come to the hospital," Paige choked out. "Providence Portland Medical."

Immediately, my mind jumped to the worst-case scenario. "Did something happen to Shannon?" Homicide detectives had enemies, I knew. There was always a chance he could be hurt by a vindictive criminal.

"No, it's not that. He's fine. He's here with me, but I need you too. Can you come? Can you get someone to watch the store?"

I contemplated for less than two seconds. Luna Medina's seventeen-year-old son was being investigated by the police for vandalism in the high school football equipment room, and his future was at risk, but the damage had taken place weeks ago, and a few hours' delay shouldn't make a difference.

"Thera's at the shop already," I said. "I have an appointment, but I'll postpone it. What's wrong?"

"Not over the phone." Her voice was a near whisper. "Just come as fast as you can. I'll be in the lobby of the main entrance."

"Okay. Sit tight. I'm coming." I pulled over to the curb and grabbed my phone from the holder to double-check directions. The Providence Portland Medical Center was on the east side of the Willamette and north of the Hawthorn District where my antiques shop was located. I'd been heading south on Cesar E Chavez Boulevard toward Franklin High School, so I'd need to make a quick U-turn on the four-lane road.

As I waited for traffic to clear, I called Elliot Stone, aka Eli Stone, a local private investigator and computer guru who was working the Medina case with me. He'd helped me save a family from death by poisoning, but this time his main goal was convincing me to partner with him on an ongoing basis. He felt his tech skills and my psychometry ability would make us unstoppable. I had to admit it was tempting, especially when any information I asked from the police department was scrutinized by Shannon Martin, my detective fiancé.

"Hey, Autumn," Elliot said. "You almost here? I'm sitting outside their house now."

"Sorry. Change of plans. The police called, and I'm not going to be able to make it until later. Can you do an initial interview and maybe reschedule for this afternoon? I'll let you know what time I can make it if they're available."

"I guess." He sounded anything but happy at the suggestion. "But I'd rather reschedule it altogether. You know I don't like meeting at clients' houses. I only agreed to meet here because of your ability."

"Fine. Whatever works." Truthfully, he shouldn't even be on the case. Luna Medina had used him to contact me after I'd rescued a biker from a serial killer, and it was me she wanted. I was guessing she hoped for that kind of miracle for her son. She didn't even know I could read imprints, unless Elliot had filled her in.

"What about checking out the vandalized equipment room at the school?" he asked. "Will you still make that appointment? It's at noon."

"I remember. Don't cancel yet. I don't know how long I'll be with the police."

"Please try to make it," Elliot said. "If Pax Medina is convicted, he'll lose everything. He's already lost his father."

As if I needed reminding. My own father's death was always in the back of my mind, and I felt for this boy. "I'm not giving up on the case. I just have to check in with the police."

"Okay. I'll do what I can."

Having lived and worked in the Hawthorne District all my life, finding the nearby Providence Portland wasn't hard once I got my bearings. Before going in, I pulled on a pair of wrist-length cotton gloves that I now bought in bulk. The ones I had today were skin-colored, which I hoped would make them less noticeable during the summer. Hospitals held more horrific imprints than I was willing to risk without a good reason.

I hurried quickly into the main entrance of the hospital, glad to be wearing one of my favorite summer dresses. If Paige wanted me in an official capacity, this was as dressed up as I ever got. As usual, I was sans shoes, and the cement was slightly cold on my bare feet, which hadn't yet absorbed significant heat from the morning sun.

Paige was pacing inside the main entrance, her shoulder-length, iron-straight blond hair poking oddly out on one side. Her normally crisp navy suit was rumpled in the front and stained with coffee. Not even after a shooting had I ever seen her anything but her usual calm and contained self. Maybe something had happened to her father or brother, who worked as detectives in another precinct. Or maybe her retired police chief grandfather had experienced a sudden heart attack.

"Autumn!" She threw herself into my arms, her strong, lean body propelling me backward. "I can't believe this is happening."

I could see Shannon farther inside the lobby, his dark blond hair curling at the ends as it always did when it got a tad too long for police bureau regulations. He was talking urgently with a burly, brown-haired man that I immediately pegged as another detective, even in his civilian clothes, so I quickly revised my earlier guess about a medical emergency. Whatever happened was being investigated.

I hugged Paige, and she slumped against me. "What's going on?" I asked, pulling back to see her face. "What can I do to help?"

"It's Matthew," she said, her pale blue eyes filling with tears. "He might be arrested for negligent homicide. He says he didn't do anything wrong, but he worked a double shift, and they don't believe him. I need you to read the syringes and everything else in the patient's room to see if you can learn anything."

"I'm so sorry."

Matthew Kellogg was a doctor Paige had been dating for eight months. With all that had been going on between our cases and Matthew's crazy schedule, we'd only gone out a few times as couples this past month, but I liked him immensely. He'd also passed all of Shannon's non-official, probably slightly illegal background checks—and apparently her father's as well, since he hadn't ordered her to quit dating him.

"He didn't do it." Paige's voice was shrill and bordering on panic. "Give the man too much drugs, I mean. Matthew's a great cardiologist, and he knew the patient was on a daily nitro-glycerin pill. He didn't give him more than he should have."

"Of course not." I stood back and gripped her shoulders. "Look, take a deep breath. I need you to explain it to me. Like it's a case."

She stared at me as if wanting to punch me, so I widened my stance and prepared to block. I still sported a black half-moon under my left eye, a remnant from my biker case two weeks earlier, and I didn't need another one before my wedding ceremony.

Abruptly, her shoulders sagged, and she nodded once, sharply. "Right, sorry. I just . . . I care about him."

"Then let me help. That's why I'm here."

"Okay." She took a deep breath. "I can do that."

"Let's go sit down."

I led her across the tile that was cool to my bare feet, over to the carpeted area where chairs lined the far wall of the lobby. Shannon glanced our way, and for a moment our eyes locked.

He looked strong, sure of himself, and determined, but I could see the concern in his strangely blue-green eyes that were unlike any I'd ever seen. Those eyes told me this was serious.

Paige settled into the padded brown chair and half turned to face me, her back toward Shannon and the burly detective. The man was vaguely familiar, but he stood sideways, and I didn't have a clear glimpse of his face. I didn't think he was an officer from Shannon and Paige's precinct.

"A man named Peter Griffin came in two days ago because of kidney stones," Paige started again, this time sounding calm, but her hands clenched tightly in her lap. "The non-evasive procedures either didn't work or he wasn't a candidate, so his doctor opted for a not very serious surgery that requires only one or two days in the hospital afterward. Matthew wasn't his doctor for that, of course, since he works in cardiology, but Griffin was on nitroglycerin for heart pain—angina, I guess it's called. Anyway, Griffin had been in such pain with the kidney stones that he hadn't brought his heart medicine, so cardiology was called in to make sure he had his normal dose and that it was safe with the surgery. Matthew cleared him. Everything went well, and yesterday he was taken off the monitors. The nurses, of course, came in every four hours to take his vitals or give him medication. Griffin was supposed to go home this morning, but when the night nurse went to check on him shortly after four am, he was flushed and unresponsive. She acted quickly, but he had a massive heart attack."

I didn't have to ask if he'd died. "The nurses only came around every four hours?"

"Well, for vitals. Because he wasn't at risk or in any danger. The last time his blood pressure was taken was sometime around midnight, and the nurse said it was a little low, but nothing dangerous. But someone saw him at three to take blood for the night panel, and they didn't report anything odd. When the results came back, though, they discovered that he had four times the normal level of nitrates in his blood. They won't know for sure until the autopsy, but they think it lowered his blood pressure so much that his organs starved—and failed."

"And he'd shown no signs of stress before that? Did anyone check on him between midnight and three?"

"I don't know." Paige glanced backward again at Shannon and the other detective. "I've been here since six, after Matthew finally called me. They questioned him for hours, and he's still here somewhere with the hospital attorney and the administrator." She stopped talking, placing her hand over her mouth as if to hold back sobs. She stayed that way for a full minute while I gazed at her helplessly.

When she eventually pulled her hand away and continued, she had regained her calm. "Everyone is looking for someone to blame. The family is claiming that Matthew must have given him too much heart medication—or told the nurses to—or that he didn't understand how it would interact with his other drugs. I understand they're heartbroken, but Matthew's a good doctor. He wouldn't make this kind of mistake. But the hospital put him on leave until the autopsy results."

"The truth will come out," I said, squeezing her arm. "The patient must have had numerous blood tests, and those will back him up and clear Matthew."

"Unless it's one of those strange, freaky things and no one ever uncovers a reason. Something like that could still destroy his career." She bit her lip, her breath coming faster. "Oh, I know that's terrible to think about when a man is dead, but Matthew doesn't deserve this. He's a good man. What if someone hurt his patient on purpose, or if someone else messed up? How will we ever know? By the time we have anything to go on, the room will be cleaned out and all the evidence gone."

Maybe Paige had been working homicide too long and now saw murder everywhere. Or maybe she simply wanted to save the man she loved from more heartache. Either way, she was my friend and Shannon's partner. She'd supported me when other officers had decried my ability as fake, and she'd been the first to offer support when Shannon had finally come to his senses and asked me out. The least I could do was use my ability to check for abnormalities.

"Of course," I said, lifting up my glove-covered hands. "Where do I start?"

She twisted in her seat to study the detective with Shannon. "Ask my brother. It's his case since he works in the East Precinct. I called him right after I called Shannon, because I knew we'd never be allowed to work the case. Quincy doesn't believe it was murder, but he does want to make sure no one else made a mistake. It's possible someone didn't record the meds and gave Griffin a double dose or something. But you might find clues that indicate someone else may be involved."

The men became aware of our attention and motioned to us. "Maybe you should go home," I said to Paige as I stood. "I promise I'll be thorough."

She shook her head. "I'm going to wait here for Matthew. He texted me that he'll be out in a while. This is ripping him in two. I'm taking a few personal days to be with him."

At any other time, that would have made me tease her. Coming from a police career family, "personal days" weren't words I'd thought were in her vocabulary.

"Okay," I said. "If you need anything, let me know."

I left her there staring at her phone, probably waiting for a text. Shannon took a few steps to meet me, his strong arm slipping around my waist, his movements taut and graceful. He was only a few inches taller than I was, his hair a color between brown and blond, slightly bleached by the sun. He kissed my cheek, and I caught the scent of his aftershave.

"My fiancé, Autumn Rain," he said, introducing me to the other detective.

"Yes, I think we met briefly once before. I'm Paige's brother, Quincy Duncan." Quincy extended a hand with an engaging smile. He was taller than Shannon by an inch but was half again as wide, his muscles hinting at a love of lifting weights. "I'm glad to have a chance to work with you, though I'm sorry it has to be like this." He flashed me another friendly, open smile. Though he was an attractive man, the only feature that resembled his sister were the pale blue eyes.

"Yeah, that's why you look familiar." I shook his hand. I remembered now that Shannon, Paige, Matthew, and I had run into him once at a movie theater. "Have you been assigned the case?" I wanted to make sure. On my last case, I'd been at odds with the detective, and though he'd come through for me in the end, it hadn't been a comfortable working environment.

He nodded. "I've made sure of it for Paige, but I have to tell you, my chief isn't happy. We've never seen a case like this that's an actual homicide, so he'd rather assign one of the newbies. It's probably a mistake, and one not large enough to be negligent homicide. Someone forgot to write down something they gave him, is my guess."

"Four times the nitrates is a little more than one mistake," Shannon said.

Quincy inclined his head. "Maybe, unless there were other interactions or conditions we're not aware of yet. Ordinarily, I'd wait for the autopsy before investigating further, but the medical examiner is backed up, and we may not get the results until late tomorrow, if we're lucky. And if I can do anything to help Matthew in the meantime, I'm glad to do it." His smile was tighter now. "Paige really loves this guy, and she hasn't had it easy in that department. She's too driven for the average Joe, and she has to maintain distance with her colleagues to avoid rumors. You didn't hear it from me, but more than a few of my fellow officers are, well, pigs. Too many are still prejudiced about female officers, especially one as smart as my sister."

Shannon's lips twitched at that, but when he spoke it was only to say, "Your sister's smarts are exactly why I think we need to make sure we cover all our bases. Matthew's a good doctor, and this is an excellent hospital. Something isn't right."

A shudder passed through me as if a wind had blown an icy current into the lobby. Shannon's gaze went to my hands, his shoulders tensed, but he relaxed when he saw nothing amiss. No, I wasn't reading imprints. I'd just felt cold all of a sudden. I crossed my arms to rub my hands up and down over the goose bumps.

"You have a sweater in the car?" Shannon asked.

But the cold feeling vanished as quickly as it had come. "I'm okay. Sometimes hospitals get to me, even without touching anything. There's a lot of emotion imprinted everywhere here."

Quincy grinned at me, and his eager expression reminded me of the first time I'd met Paige. She'd been hungry to see me at work, and so was he.

"Let's get to it," I said.

Ten minutes later, we were in a surprisingly large hospital

room blocked not by yellow crime tape but with a *Do Not Enter* sign. I hadn't expected the body to be there, but the bed wasn't either.

"Where's the bed?" I asked. "He could have imprinted on that before he died. I need to see it."

Quincy nodded. "We'll have to ask the nurse. The medical examiner's office came to collect the body once the hospital reported the suspicious death, but I would have assumed the bed would have come back here afterward."

"Maybe they disinfect the bed before returning it," Shannon said.

They stared at each other for a moment before Shannon added, "Since it's your case, I guess you'll have to ask the nurses. And sooner rather than later so the bed doesn't get lost. I'll make sure we don't disturb anything in case Autumn uncovers something criminal."

What Shannon wasn't saying was that there was no way he'd leave me alone. I was getting better at extracting myself from nasty recurring imprints, but he remembered too vividly how an overdose of imprints less than two months ago had robbed me of my ability altogether. It was why I'd taken to wearing gloves when I wasn't reading imprints.

Quincy glanced my way. "Don't finish before I get back. I want to see this imprint thing at work."

"After we're finished, we should probably block off the room until we have the autopsy results," Shannon added. "Just in case CSI ends up needing to go over it."

"I still say the death was probably due to a clerical error." Quincy started for the door. "But we can do that."

"I'll also need to check with a nurse before looking at the empty syringes," I said, motioning to the red disposal unit.

"Okay, I'll be right back with someone." Quincy gave me a final, reluctant glance before leaving the room.

When he was gone, I pulled off the gloves and tucked them into my purse before hanging it on the door hook. Next, I removed my three antique rings that gave off comforting imprints. My engagement ring was locked in the safe at my shop so I wouldn't accidentally leave negative emotions on it while chasing imprints, but these would help me settle down afterward. For now, I put them in my dress pocket.

"So far, no imprints on the floor," I said, looking down at my toes. "But that might have as much to do with the shoes required sign on the door downstairs as it does with those funny, blue non-slip socks they make patients wear."

"Good to know you at least saw the sign." Smiling, Shannon lowered himself to a chair to watch me work.

"Oh, I saw it." Since it was a private hospital, they could enforce the policy, but going without shoes wasn't against the law, not even in government buildings, though officers had threatened to ticket me before. Because most shoes threw out my back, I'd done without them for most of my flower-child upbringing, and now it was part of who I was.

Shannon laughed. "Right. Anyway, I already went over this room with Paige earlier, and nothing seems out of place."

"Poor Matthew if this does turn out to be some sort of freak mistake." This would haunt him, especially if the death remained unexplained.

I held my hands over the sink and computer area. The tingling of my fingers told me there were imprints everywhere. "There's a lot here," I told Shannon. My stomach twisted at the thought of reading so many scenes and emotions. I'd eaten a double breakfast knowing I was investigating today at the high school, but I was going to need more sustenance by the time this was over.

Shannon leaned forward in his chair. "Maybe they're not recent imprints. Unless it turns out they've had other questionable deaths on this floor, you only need to go back two days." He sighed. "Great, speaking of that, I guess we'll have to research if there were other questionable deaths, won't we?"

I nodded. "Yep, but for now, I'll limit it to last Saturday."

As I read imprints, I always see the most recent one first, and my mind pulls up an imaginary calendar narrowed to the date and time of the event. Imprints older than a few months were more difficult to pinpoint exact times, but general dates were accurate enough for most investigations.

I checked the sink in several places with the knuckle of my right hand, finding nothing earlier than a week ago—and that was from the sister of a patient as she refilled her water bottle. The computer keyboard, the monitors, and the walls also showed nothing recent except vague hurry. In contrast, the medicine drawer held a vivid imprint from a month earlier when a nurse clumsily opened it as her patient screamed in pain.

I'd been lucky that so far the most recent imprints from the patients or their families had been hopeful or positive. It seemed most people placed in this room had recovered.

"I'm guessing the gloves the staff wear cut down on imprints," I said, moving to a small couch against the wall. "So even though there are a lot of imprints, the ones from the hospital staff are older. Most of what I'm finding is from patients' families, some dating back to last week but some also from months ago. It helps not to have to read more than the first one or two."

The couch tingled with a strong imprint. I touched it

gingerly, finding a happy imprint from last Saturday. I let it play out.

He was going to be all right! Yes, they'd told me it was only minor surgery, but I'd worried that his previous bouts of bleeding ulcers might cause complications.

"Peter," I told him, "this is proof that you're still working too hard."

He tilted his head back and laughed, looking every bit as handsome as when we'd married thirty-two years ago, despite his now salt and pepper hair. "I don't think kidney stones are caused by stress. Anyway, you'll be glad to know that I've been listening. I was going to wait to surprise you, but now's as good a time as any." His smile grew wide. "I bought tickets last Thursday for that trip to Venice you always wanted. We leave in four weeks."

Excitement flooded me. "Really? But what about the product launch? You still have two months left."

"Now that we're in production, it's all up to marketing and shipping, and I have good people over those. I can leave for two weeks. Then I'll be back for the launch."

"Good," I said, leaning forward to push myself to my feet. "Until Venice, then. I'm holding you to it."

The imprint cut off abruptly as whoever had made it—presumably Peter's wife—stood and her hand lost contact with the couch cushion.

The hopeful scene was quickly replaced by a resentful imprint from a man wishing he were at work instead of his mother's bedside after her gall bladder surgery last Wednesday. I withdrew my hands quickly, glad when the blatant self-concern of the imprint was covered by a rush of pity for the old woman. My pity, not the spoiled son's. Sometimes it was hard to compartmentalize.

Peter Griffin's wife had left another brief imprint on the bedside table that had been moved to the side, but it didn't seem important. Nothing radiated from the two portable shelves that stood against the wall.

Shannon popped to his feet. "Here's the chair."

I touched it with the tip of a finger, and instantly my breath was ripped from my chest.

I gripped the armrests as I collapsed into the chair, unable to remain on my feet a second longer. Peter couldn't be dead. His handsome face looked peaceful, as if sleeping, but his cheeks were beginning to swell. That threw everything off. He didn't look like my Peter. But one thing was certain: the man in the bed wouldn't be going with me to Venice.

Grief flooded me at the thought. I'd found the flight reservations in his office at home, in a manila envelope with hotel information. On the outside, he'd written, Until we meet in Venice. *It was a silly thing I'd started saying to him this past year whenever he worked late, and he'd joked right back.*

There'd be no more joking now.

Tears leaked down my face. "I don't understand," I said to his cardiologist, the kind-eyed Dr. Kellogg. "They said he was fine. He was supposed to go home this morning. How could his heart just stop?"

It seemed more unreal now that I'd said the words aloud. My husband was strong. He had always been strong. He had never needed me or anyone else. How could he be dead?

"We don't know exactly what happened," Dr. Kellogg said, his voice wavering slightly. "We tried to resuscitate him. We shocked his heart. We did everything we could. I've double-checked his meds, and there is nothing that indicates why his blood pressure dipped so low. We won't know more until we get the results of the autopsy."

They were going to cut Peter open. More tears escaped my eyes and slid down my face. I didn't bother to wipe them away.

Dr. Kellogg retreated a step, then two. "You take as long as you want with him. Let the nurse know when you're ready, and we'll take care of the rest. We'll need to know what mortuary you'll be using."

"How do we know your doctors will even report what they find in the autopsy?" said a male voice behind me.

I turned to look up at my son Niklas, who had spoken. He stood next to his brother, Stevan. I was glad to have both my strong sons at my side. Niklas gave me a tight smile and put a comforting hand on my shoulder.

Dr. Kellogg paused at the door. "The hospital has already called the medical examiner. That's protocol in a situation like this. They'll be thorough. We all want answers."

At least the man didn't talk about closure, although he probably wanted to. He looked exhausted, and for the first time I wondered how long he'd been at work. At least since Peter died during the night—and probably longer.

No, Peter couldn't be dead. This couldn't be happening. It was all a terrifying dream.

A weight seemed to crush my chest. "I need a breath of air," I said. "Please help me up."

Niklas bent down and put an arm around me. "You don't have to worry, Mom," he whispered in my ear. "He'll never hurt any of us again."

The heartbreaking imprint vanished, leaving me bereft and more than a little confused. It seemed Peter Griffin wasn't the perfect husband or father the casual observer might believe him to be. It was clear that at least one of his sons didn't seem to be mourning his death.

"You okay?" Shannon's hand gently massaged my neck.

I nodded but didn't speak because another imprint was beginning, also from someone visiting Peter Griffin, this time while the man was still alive.

"You just get well," I told Peter. "I'll make sure the finances are ready for Futura's release." I needed to hold him off until the launch. Then I could replace the money, and he'd never know.

"I still want to see the books," Peter insisted, his square jaw lifting slightly.

Dread filled me. I had to prevent that at any cost. Good thing I had an alternate plan. "Of course. Any time. Well, I'd better get going and let you rest."

"I am a little tired. I appreciate the visit, Robby. Good night, and thanks for the card."

I lifted my hand from the chair with a sigh.

"What is it?" Shannon asked.

"Peter Griffin's family might not be all that sad about his death. And a man named Robby from his work came to visit at nine-thirty last night. He definitely had a secret he was trying to keep from Peter."

"A secret important enough to kill for?"

I couldn't deny that the mysterious Robby's alternate plan might involve murder. "I don't know, but we owe it to Paige and Matthew—and Peter Griffin—to find out."

Chapter 2

I read the imprints on the chair again, not to see if there was anything new, because there never was, but to make sure I didn't miss an earlier imprint from the time Griffin was in the hospital. After the first two imprints, the next was from Thursday, so I lifted my hands, glad to be done with the chair.

I'd finished with the bathroom and was eyeing the garbage container next to the sink when Quincy returned with a stout, middle-aged nurse in tow, whose nametag read Freya. Her smooth hair was cropped to her chin, curling slightly under, and her face was frozen in a scowl that seemed to deepen as she caught sight of my black eye. If I'd have to guess, she didn't like me at all—or maybe any of us.

"Bad news," Quincy announced. "The bed apparently went somewhere for maintenance because they want to be sure nothing was wrong with the back-up call lights on the bed. But they're tracing its whereabouts. I've told them not to clean it."

It wouldn't matter if they did, since no amount of cleaning removed imprints. I had recently discovered that heat did affect them, however, though I hadn't done enough research to know how much heat. This meant that a clothes dryer might be part of why clothes weren't good imprint carriers, and not only because they lost bits of fiber with each washing.

"I need to check out the medical waste, any syringes, and the garbage," I told the nurse. "I might need to touch some of them. Is that safe to do with my bare hand?"

She nodded without surprise, and I realized Quincy must have explained what I was doing. "It should be, as long as it's not a needle. We're really careful here, and he wasn't taking anything that should hurt you. He also didn't have any blood-borne illnesses, so even the needles should technically be safe, though you should be careful not to prick yourself." Freya smiled suddenly, transforming her entire face. Maybe she didn't hold a grudge against me after all. "But please don't do that."

"I won't," I said, smiling back. "Mr. Griffin would have been more likely to imprint on the bed or a wedding ring while he was getting a shot or IV, anyway." I looked at Shannon and Quincy. "Why don't you guys get some gloves on and spread the contents of the garbage out on something while we're doing the medical waste?"

"I'll get you some garbage bags to lay it on," Freya offered. After doing so, she pulled on neoprene gloves, despite her assurances about the safety of the medical waste, and opened the red container on the wall. I held my hands above the spent syringes. Nothing radiated from them, which didn't surprise me precisely because of the gloves.

"Nothing here," I said. "You can put it back."

The nurse did so, her grim expression once more on her face. "It's just so sad. I took care of him yesterday, and he was a really sweet man. Not demanding like some of the patients. His wife was here most of the day with him. They were talking about a trip."

"To Venice," I said.

"How did you know?"

Quincy's laugh boomed loudly in the room. "I told you, she's psychic."

"I'm not psychic." I gave him a hard look, even though I was used to the moniker. My idea of psychics was people who saw the future or read people's minds. "A section of my brain is more developed, is all. It's an ability, like a knack for playing the piano."

He waved the words away with a meaty, glove-covered hand. "Yeah, yeah. You're the next evolution—that's what Paige told me you'd say. Lucky you." He winked at me to soften the words, and for a moment, I had the distinct feeling he was flirting with me.

Ignoring him, I turned back to Freya. "You talked to the night nurse when you came in?"

She nodded. "We always go over each patient."

"Did she have any indication that Mr. Griffin might be in trouble?"

"Evelina said the last time she tested his blood pressure, it was a little low, but nothing to be worried about. Nothing dangerous. Especially for a man in such good shape." She frowned and looked thoughtful. "I do remember her saying she gave him a painkiller at one. He was complaining of a head-ache. He said it was probably because he hadn't slept well, so she tried to leave him alone and only peek in on him quietly. Of course, they'd have woken him up for the blood draw at three, and by four . . ." She shook her head. "He should have used the call light if he felt so bad. Low blood pressure has a lot of symptoms."

"Is that why you think the call light on the bed might be broken?" I asked.

"Well, it didn't seem to be, but when someone dies like that, the hospital attorney likes to cover all the bases. Especially when the regular remote call light was on the floor when she came in, like he'd dropped it. Or threw it. But an alarm sounds if it's detached from the wall, so that wasn't the problem. We sent it out for testing to make sure it was working well."

"I'll need to see it," I said. "If you can track it down for me."

She nodded. "I've got a call out."

I moved to survey the garbage the men had laid neatly on the floor. Wrinkled paper towels, a fork, a water mug, and paper cups were there, but no get-well card from the mysterious Robby. "Did the family already take Mr. Griffin's belongings?" I asked the nurse.

She nodded. "When a patient passes, we typically bag all the clothes, gifts, and other belongings for the family. Sometimes they'll throw a lot of it away before they leave—you know, like the lotion and comb and lip balm the patient was using here. But his wife didn't even open the bag. Mr. Griffin also had a gym bag they'd brought in with extra clothes and reading material. His phone and tablet were in that."

"I see." I was sorry not to have the items to touch, but if someone at Griffin's work had poisoned him, or if hospital personnel had made a mistake with his care, I didn't think his personal items would be likely to hold condemning imprints. But it might be something to follow up on later when I went to talk to the widow, especially if her son Niklas had touched them.

"What's that?" I pointed to a small, white box Shannon was placing in the row of organized garbage. It was barely larger than my palm but looked pristine and white, like an unmarked donut or bakery box.

The nurse shook her head. "Probably a treat someone brought him. You'll have to ask Evelina. I'd bring her in, but they finally let her go home." She clicked her tongue in apparent sympathy.

"How soon are people allowed to eat after surgery?" Shannon asked, squatting down to lay out the last of the garbage.

"Depends on the surgery," the nurse said. "His was minor, so it wouldn't have been long." She tapped on the computer keyboard and pulled up a record. "Looks like he was nauseated after his surgery, but by dinner on Saturday, he was eating normally. And yesterday while I was here, he had all three meals."

I squatted to examine the white, unlabeled box. Even before I touched it, the lack of tingling told me there were no imprints. Removing the top, I saw four empty paper liners, the kind that would hold gourmet chocolates. No imprints met my search here either, but I swept up the tiniest bit of brown flake and sniffed it.

"Smells like chocolate."

"A lot of people bring food and treats to our patients, even though we have a great menu for them to choose from." Freya pulled off her gloves and checked her phone. "I'm being paged. Will you be all right here without me?"

"Yes, but we would like the number of the nurse from last night," Quincy said.

"Of course. The president of the hospital has authorized me to give you anything you need. They're putting together a file now. And I'll keep tracking down that bed." She nodded and exited the room, relief apparent on her face.

The minute the door closed, Shannon stood and looked at Quincy. "I think you need to get a team out here and dust this chair for prints. Maybe the rest of the room too. We might need to prove someone else was here and had the opportunity to kill Mr. Griffin."

"You found something?" he asked.

I filled Quincy in about the imprint left by the man from Mr. Griffin's work, as well as the comment from his son.

"So," he mused. "Someone might have hurt Peter Griffin, and we can't rule out the family. This is looking like it might become an interesting case after all."

"It still might be an accident," I said. "Like two nurses giving the same meds."

"Maybe. The hospital is conducting an internal search now. I'll get a court order for their records. And for their security footage. Also, from what the nurse told me, anyone coming here after ten has to check in with security and get a wristband, so they'll be on the check-in list." Quincy's eager smile grew that much wider. "If this turns into a real murder case, maybe I won't be doing the grunt cases for the next two months to make up for pulling favors with my captain."

Shannon gave a disgusted sigh, but I could see right through this big man's bluster. Quincy was worried about his sister and her boyfriend or he wouldn't be here.

I turned back to the garbage, holding my hands above it. Nothing radiated imprints, which was normal for casual garbage. You didn't feel much about something you were going to throw away, or use it long enough to leave imprints. Only one of the cups held a hint of sadness.

"I'm finished," I said, going to the sink and scrubbing my hands clean.

"Even if you don't process this stuff until after the autopsy," Shannon said to Quincy, "we should probably take it into evidence."

"Already ahead of you." Quincy began shoving it into an extra garbage bag. He was all business now, reminding me of his sister. "If we end up processing it, I'll need Autumn's prints for elimination purposes."

Shannon tossed in the white box. "We already have them on file."

When the room was relatively in order again, Quincy began unrolling crime scene tape from his pocket. "Guess it's better late than never. I'll have to wait for the autopsy results, though, before my chief is going to okay a forensic team here."

A sound at the door startled all of us, and we turned to see Matthew Kellogg standing there. I often teased Paige that her boyfriend's attractiveness rivaled one of the doctor actors in a television soap, but today he looked nothing like himself. Stubble shadowed his haggard face, and his brown eyes were bloodshot. His dark hair stood up on both sides. His tall, lean shoulders slumped, and all his clothes were rumpled as if he'd worn them for a week. He'd looked despondent in Brigit Griffin's imprint of him, but now he looked infinitely worse. Misery shrouded him like a physical mantle.

"Thank you for coming," he ground out. His eyes shifted to Quincy. "I know you're pulling all sorts of strings for Paige and me. I appreciate it."

I moved toward him, reaching out to adjust the twisted collar on the white jacket he wore over his wrinkled green scrubs. "Of course, we're here. You should go home and rest. Paige is waiting for you downstairs."

His eyes locked onto mine, and when he spoke, it was as if he hadn't heard. "I've been over everything ten times. I've pulled in second and third and fourth opinions. The hospital administrator and I questioned all the staff. We can't find any errors or anything else that might explain what happened or why there would be so many nitrates in his system. It doesn't match with the previous blood draws. We gave him one extended-release capsule every day, exactly like he gets at home. He'd know if someone here wanted him to swallow another pill. But even extra doses of nitroglycerin wouldn't explain why he died like that. It should have been caught in time. There's got to be something more we're not seeing."

I couldn't promise anything, but I wouldn't let him go on stabbing around in the dark. "There might be something else," I said. "I found a few imprints that don't add up. Give us a few days to see what we can do."

He barked a laugh that sounded more like a rough cry. "All I've got is time. I'm suspended until after the inquiry. But I know how this goes. They can't afford a drawn-out lawsuit, so if nothing turns up, I'll be part of the settlement offer to the family. Guess that's why they insist on so much malpractice insurance. Not that I blame them if they hang me out to dry. They have to protect the hospital." His jaw clenched and unclenched. "I've lost patients before, but not like this. Not for no reason." He swallowed hard, the sound noisy and painful in the silence of the room.

Quincy moved up beside us. "Go home with Paige," he said gently. "She's waiting downstairs."

Matthew nodded and turned around, looking like a sleepwalker.

"So what's next?" Quincy asked when Matthew was gone, waggling his thick eyebrows at me.

I considered for a moment. "I'll need to talk to Peter Griffin's colleagues at work, and his family. Someone should also talk to the nurse from last night. We know there were too many nitrates in his body, presumably from heart pills, so we start there. Who knew about his heart condition, and how could he have overdosed?"

"Anyone from his family could have brought Griffin's own nitroglycerin pills from home and dissolved them in his water," Shannon said.

I frowned. "He would have noticed the taste if it had been dissolved in water."

"Maybe it wasn't water." Shannon raked a hand across his hair. "He could have a soft drink addiction. Or maybe it wasn't pills they used."

"My dad has a quick-acting nitroglycerin that dissolves in your mouth," Quincy said. "He uses it when he's under stress or plans to exercise. So it wouldn't be all that hard to put into food."

I groaned. "Maybe let's not go around announcing that Dr. Kellogg's girlfriend might have access to her dad's meds."

"Thousands of people have access to heart medications belonging to others," Quincy said with a snort. "What they don't have is motive, and neither do Paige or Matthew. And you already uncovered something suspicious at Griffin's work and something weird going on with the family."

"What work did Peter Griffin do?" I grabbed my purse from the hook on the door.

"Tech firm," Shannon said. "He's a partner in a new startup called Futura."

"That makes sense with the imprints I read."

Quincy waved his yellow tape at us. "I'll get this wrapped up, and then I'll head back to the precinct to start researching, starting with hospital personnel background and surveillance tapes. We'll have a list with the night visitors, but I'll add everyone known to have visited Peter Griffin during the day as well."

"I'll do background on the family," Shannon said.

"If you go see them, I want to go too." I stepped over a string of Quincy's tape that he'd laid over the threshold. "But I'm more interested in Griffin's workplace. I want to know what product they're releasing in two months." The imprint about the money was the most compelling to me, even more so than the family. The second imprint from the chair had clearly indicated that the visitor was willing to do whatever it took to make sure Peter Griffin didn't discover his secret.

Maybe even murder.

"Your PI buddy might be able to dig up dirt on the company," Shannon said.

Quincy chuckled. "PIs do seem to know where all the bodies are buried. I have an info sheet on Griffin with what I have so far. That should get you started. I want to know what everyone finds, though. Remember, it's my case."

"It's for Paige," I corrected. I was not doing this for him, and not even for the grieving Mrs. Griffin.

"Right. You know what I mean." Quincy winked at me. That was twice now, and it was odd.

I stepped into the hallway as a gust of cold air blew down the hallway. I stepped back, only to feel more cold to my left, as if an invisible presence stood there. I reached out a hand but felt nothing.

"What is it?" Shannon squinted at the wall next to us.

"I'm not sure." I removed my gloves from my dress pocket and pulled them on.

Shannon rode down with me to the lobby. There, he kissed me goodbye, rubbing a thumb lightly over the bruise under my left eye. The rest of my scrapes and cuts had healed nicely, but this black stain persisted despite the arnica I rubbed into it three times daily.

"We still on for the wedding?" he asked lightly.

I knew he was asking because of Paige, but I didn't hesitate. I'd learned my lesson after my tangle with a serial killer. "Yes. We'll be able to help Paige and Matthew before then."

He inclined his head. "Paige would kill me anyway if she found out we changed our plans because of her." He paused and added, "And no, Paige doesn't know yet. You tell Tawnia?"

I shook my head. "It's only been two days since we decided."

"The sooner you tell her, the better."

I held back a grimace. My twin would be happy for me, but after spending the first thirty-two years of our lives apart, she'd been making plans for my wedding since before I'd accepted Shannon's proposal. I'd been the maid of honor for her wedding, and finally it would be her turn.

"I'll do it today," I promised Shannon. He kissed me again quickly on the mouth, causing a couple of watching children to giggle, and then headed for the parking garage where he'd left his vehicle.

I'd parked out front instead of in the garage, and the moment I was outside, warmth poured through me. Before that moment, I hadn't realized I was still cold. The cement had gathered heat in the nearly two hours I'd been inside the hospital, and I stood for long seconds, allowing the warmth to seep up through my bare feet. I always felt grounded when I paused to experience the city this way—through concrete, dirt, or whatever the medium—as if I were a part of Portland and it was a part of me.

My link with the city wasn't the only one I felt. I also experienced a thread of connection with my sister and her daughter, and more recently, my biological father. These connections would thicken with approximation, warning me of their presence. I'd felt it with others not related to me, but blood and emotional closeness strengthened the bond. Before today, I hadn't been sure I'd felt it with Shannon, but I could sense him receding from me now, our connection stretching thinner until it was surely in my imagination. Maybe after the wedding it would be stronger, but did I really want that? Shannon had a dangerous job, after all. Twice before, when my adoptive parents died, I'd felt connections sever. It was something I didn't ever want to relive.

Blowing out a breath, I called Elliot Stone.

"Tell me you're on your way to the high school," he said. "And why don't you answer texts?"

"I was reading imprints, that's why." I started across the parking lot to my car.

"It's almost noon. Too late to cancel."

"I can head over there now, but I need a favor. Information."

"Yeah?" Amusement colored his voice. "See how well we work together? You're already coming to me for help."

"It's for a friend," I said.

"I thought it was the police you went to see."

"She's a homicide detective. Paige Duncan. She works with my fiancé."

"Yeah?" His tone sobered. "What happened?"

I'd reached my car and began fishing for my keys. "Peter Griffin, age sixty, a partner in a start-up tech firm called Futura, died of a sudden heart attack early this morning after routine kidney stone surgery on Saturday. There's some indication of an overdose of his heart medicine that may have been tampered with, and Paige's boyfriend is probably going to be blamed because he was the cardiologist over Peter's care during his hospital stay. But I found imprints that indicate something more might be going on besides a simple medicine mix-up. One involves a man named Robby, who might be an employee at Futura. The police are sending me more info, and I'll get that to you, but isn't what I gave you enough to go on for now?"

"Plenty. I can start a search remotely now, and check with my contacts later. But you are coming to the school, right?"

"Yes. I'm leaving the hospital now." My engine roared to life. "Or will when we hang up. But how'd it go at the boy's house this morning?"

"They were fine with rescheduling when I said you were working with the police. But the mother's anxious because she thinks they're going to charge her son. She only has today off from work."

"We'll see her," I said. "Gotta go if you want me on time." I looked at the dashboard clock. "Scratch that. I'm going to be ten minutes late. Make nice with the principal for me, okay?"

Elliot was grumbling something when I hung up.

Chapter 3

Black and white spray paint slashed across the walls, floors, and ceilings of the equipment room. Lines zigzagged over arm pads, body shields, and football dummies. Distorted smiley faces leered out at us. The jumbled mess held no hint of organization or artistic beauty sometimes found in the graffiti on walls or bridges around town. Even the words of profanity that emerged from the chaos were so poorly executed that imagination had to fill in for the blotches of paint or for a thin line that abruptly disappeared altogether.

The paint was only the beginning. Every single piece of equipment not made of metal had also been slashed repeatedly until the stuffing inside was coming out. Sooty dust layered every surface, though I suspected this might have come from the forensic team.

Elliot Stone whistled under his breath. "Someone was angry." He put his big finger inside a rip running down the entire length of a body-sized blocking pad. The computer-guru-turned-private-investigator was wearing slacks that looked at least a decade old and a blue, short-sleeved shirt whose buttons strained over his ample chest and stomach. He wore a beard that was close to needing trimming and glasses that magnified his green eyes.

"It's over a hundred thousand dollars of damage," said Baird Tillmon, the Franklin High School principal.

The stench of new paint was overwhelming, even after two weeks. "That much?" I found it hard to believe that Franklin could invest that kind of money in sports equipment when Elliot had told me on the way here that half the student body was on free or reduced lunches.

"Are you kidding?" Tillmon nodded vigorously enough that I could see the small balding circle on top of his graying head, despite his tall height that rivaled Elliot's. His hair was cropped short, and even though it was summer, he wore a long-sleeve, button-up shirt with a tie. He was lean and handsome in a scholarly way, with thoughtful brown eyes and a thin nose. "Each of these chute boards and dummies cost a hundred bucks, and the larger blocking pads are double that. The sled doesn't look too damaged under the paint, but each of the dummies on it are six hundred new. No, we didn't pay that much, but that's what the replacement cost will be. Our coach is good at getting donations and looking for sales, and most of this is stuff he's begged or wrangled from donors over eight years. He's brought our team from obscurity to a real contender for the high school championship in the years he's been here. That means a lot to our kids. The football team has united us, and this . . ." He raised his hands, turning slowly. "This is going to upset the entire student body."

"Good thing it's summer break then," Elliot said, pushing up his glasses. He looked uncomfortable in this school setting, and I guessed he might have bad school memories that haunted his past. I knew I did.

Principal Tillmon blinked. "Yes, I guess so. I suppose if we can get enough of the paint off, we might be able to use duct tape to get us into practice next month and maybe through the season. That is, if Ricardo Valdez doesn't quit on me. He's my head coach."

I reached out to touch the light switch on the left side of the door. No recent imprints there. "He hasn't seen this yet?"

"No, he's on vacation with his wife's family in Spain until Friday. I'd been hoping to figure out who's responsible before then, but so far the police haven't made an arrest." Tillmon's gaze rested momentarily on the bruise under my left eye.

"And you think it's Pax Medina." I walked over to one of the football dummies attached to a large metal frame, the one Tillmon had referred to as a sled. The stuffing on this dummy was held in only by a thick X of black paint.

"Police found cans of black and white paint in his car."

I exchanged a look with Elliot. He hadn't told me that, but then again, we hadn't met with the boy yet, so maybe he hadn't known.

"What about fingerprints?" I asked. "Are the police finished here?"

Tillmon shrugged. "I think so. They haven't been back in two weeks. They had a team go over everything then. They dusted and took pictures. But with all the prints here, they said it was unlikely they'd find anything that could positively identify the culprits."

"Why did they focus on Pax?" I asked, moving a bare foot over an unmarred section of the cement. No notable imprints on the floor. Yet.

Tillmon's gaze strayed to the tips of my toes, just visible under my dress. "Uh, they figure it was done sometime on

Thursday or Friday night, two weeks ago. Well, a few days more than that now. Anyway, Pax had access. He works for us here as a janitor, along with three other teens. They clean and paint and repair things all summer under the supervision of the head janitor, getting it ready for school to start. Pax doesn't have keys to the building, but plenty of opportunity to leave something open. He also stays after all the other kids leave to practice the piano. The police started interviewing all the kids on the Saturday morning after the damage was discovered, and they saw paint on Pax's hands."

"His mother said he's been suspended from work," Elliot stepped over one of the body shields that had been strewn on the cement floor of the equipment room to stand next to the principal. "That's a lot of money lost for a kid like that."

Tillmon frowned. "It was supposed to be until we determined if he's responsible." He heaved a sigh that seemed to involve his entire body. "It's a shame. Pax has always been a good kid. But with the paint cans they found in his car, and how everyone knows he only plays football because of pressure from the coach and other students, the police seemed to think it fits. I got the impression they're waiting for a few more things before they charge him. If they do, Pax will be suspended."

Elliot looked hard at me and then at my hands, a sure signal he wanted me to dive into the imprints. But I liked to have some background knowledge to understand the imprints I'd find. I also usually preferred to meet with a client before I started investigating, to make sure he was actually innocent, but the death of Peter Griffin had taken that opportunity from me. The way things stood now, the boy could actually be guilty.

"He's that good at football?" I asked. "That his peers put pressure on him to play?"

Tillmon folded his arms across his chest. "He's that good. He can throw, he can catch, and he's not afraid of tackling or being tackled. He's not the star player or anything, but only because he doesn't want to be. It's basketball he really loves. That and playing the piano. He's extremely talented, especially for a low-income kid from a single-parent home whose mother has to work full time. I don't understand, though, why he'd risk his future. He has a stab at several prominent scholarships."

I placed a finger on a tiny section of a football dummy that hadn't been painted. No imprints there. "Do you really believe he did it?"

"If you'd have asked me before they found the paint cans, I'd have said no way." Tillmon unfolded his arms. "Look, I let you in here because the police verified your identities and because Mrs. Tillmon asked me to let you see the place for yourselves. I want to believe there's another explanation for the paint the police found in Pax's car, but as you can see, there isn't much to go on."

"I'm actually just beginning," I said. "I have a different skill set from the police."

Principal Tillmon's brow furrowed. "How long will it take? I have other appointments."

"Oh, you don't have to stay." Elliot gestured toward the door. "We know about the chain of evidence. If we find anything we think the police missed, we'll let you know."

Tillmon blinked at the dismissal. "Okay, then. I guess I'll leave you to it." He walked to the door, hesitantly, as if not sure he should allow us to stay in the room without him.

When he was gone, I started with the football dummies attached to the sled, targeting the few inches of surface not covered with paint. Only a half-dozen imprints remained uncovered, mostly anticipation and frustration. Nothing clear, and nothing that didn't take place at least six weeks ago, which put the most recent imprints at mid-May.

Slowly I explored the metal base of the sled, catching an intense moment of anger directed at the coach, but again that had occurred last May. "I don't think much of this has been used since school let out," I told Elliot, who was looking at something on his phone.

"Makes sense. They had practice and tryouts during the spring, and now a summer break before they start practicing again next month in August."

I moved to the scattered body shields. Running my hands above them, I waited for the tingle that meant a strong imprint. There. I dropped a finger on it.

Stay firm, I told myself. Don't let them push you out of the way! The coach was watching. This was my big chance.

The other student crashed into me. My feet danced under me as I gave way and fell hard. I heard a snicker behind me and bounced to my feet, but everyone was already looking away.

I'd failed. No way would the coach let me be on the team now. Unless it was to bring the rest of them water. Anger and humiliation coursed through my body.

I felt bad for the kid, whoever he was, and hoped he'd judged himself too harshly.

On some of the equipment with thinner coats of paint, I could still read imprints, but the shields with more paint muted them to the point of uselessness. I found three similarly worried imprints before moving on to a plastic garbage can full of spray-painted footballs. The balls held a myriad of short bursts of emotions during plays or practices, moments of intense triumph or utter despair. Then came one imprint that was longer than the rest.

"Just want to ask you to give him a chance," Principal Tillmon said to me. *"He's a good kid, and he worships you."*

I gripped the football more tightly. What I wanted to say was that the kid was all bluster and no game, but Tillman was my boss, no matter how I looked at it. "I won't play him unless he earns the spot," I insisted. "Or unless everyone better than him gets sick. I've worked too hard to get this team where it is to let it fall apart."

Tillmon nodded. "I'm not asking you to. Just let him work out with the team. Teach him what you can. He might surprise us. In the meantime, it keeps him out of trouble."

So Principal Tillmon was a believer that hard workouts and team membership might turn a troubled kid around. Maybe he was right, and the coach was willing to play along—at least to a point.

"Something important?" Elliot asked.

The moment had occurred three and a half months ago in March, and it didn't seem to be related. I shook my head. "Not really. Just the boys worried about not making the team for this year, and the principal asking the coach to let a boy play. Probably standard stuff."

"Well, keep it up." He held up his phone, faced in my direction. "The principal was right, by the way. Even used, this stuff is expensive. They might be able to strip the paint, though."

"The vinyl covers can probably be repaired." I'd done it before on vintage items. "Wouldn't look pretty, and I'm not sure how long it would hold up."

Elliot was about to reply when shouting in the hallway

outside the equipment room interrupted our conversation. We were hurrying to the half-open door when it burst open to reveal a tall, Hispanic youth, who was visibly upset, with Principal Tillmon close on his heels.

"Pax, you can't be here," Tillman said. "The best thing you can do is to stay away."

Pax twisted his head to look at the principal. "But I didn't do it! I swear I didn't do it. I need to see what I'm accused of doing."

His mother, Luna Medina, appeared behind him, looking short compared to the two men. Her long, black hair hung down her back in a tight braid and sweat beaded her forehead. "Please, Pax, let's go home," she said in English much more heavily accented than when I had talked to her during my last case, as if worry had stolen her fluency. "We will fix this. Don't worry. I believe you, son."

Pax didn't look at her. "I just want—" He broke off, his mouth opening in shock as his eyes finally took in the room. His flush deepened. "I didn't do this," he said, his voice weakened now. His gaze shifted to Elliot, and his voice grew stronger. "But I don't need your help, Mr. Stone. Like I told my mother when you came this morning, we can't afford it."

"We can't afford for you to lose your scholarships," Luna countered. "You don't worry about it. I will take care of everything."

"You both need to leave now," Principal Tillmon said firmly.

Luna gave him a scathing glare. "You know my son didn't do this." She shook a finger under his nose. "He would never do anything to risk his basketball or the piano."

Tillman stared back and forth between mother and son, both flushed with chests heaving. Finally, he nodded. "I do believe that. And I'm sorry about the suspension."

Pax's jaw jutted forward. "Then why can't I at least come in to practice?" Aside from the challenging expression, he was a good-looking teen. He was nearly as tall as the principal, with large brown eyes, well-formed brows, and unblemished brown skin. He was on the slender side, but the muscles bulging under his T-shirt probably earned him a lot of admiring looks from female students.

"It's only until they find who did it," answered Tillmon.

"Unless it's me they pin it on." Pax glanced at his mother, his eyes panicked. "I'll lose too much if I don't practice."

"You can play the piano at church." His mother placed a comforting hand on her son's shoulder. I could see him calming under her touch. Whatever anger had brought the teen here, they had a good relationship.

"Hi, Pax," I said, stepping forward and extending a hand. "I'm Autumn Rain."

He stared at me for a moment before raising his hand like a limp noodle. He'd have to fix that handshake if he planned to go anywhere in life. I squeezed his hand firmly to show him how.

He didn't appear to notice. "I didn't do this," he repeated.

"Then may I see your necklace?" On a thin black rope around his neck, he wore an arrowhead that would surely have good imprints.

He stared at me for a rebellious instant, but at a wave from his mother, he mumbled something under his breath and removed the necklace, extending it to me. Obviously, Elliot had told his mother about my ability, which was fine by me.

I didn't take the necklace from him but placed a single finger on the arrowhead. It wouldn't pay to get caught up in too strong an imprint.

Mom shouldn't have hired the investigators. I didn't do it—and somehow the police would have to realize that—without losing all our savings. I should never have listened when Opal got it into her head about fixing the pointers, or I should have at least tossed the paint when we were finished. She'd vouch for me, but I couldn't drag her into this. Her parents would kill her.

This most recent imprint was from less than an hour ago and was proof enough to me that Pax believed in his innocence, though he did have something to hide, something that hopefully wasn't connected. The imprint vanished, followed by another, even stronger one.

Opal was so beautiful, staring up at me with those huge blue eyes in her pale, delicate face. I was drowning, drowning—and loving every moment of it. Her moist lips called to me. Her long, dark hair begged me to stroke it. Did I dare? I swallowed hard, fighting the urge. Soon.

"Sure, I'll help," I said. I'd do anything for her. I'd felt that way since the moment she'd walked into the music room the week after school had ended.

The imprint had come from Thursday morning, two weeks earlier, presumably before the vandalism. They'd both been here in the school hallway—I recognized the brick wall.

Additional glimpses of the girl followed as I watched their friendship unfold like a backward movie. They were together outside on the track eating lunch, talking in the hallway, or laughing as they shot baskets in the gym. The scenes with the girl were interspersed with others of him gripping the arrowhead as he sat at a piano intently studying a difficult passage of music.

The only negative imprint was last May, apparently before he'd met the girl, when Pax took a ribbing from some of his football buddies about missing practice and the coach made him do laps while the others played on the field.

This was followed—or preceded rather, in the timeline— by a triumphant basketball game, where the students had lifted Pax on their shoulders after he'd scored a winning point. His joy lifted me into a dizzying high.

When the imprints began to repeat, I lifted my finger. "Okay, I believe you didn't do this damage. But why did you have spray paint in your car?" No matter what he'd wanted to hide, it would have to come out. And I was going to talk to Opal, whoever she was.

Pax stared at me, placing his arrowhead into his pocket instead of around his neck. "I was helping a friend with a project."

"What project? What friend?"

Pax clamped his mouth shut.

"If you have an alibi," Elliot said, "we need to know."

"Why?" Pax shot angrily. "I didn't do it!" He swung his arm out at the equipment room. "This was a ton of cans, not two tiny ones."

I looked at the principal, who nodded. "The police found more than a dozen cans in the Dumpster outside. Not all the same brand, either."

"Do you know if they contained any fingerprints?" Because I hadn't found imprints from Thursday or Friday the week of the vandalism, not even on the doorknob. My guess was the perps had worn gloves, which nixed both fingerprints and imprints. Though if the perps hadn't worn gloves when they purchased the paint, imprints could still be on them, even if they wiped off fingerprints before coming to the school. I wondered how easy it would be to get the cans from the evidence lockup or wherever they were.

"The police didn't say anything to me about fingerprints. They did say they'd be contacting local stores to see if surveillance cameras saw anyone buying that much paint." He looked nervously around the room. "Are you finished in here?"

"Not really, but I'd like to take a break and talk to Pax and his mom. We can do that outside."

The principal looked relieved. "Okay, then. I'll be in my office if you need me." He gestured for Pax to leave, which the boy did after a final bleak glance at the equipment room.

Elliot walked with Luna and Pax down the hallway, while I paused briefly to run my hands near the walls outside the equipment room door. Whoever had done this might not have put on the gloves before going inside with a bag of paint cans.

Tillmon finished locking the equipment room door and watched me with unveiled interest. Nothing popped out at me, so I nodded at him and hurried after the others.

"Uh, could you wait a minute?" Principal Tillmon said.

I turned back toward him. "Yes?"

He toyed with the key in his right hand. "Look, I know the Medinas don't have a lot, and I'd like to help with financing your investigation. Not officially as the school, but from my own funds. I can contribute a few hundred dollars if you'll knock it off her bill. I know the police have their hands full with far more important crimes, so maybe you'll get to the truth better than they can. If Pax didn't do it, I don't want to see him suffer."

My phone buzzed in the handbag I had looped over my neck and one arm. Ignoring it, I tilted my head to study him. "That's really nice of you."

He shrugged. "It's not completely altruistic. If Pax did it, the only thing we'll get out of him is work getting the paint off, but if it's someone else, or if a group of kids are responsible, their parents might be able to reimburse the school for the damage and make sure I don't lose my coach."

I didn't really buy that explanation because Luna seemed determined to do whatever it took to get her son free, but I let the principal have it. "I'll keep that in mind," I said.

Talking about reimbursement made me uncomfortable. I had never charged a fee for reading imprints, though I did encourage people to buy an antique from my shop. That was one of the reasons I dragged my feet about joining Elliot. I envied his ability to research and his extensive contacts, but as the daughter of two bona fide flower children who had been known to let complete strangers crash for weeks on end at their apartment, I didn't want to bankrupt people who were already struggling.

I caught up to Elliot and the Medinas as they exited the nearest door, which was nowhere near the front where we'd come in. We were following Pax now, as he took us outside to the track that surrounded the football field. It was early enough that the building's shadow shaded part of the empty track on this side, while the stadium opposite was in full sun. Across the field, I could see the statue of Benjamin Franklin, the school namesake, looking out over the playing turf.

Pax stopped walking and turned toward us, folding his arms, his face tight.

"You must tell them everything," Luna told her son. "They only want to help. You must get those scholarships."

Pax licked his lips. His shoulders slumped and a hint of despair came from his dark eyes. I could tell he didn't plan to say anything to help his case, not if it risked the girl, Opal.

"Why don't I tell you what I know instead?" I said gently.

Pax met my gaze and did a tiny doubletake as he appeared to notice my black eye for the first time. Or maybe it was my heterochromia that surprised him. In the outdoor light it was probably very clear that my right eye is hazel, while the left is blue.

"Okay," he said.

"A girl named Opal asked you to help paint something—sprinkler pointers, I think they were. You said yes. That's what the paint was for."

Pax's arms unfolded, his hands dropping to his side. "How do you know that?"

I lifted both hands. "It's my gift, and why I'm able to discover things no one else can. Your emotions are imprinted on your arrowhead. I know you care about Opal, and I'm pretty sure she feels the same about you."

"Wait," Luna broke in. "Is that the rich girl I saw you with here last month? I told you to stay away from her."

"You're wrong," he said, taking a step back. "She doesn't feel that way about me. We're just friends. I'm teaching her to play the piano. And I haven't seen her since they made me quit work." His tone was vehement, but his eyes held hope.

"I bet you've texted," I said.

"We need to talk to her." Elliot drew out his phone. "Give me her contact info. If she can give you an alibi, all this goes away."

Pax shook his head. "I'm not getting her into trouble."

"Does that mean you did something you need to hide?" Elliot demanded.

I scowled at him and made a tiny slicing motion across my neck. He really needed to work on his people skills. Couldn't he tell the boy was ready to flee?

Come to think of it, Elliot also looked flushed, as if far more upset than he should be about the boy's refusal.

Pax stared at us, his eyes wide and his mouth ajar. "I-I—" Breaking off, he turned and sprinted away through the gates and along the side of the school. No way I'd catch him, and Elliot probably hadn't done any running since he himself was that age.

Luna gave an exasperated sigh. "He *will* talk to you. Can you come by later? It's my only day off."

"Sure," Elliot said. "Let me know when you track him down."

"I don't really need him now," I said. "I know he didn't do the damage in the equipment room. But he is hiding what he did with Opal. Do you know her? She's the one I want to talk to."

Luna's brown face darkened. "I saw her with him here when he forgot his lunch one day. I don't know her name, but I know her type. Rich girl with fancy clothes who wants to be around my boy only because he plays the piano like an angel. Or because he can shoot a ball into a basket. Her parents will hate him. They will want some rich doctor or lawyer for their precious little girl. She will break his heart."

I'd only seen Opal through Pax's impression of her, so I couldn't say for sure that Luna was wrong. "If we can't find her, I may need to come over and look around your house to see if there are any clues about who she is."

"I bet he has her number on his phone," Luna said. "I will *make* him tell you."

I didn't bet on her odds of making him do anything, not if he really thought he was protecting Opal. I didn't want her to ruin her relationship with her son. "Don't push him too hard." I looked at Elliot. "Eli here will talk to Mr. Tillmon and see if

Opal goes to the school or works here. She has been here at least half a dozen times this summer, so there's a connection. We may not need to get the information from your son."

Luna's sturdy shoulders sagged abruptly, and tears glistened in her eyes. "Thank you for helping me. I will let you know when I find Pax. Maybe he will be ready to listen then." With a dip of her head, she walked slowly away from us, following the same path her son had taken.

Elliot grinned at me. "See," he said, scratching at his beard. "We make a good team. Are we going back to the equipment room?"

I shook my head, reaching for my phone to check the text that had come in earlier when I'd been talking to Baird Tillmon. "I'll go back if we have to, but I'm sure they were wearing gloves. We need to find suspects and talk to them around their own belongings."

"Then I'll work on finding this Opal. And I'll get a list of the football team."

I liked that his mind went in the same direction mine did. "Maybe the basketball team too. Maybe someone there had a beef with the football team or the coach."

"Right."

I looked down at the text and grimaced. I'd been hoping it was from Shannon with more details about Peter Griffin, but it was my sister, Tawnia. She was at my antiques shop looking for me.

"Bad news?" Elliot asked.

"Not really." I just had to find a way to break it to my sister that I was getting married in less than three weeks—and before we could begin planning, I had to solve two cases, one of which might be murder.

Chapter 4

"*Y*ou're getting what?" Tawnia's voice spread throughout the entire shop, a little more shrilly than usual. Good thing it was slow this afternoon so the only person around was Thera, the employee I shared with my best friend Jake Ryan, who owned the connected herb shop next door.

I grabbed my sister's hand and pulled her into my back room that ran the width of my shop behind the counter. "Yes, I'm marrying Shannon." My stomach did a happy dance at the mention of the word. Or was it a nervous lurch? I didn't care. I was getting married regardless of my stomach. "I thought you'd be happy."

"Well, yes." Tawnia leaned over and laid her sleeping ten-month-old daughter into the portable crib I keep in the back room, crammed between the door and my easy chair. "But I also thought I heard you say three weeks." She straightened, hands on her hips. "And that can't possibly be true."

I met her stare head-on. That's the only way to deal with my twin. Looking at her was like looking at a picture of myself, not a mirror image, as everyone always suggested. Except she had dark hair that was past her shoulders while my hair was short, and she also didn't have the scar I sported at the outer corner of my blue left eye. She shared my heterochromia, though, as did our biological father, and despite my hair being dyed red on top, my customers often confused us.

In other things we were barely alike. I liked to cook healthy foods and wear comfortable clothes, while she relied on junk food, could burn meals even in a microwave, and liked to wear suits and dressy outfits. I liked old things while she preferred new. She worked as an artist for a local advertising firm and could draw well enough that the resulting image looked like a picture, and I was good at refurbishing old furniture. One thing that tied us together more tightly than our shared genes and our lifetime search for each other was that we were both madly, passionately, and forever in love with her daughter, Destiny Emma Winn, who, biologically speaking, was as much mine as hers.

"Destiny can be a flower . . . eh, baby," I said. "She's just about walking."

"Barely," Tawnia said with a slight roll of her eyes. "And only because you and Bret keep practicing with her. Don't you guys understand that the sooner she walks, the sooner she'll be running around and climbing up on things? Then she'll want to start play dates and dressing up and putting on lipstick, and I'll miss her being a baby so much that I'll probably have another baby, and she'll feel neglected and get into even more trouble."

I laughed at my sister's proclivity to invent wild stories, a trait she shared with our biological father. "She's already climbing, and walking will only help that because she'll have somewhere to go besides up. And she'd love a little brother or sister." I didn't confirm that the lipstick would be coming sooner than we both wanted.

"But three weeks?" Tawnia grabbed my hands, now free of the gloves. Her gaze penetrated mine. "What about your black eye? It might not be healed by then."

"It's only a little bruise now, and you're good at Photoshop, right?"

"Well . . ." she said. I could tell by the smile tugging at the corners of her mouth that she was almost finished freaking out.

"Anyway, I'd have thought you'd be glad I set a date."

She took a deep breath and nodded once, sharply. "Okay, let's start planning. But keep using whatever herb concoction you're putting on that bruise. I'm good, but I'm not a miracle worker." She thought for a moment. "I assume you still want to have the ceremony in the meadow where your mother and father married, so you need to check with the owner. Wasn't it some guy your dad knew? And you need to make sure the dress fits. I'll take care of food."

I gaped at her. "No way. Not the dinner." I wasn't heating up any junk food in a microwave to serve in that beautiful meadow. I was going to have herbal teas and a self-serve dinner buffet of organic dishes.

She glared at me. "Relax. We'll cater it. You can approve every item. As for flowers and everything else, I'll find samples to choose from."

It was sounding more complicated by the moment. I walked over to the half-size refrigerator in the corner by the bathroom door and extracted half a sandwich left over from Saturday. After the morning I'd had, I was starving.

"Can't we buy a few bouquets at the market?" I said, my words a bit garbled because of the sandwich. "I can't afford catering. I literally have less than a thousand dollars in my bank account. And half of that I'll need to save to put toward the shop mortgage."

"Don't worry. We'll figure it out. And Shannon will be helping. After all, it's his wedding too, and he's responsible since neither of you have parents who are footing the bill." A thoughtful look crossed her face. "Although, I bet Cody would be willing to help. And I am too, of course."

Cody Beckett was our recently discovered biological father, who looked like a homeless man but was really a real estate guru and a sought-after artist of sculptures made from giant tree trunks and metal pieces of junk. He sometimes took a year to finish each of his specialty pieces and made more with one than I did in five years of nine-hour days at the shop.

He would be willing to pay for the wedding because he still felt culpable for the crime he'd enacted on our mother while under the influence of drugs he'd taken to blot out his psychometry gift, the same gift I shared. But I'd forgiven him, and I wouldn't ask him to pay another dime.

I swallowed a bite of sandwich that was a bit too large for my throat. "Don't," I said, gagging slightly. "I'm at a good place with Cody right now. I don't need anything from him." At least nothing that had to do with money. I was, however, feeling more attached to him than ever, which I didn't like to admit, not even to myself. After all, he was the only parent I had left. Not like Tawnia, whose adoptive parents were still very much alive and in her life.

"Yeah, I understand. He still feels guilty."

And he was guilty, even if there had been extenuating circumstances.

Tawnia headed out of the back room, making a beeline

toward my computer on the counter. My counter was about half the width of the shop, located in front of the back room, which allowed us to see the entire store, except for a few places where tall shelving blocked our view.

Near the door, Thera was talking with long-time customer Charlie Horton, a slender man in his late forties, whose day job as an electrician kept him fit. He was a baseball card collector of the highest level and owned a Shoeless Joe Jackson card worth over six hundred thousand dollars. I had nothing that costly, but still he came every week to see if I'd found anything he could add to his collection.

"Hey, Charlie," I called. "I saved you some new cards."

"Thank you." He gave me a wave and followed Thera to the baseball card cabinet.

Tawnia pulled herself up on my counter stool and began bringing up websites, humming to herself. I hoped she knew me well enough to be helpful, because the black-tie wedding she'd had at an expensive downtown hotel had been classy, but so far from my experience that I'd felt uncomfortable all night.

Stuffing the rest of my sandwich into my mouth, I unlocked the safe under my counter to retrieve my engagement ring. The thick band was set with small stones of two alternating colors, our birthstones, and was a copy of an antique ring I'd loved and hadn't been able to afford at auction. The nearly overwhelming imprints of love Shannon had left on it strengthened me, and the tension that had built up from the imprints I'd read seeped from my body.

I checked my email on my phone to see if Elliot had sent me initial information on Peter Griffin or the girl, Opal, and there were two emails from him and one from Shannon. I opened the one from Elliot with the subject line *Opal*. He'd found three girls at Franklin, and had included pictures from the yearbook, but none of them were the girl I'd seen in Pax's imprints.

The next email was information on Peter Griffin's business, Futura. The company was planning to release a pair of smart glasses, also called Futura, that would enable people to have a continuous augmented reality. Users could search for information, play games, or get updates—all while appearing to do nothing. The current release could connect to the Internet directly with a data plan or through a phone hotspot.

They'd solved many of the reoccurring problems that had plagued other attempts at smart glasses, like aesthetics, loading issues, and radiation. Tiny low-level lasers projected the images directly into the eye, so even if you didn't see well in real life, the display was crystal clear. To me, it sounded like science fiction. Peter owned the largest single portion of Futura at thirty-one percent, with twenty percent belonging to his partner, fifty-five-year-old Titus Grey, and the other forty-nine percent to investors. Elliot couldn't find the number for the total investment dollars, but by all accounts, the company was months away from billion-dollar profits.

I was still immersed in reading when another customer came into the store and angled toward the Fisher-Price toy case.

"I'll take care of her," Tawnia said, looking up from the computer. "Meanwhile, you pick some flowers from these pictures. This is a great place to get them in bulk. I can arrange them in vases for the tables." She vaulted off the stool and hurried toward the customer with a smile on her face.

I slid over to the computer as she left, clicking on my email and forwarding the information about Futura to Shannon and also to my under-the-counter printer. Then I opened Shannon's attachment with the subject line *Griffin family info*, thinking to print that as well, but something in the body of Shannon's email caught my attention. Peter Griffin's life insurance was over two million dollars. Remembering Niklas Griffin's whispered comment in his mother's ear, this bumped the family to the top of the suspect list. They'd had access to Peter's medication and plenty of time to research interactions.

Shannon had included a picture of Peter and Brigit Griffin posing in front of a fireplace. The new widow was a beautiful, mature woman with short blond hair and tasteful makeup. She looked like someone who would be married to the dashing and virulent Peter Griffin. But was their marriage a farce? What had Brigit's son meant by his comment about Peter in her imprint?

"Autumn Rain, what are you doing?" Tawnia's voice made me start. Her hands were back on her hips.

"Stop that," I said, slapping at her. "You scared me."

"You're supposed to be picking out flowers." She peered over my shoulder at the picture of Brigit Griffin. "This looks like a case. I thought that while we're planning a wedding, you wouldn't be wrestling with any would-be killers or running from mob bosses."

That made perfect sense to me, but sometimes the world didn't work out that way. "No serial killers or organized crime this time," I said. "I'm just helping out Paige's boyfriend." I gave her a quick rundown of my morning, including my stop at the school.

"So two cases, not one."

I nodded. "Yeah. And if you happen to draw anything unusual . . ." I let the sentence trail off.

Tawnia was what I considered a real psychic. At certain times, she was able to draw people she'd never met in events that always came true shortly after she drew them. Or maybe they were already true as she drew them. She didn't have much control over the ability, however, and as with many creative people, stress was a good way of stopping her from drawing anything.

Tawnia started to laugh, which made me stare at her in surprise. "What?" I said.

"You already know what flowers and food you want, don't you?"

I nodded. "Gerberas. I want it to be as close as possible to Summer and Winter's wedding, and that's what they had." I paused before adding. "You know, they were our age when they adopted me." Thirty-four. They'd been married for six years by then.

"Summer and Winter," Tawnia repeated, and I knew she still found it strange that I'd called them by their first names. It was one more way our lives had been different in our two separate adoptive homes. I'd stayed with Winter and Summer, who'd housed our birth mother, while Tawnia had been sent to the adoptive family who had paid for our birth mother's medical bills, even though my mother had changed her mind before our birth and her unexpected death. Two babies instead of the expected one had solved the adoption agency's problem, but it had cost us dearly.

"Tell you what," Tawnia continued. "You concentrate on helping Paige and that poor boy, and I'll go through the pictures of your parents' wedding." She held up a finger and added, "But we're adding a few embellishments because you have to remember that Shannon's parents will be there too, and they're not hippies."

She was right. "Agreed. There aren't many photos anyway,

but I've seen it in their imprints." Why my voice chose to go all wobbly right then wasn't from any desire on my part.

Tawnia's hand closed over mine. "I know. You've told me all about it. We'll make it perfect."

"And simple," I said.

Her grin widened. "I can do simple, but only for you."

"Thanks."

She gave me a brief hug. "I'm going to work on an art project in the back until Destiny wakes, and then on my way home, I'll go to your apartment and get your photo albums and draw a mockup of the wedding setup. Unless you think Thera needs me here while you're out on this case."

I shook my head. "Jazzy's coming in later when it usually picks up." Tawnia had been filling in too much for me as it was, which was another reason I was considering joining forces with Elliot. I needed to be reimbursed for the time I was away from the shop so I could hire more help.

"Okay, then. You let me know." She gave my hand a squeeze and disappeared into the back room.

I sent Shannon's information about the Griffin family to my printer as well, loading more paper into the tray before turning to the counter as Charlie approached, four plastic-protected baseball cards in his hand.

He raised his grizzled head to smile at me. "Thanks for saving this new batch. I want all of them."

A little thrill spread through me because I'd found the cards for almost nothing last weekend, and even after giving him a good deal, the markup meant I'd have the rest of my mortgage for the month. From here on out, everything could go toward the wedding.

"So how are your online sales?" Charlie asked.

"Coming along," I said. "Jazzy is now on commission. And it's really taking off. You were right to encourage us."

I'd been slow to the digital age, selling online only occasionally when I'd had large ticket items and no local interest, but all that had changed after letting Jazzy loose on eBay and Facebook. For a fifteen-year-old runaway I'd helped rescue from a child trafficking ring, she'd turned out to be more reliable than I'd ever anticipated. A lot of that, I knew, had to do with her attorney foster mother, Claire Philpot, who had actually paid Jazzy's wages during her training here at my shop and Jake's next door.

After finishing with Charlie, I grabbed my phone that was buzzing like crazy. "Hello?"

"We're on our way to visit the Griffins," Shannon said without preamble. "Want to tag along?"

"We? I thought Paige was with Matthew."

"Quincy is meeting me there. We're both very interested in them now that we know about the life insurance policy. I can swing by for you."

"Text me the address. I'll meet you there."

"Are you sure?"

"If that's a subtle hint about my directional impairedness, I'll have you know my Google Maps is now showing right side up." It made a huge difference in finding addresses, and all it had taken was deleting the cached data and doing a little waving with my arm.

"Okay, but call me if you get lost."

I hung up without a response and was glad that he still sent me the address so I wouldn't have to wade through the papers he'd sent to find it.

I looked up to see Thera coming toward me. A string of

large blue beads wound around her neck, and her long white hair twisted elegantly up on her head. Before Winter's death, she'd been a former Herb Shoppe customer, a divorcee with perhaps designs on becoming more than friends with Winter. I'd thought of her as the blue lady because she'd always worn calming blue. She'd been an unwavering friend and a huge support to me since Winter's death and had worked for both Jake and me for the past two years.

"So, you finally set a date." Her hazel eyes glowed. "Guess that means you and Shannon really are getting married."

"I take it you overheard Tawnia's scream of surprise." I grabbed the finished stack of printouts and shoved them into my bag.

Thera laughed. "Oh, yes. I think Jake must have heard her next door. I'm happy for you."

"Thanks. I am too."

"Let me know if you need help planning things. Three weeks isn't a lot of time, and you're obviously occupied with your new case."

"Cases, actually." I filled her in briefly, and then added, "I'd thought Paige would help Tawnia and me plan, but now I'm a little worried it'll get out of hand."

"Hmm." Thera fingered her beads. "I'll talk to Tawnia and put in a word."

I glanced at the double doors that connected Autumn's Antiques with the Herb Shoppe next door that had once belonged to my adoptive father, Winter, but now belonged to my best friend and former boyfriend Jake Ryan. "And in case Jake hasn't heard we've set the date, I'd like to be the one to tell him."

"You'd better hurry. Things like that spread fast."

The woman who Tawnia had helped earlier reappeared through the connecting doorway, a bottle of vitamins from Jake's in her hand.

"She must be back for the toys she was looking at." Thera was already moving toward the woman as she spoke.

I put my engagement ring back into the safe. Feeling its loss, I fished in my pocket for the three antique rings I'd taken off at the hospital. Their positive emotions made me feel immediately better.

I'd reached my car when the phone rang again, and Elliot Stone's number appeared on my screen. "I can't talk long," I said, answering. "I'm on my way to Peter Griffin's house. Is this about Pax? Because in case you didn't see my message, none of the girls you sent are the Opal he's protecting. She might be from another high school. Probably one close by because she's been to Franklin a lot."

"I'm checking the yearbooks now," he said. "It would help if we had an image I could compare with. I should have asked the mother for the kid's phone."

Belatedly, I thought about Tawnia. I'd asked her to make a composite sketch before. "I can have a sketch made," I said. "Might be a while, though. I thought Opal would be at the school, maybe even working there with Pax. Did you ask about that?"

"The principal gave me the names of the kids who work with Pax. There's no Opal. But I guess they might know her."

"Okay, well, keep working on it. Or I can go to Pax's house later." I started my engine.

"Wait, that's not why I called. I just got off a video chat with Peter Griffin's partner. I had to track him down at his home since they're closed today because of Peter's death. He's hiring us."

"What?"

Elliot chuckled, and I could imagine his satisfied smirk. "That's right. It's only contingent on if Peter Griffin's death was a murder and if we either clear Futura's employees or discover that someone there is responsible and why. I told him about our suspicions. The company has everything staked on their product release in two months, and he's jumpy. You have a meeting with him tomorrow morning at nine-thirty. I hope you can get away from your store then."

"How did you manage all that?"

"Well, I knew you wouldn't take money from your friend, but if we don't recoup losses, neither of us will be able to give one hundred percent. So I found someone this case means a lot to, someone who is willing to pay. This way you can call in extra help for your store, and I can pay my rent. We might be able to approach the family too, with the same kind of deal. I think they'll want the truth."

"Unless they're behind it. They have a two-million-dollar life insurance policy on Griffin. Anyway, I'd rather not work for the family." I stared at the traffic going by, not really seeing it, but instead hearing again Niklas Griffin's whisper in his mother's ear: *"He'll never hurt any of us again."*

"Does the insurance policy have a suicide clause?" Elliot asked. "Peter Griffin also had access to his own drugs, so we still have to eliminate the possibility that he hurt himself. Wanting to die could explain why Peter didn't call for a nurse, and why the call remote was on the floor. Maybe he was afraid he'd change his mind at the end."

"I don't really believe he killed himself," I said. "Peter Griffin just bought tickets for a trip to Venice with his wife. That doesn't sound like a suicide. But I'll let you know what I find out at the Griffin place. Keep digging. On both cases."

"Speaking of that, there's one more little-known fact I discovered about Peter Griffin and Futura. This isn't his first business. Some years ago, he had another start-up called Armed that failed utterly. They were trying to develop a smart watch to replace cell phones. The watch was supposed to project a holograph image over a person's arm. Supposedly, they could scroll through it, click, and otherwise use like a phone. They collected over five million dollars for development but were never able to get beyond the initial stages. The company went bankrupt. I think a lot of media effort has gone into making sure the two products and companies are not connected. My programs searched twenty pages in the search engine to find even a whiff of it."

"So what you're saying is that Griffin might have even more enemies besides those in his family or current workplace."

"That's exactly what I'm saying. Peter Griffin's death might not be related to a current problem, but to pay him back for losing someone's money. And someone like that might have had the foresight and means to plant evidence pointing to your doctor friend."

I sighed. "Then we better find out whoever did this before anyone else gets hurt."

Chapter 5

The Griffins lived on Riverside Drive, about twenty minutes south of my shop and on the west side of the Willamette River. It had been nearly two years since the Hawthorn Bridge bombing and Winter's resulting death, and I thought about him as I crossed the river. He'd be happy that I'd found Tawnia and let Shannon into my life, but getting married without him was something I never imagined I'd have to do. He'd been a constant in my life, especially after losing Summer to breast cancer when I was eleven. Now I'd stand with Shannon in the same meadow where they had pledged their lives to one another, a pledge Winter had remained faithful to until the day he'd died.

I thought I could do the same with Shannon. After all, we already knew how to fight and makeup, and making up was everything. But Winter wouldn't be there to give me away—or to give his blessing, rather, because if he were here, he'd probably tell me that only I could give myself away. And he'd be right.

I'd reached Riverside Drive, and the houses—few and far between now—were nestled between full-sized white oaks, bigleaf maples, and red cedars. I doubted any of them were worth less than a million dollars.

When I reached the Griffin address, Shannon and Quincy were in separate cars parked near a wall of trees that covered my view of the house. I pulled up behind Shannon, catching only a glimpse of gabled roofs and brown brick as I hurried to meet him.

"Glad you made it." Shannon smiled and slipped an arm briefly around my waist as he leaned over for a kiss.

"You mean that I didn't get lost."

Shannon's grin didn't falter. "That too. What took you so long?"

"I was talking to Elliot."

Parked ahead of Shannon, Quincy slammed his car door and came to meet us. I waited until he was within hearing range to say, "I sent you both the information Elliot found on Griffin's company, but he just found something else that we might need to look into. Apparently, Futura is Griffin's second attempt at a start-up. The first one failed miserably and lost at least five million investment dollars."

"If he can get investor or employee information," Quincy said, "I'll compare it with the security sign-ins at the hospital. Someone might not be happy about losing their savings."

Shannon motioned us toward the entrance of the Griffins' drive, and we moved in that direction. "If this was a planned murder, I doubt they'd check in," he said. "Or at least not to see Griffin. We'll need to watch the security footage."

Quincy gave a small groan. "Right. That'll take time. Griffin was there all Saturday and Sunday. I'll send you both a link to the footage, but keep in mind that we'll have to identify at least some of the possible suspects first, or it'll be a waste of time going through it. The good news is that there is only one public way to that floor, so we'll be able to see everyone. And Paige is chomping at the bit to help, so we can always have her go over the footage while she's on leave."

The house came in sight as we entered the drive. After my glimpses of the other nearby mansions, this one was a bit of a disappointment. It was big, all right, but rather plain, and the white rain gutters and white decorative strips across the window clashed with the dark brown of the house. The yard was short, and if they had their windows open at night, I bet they could hear passing traffic. There were no flowerbeds except one between the walk that angled from the drive to the front door, and this was entirely filled with a red flower I didn't recognize. The porch was wide enough to accommodate a double-door entry, but it too was plain brown. The house had no personality, and I wondered if that reflected Brigit's or Peter's choice.

I slipped my antique rings into my pocket before checking the doorknob, but there were no important imprints. Quincy rang the bell, which chimed a little presumptuously. After a short delay, a tall, lean man with short brown hair and a five o'clock shadow opened the door. His green eyes in his narrow face were sad. I guessed he wasn't quite thirty, but his expression added years to his face.

"You the detectives?" he asked. The sound of a piano came from the background, and I recognized the tune of "Twinkle, Twinkle, Little Star."

"We are." Quincy showed his badge. "You must be Stevan Griffin. I'm Detective Quincy Duncan. We talked on the phone." Stevan was the Griffins' younger son, and the fact sheet Shannon sent said he was twenty-eight, so I hadn't been that far off in my estimation.

"Yes. Come on in. My mother's expecting you."

Stevan gestured us into a wide, stone-floored entryway, where a huge staircase led upstairs. An enormous crystal chandelier filled the vaulted entry, burning brightly even though a large window above us let in plenty of light. He angled to the left, going into a majestic sitting room, and we followed.

The room was beautiful, up-to-date, and had a definite personality. Off-white and teal furniture, leather, velour, elaborately-carved wood, and gilt picture frames were the order of the day. The high-pile beige carpet was so soft and plush that my bare feet sank into it, my long dress brushing the fibers and hiding my feet altogether. A woman I barely recognized from her picture as Brigit Griffin sat in the middle of an off-white leather couch, holding a little girl who was not much older than Destiny. Another little girl was at the white baby grand piano with a brown-haired woman. The child was plunking out hesitant notes on the piano, following the guidance of the woman.

They all looked up as we entered, and the piano squawked a discordant note as the child turned toward us.

"They're here," Stevan said unnecessarily.

The woman at the piano moved quickly to the couch and took the child from Brigit. "I'll give the girls a snack and put them down for a nap upstairs," she told Stevan. "Call me if you need me." With a sympathetic smile, she took the hand of the other child, who had stood from the piano, and led her from the room.

"My wife and daughters," Stevan said.

Brigit delicately patted fingertips under her eyes. "They're a comfort," she whispered, her voice barely registering. "I wish

Peter had spent more time with them instead of waiting for them to grow up." Her eyes—green eyes like her son, I saw now—met Stevan's. "You have to remember that."

He sat down next to her and took her hand. "I will, Mom. But now these officers are here to talk to you."

Her eyes wandered over Shannon and Quincy, who were dressed similarly in single-color button-down shirts—blue and white respectively—and dark dress pants. They both looked like cops, especially with their shoulder holsters and weapons.

Her gaze landed on me—and changed. "You're not a police officer, are you?"

Apparently, I didn't fit her idea of a cop in my summer dress, though I too wore a Glock 26 in an ankle holster she couldn't see. "I'm a police consultant," I said.

"She's here only to observe," Quincy added without his usual flirtatious grin.

Shannon's lips quirked, and I stifled a laugh. If Quincy thought I was going to keep silent, he was in for a surprise.

"Please, if you'll have a seat." Brigit gestured vaguely with a slender arm.

Quincy settled in an armchair while Shannon and I took the loveseat opposite the couch.

"We're very sorry for your loss," Quincy said.

I bristled internally. Hearing the phrase come from Quincy's mouth reminded me of all the well-meaning people who'd said the rote—and therefore meaningless—words to me when Winter had died. "Sorry," yes, that was good, but not the rest strung together like that. *Sorry for your loss* . . . those words did nothing to describe the horrible pain I'd suffered or the emptiness of no longer feeling Winter's connection. They had been like a sword plunged into my heart. Tears threatened, but I steadied myself by fingering my antique rings in my pocket, letting the positive imprints calm me.

Brigit's jaw worked, and a tear slid from the corner of one eye. She didn't appear to be wearing makeup, which explained the difference from the photo I'd seen, but even without the color, she was a refined and beautiful, if sad, woman. "Thank you," she said finally, inclining her head.

"I've been investigating records at the hospital," Quincy went on, "and as a part of that, we need to see your husband's medicine."

I sat up straight. "We'd also like to look at the items you brought home from the hospital," I added quickly. If someone else had visited him with malevolent intentions, Peter's belongings might hold telling imprints.

Ignoring me, Brigit stared at Quincy. "His medicine? But why?"

"Your husband had a high level of nitroglycerin in his system, and we want to rule out where the medicine might have come from. As yet, the hospital hasn't been able to find any reason or way Peter could have received the nitroglycerin there. Each dose of medicine is recorded as it's given, and the earlier blood tests showed he was at a healthy level."

Brigit's tears began to fall more rapidly. "What are you saying?"

In the instant of her distress, a coldness blew into the room. It was so intense that I expected the curtains to flutter. But they remained motionless. Still, it felt as if something—or someone else—was there in the room. I wanted to think such a thing was impossible, but I already believed the impossible. Could this be a new aspect of my ability? It had taken me thirty-two years to start reading imprints; maybe using my ability was causing it to evolve. But what exactly did it mean?

"We're just investigating," Quincy assured her. "We have to check everything."

"No. You think it was suicide!" she said, her cheeks flushing. "Well, I'll tell you something. Peter would never have done that. He loved himself far too much."

"Mom." Stevan put his arm around his mother. "They're just doing their jobs. Go get the pills, okay?"

"Okay. I'll show them." She hurried from the room, and I heard her going up the main staircase.

I was immediately interested. People usually felt strongly about their medicines, and I expected to find good imprints when she returned with the bottle.

The cold seeped away, either dispersing or leaving with Brigit. But unless I followed her, I couldn't say which.

"You knew about your father's heart medicine?" Shannon asked Stevan when he reseated himself on the couch.

"Yeah. He started taking it about three years ago. As far as I know, it helped his pain."

"Did everyone in the family know about it?" Quincy asked.

"I don't think my older brother did. He and my father haven't been on good terms, at least until lately." Stevan's lips pursed momentarily. "I don't think he would have told Niklas. My father doesn't—didn't—like to feel weak."

I stood up and approached the gas fireplace between the loveseat and the chair. A large painting of the Griffins when their boys were teens hung on the wall above the elaborately carved white mantle. The picture was too far away to touch without being obvious, so I moved to one of the decorative bookcases on either side and touched the edge of a gilt-framed picture of the boys. A feeling of pride, and that was all.

"Is there anyone you know who might want to hurt your father?" Shannon said.

Stevan was silent for a few moments, and I glanced over my shoulder to see him sitting on the couch with his forearms resting on his thighs, his eyes locked on hands that were clasped in the space between his knees. I took the opportunity to touch a few more items, but the only recent imprints seemed to be from a cleaning lady.

"No," Stevan said finally, looking up at Shannon. "I don't think so. I mean, sure, his competitors didn't wish him well, but they didn't know he was in the hospital, much less that he was taking heart medicine."

"What about at work?" Quincy asked. "I understand that you work at Futura with him. In what capacity?"

"I'm basically over marketing, but I'm also my father's right-hand man. I take care of anything he needs me to do, from hand-holding investors to figuring out what the hold-up is on materials. He's a genius with business." He stopped talking. "Was, I mean. I still can't believe he's gone."

"And everyone at work liked him?" Quincy asked.

"Not just like," Stevan said. "Everyone there worships him. He's the reason our product is going to be a success. He found the investors, he has the tech connection, and he's the face of the company."

"But not the creator of the smart glasses themselves?" Shannon asked.

Stevan sat back and folded his arms. "No. His partner, Titus Grey, is the tech genius behind Futura, but he'd still be in his garage if not for my dad. There was no trouble between them. In fact, Titus is devastated. We all are." Tears gathered in his eyes. "I don't know how we're going to do this without him, but we will. For him, for everyone at Futura."

"How much is Futura worth?" Quincy asked.

"The company?" Stevan shook his head. "Right now, we're up to our ears in debt, but we've already got enough preorders to cancel all of that. There's nothing out there like our glasses, and even conservatively, we're looking at billions of dollars of potential profit, with nowhere to go but up."

"Aren't there a lot of smart glasses out there?" I asked. "Or couldn't someone copy yours?"

Stevan frowned and shook his head. "Not without our files. And if there was anything available that even approached our product, we would have heard something about it by now. But if someone did come up with something that could compete, it might start a price war, which could hurt us in the end."

I arched a brow. "Also to the tune of billions?"

"Only if they could undersell us, and I don't see how they could do that. They'd have been forced to invest hundreds of millions of dollars in research and development, just like we have."

Hundreds of millions, I thought. *Not just a measly five million.*

"And your father's share of the business goes to who?" Shannon asked.

"My mother, I believe," Stevan said. "It all goes to her. He did say something about changing his will, but it was probably just talk. She's stayed by him all this time, supporting him even though he's put her through a lot with the ups and downs of his businesses."

Shannon exchanged a glance with Quincy. One of them better ask it, or I would. Neither spoke, so I said, "What about your father's previous business? What about Armed?"

Stevan blinked at me, and I had the feeling he didn't want to respond. "What about it? That was years ago."

"Why did it fail?" Shannon asked.

Stevan stood and took a few steps toward the baby grand. "The tech wasn't solid. My father was taken in by a dream that is impossible with our current level of technology. It's not even within reach. As I said, he's not a tech guy. When he realized it wasn't going to work, he tried to hire other people who could make it work, but finally, he had to cut his losses."

"Five million is a lot to lose."

Stevan scowled, and for the first time I saw a resemblance to his charismatic father. "That was only investor money. He lost a million of his personal funds as well. It wasn't a good time for him, but he did what he could." He hesitated before saying, "But look, that's old news, and it has nothing to do with Futura. We've worked hard not to have the two products connected. We're two months away from launch, and our smart glasses are going to outpace anything that's on the market now or what's currently in development. If there's any bad publicity . . ."

"We don't plan to bring it up," I said, when neither of the detectives stepped in. "But could anyone from that old company still have a grudge against your father?"

"No," he said. "Everyone understood the risk. Most of the investors were either very wealthy and didn't miss the funds, or they were small online investors who didn't lose much more than the promised prototype. There were a few who'd invested more, a couple of them who worked for the company. My dad paid them back."

"He paid them all back?" Doubt dripped from Quincy's words.

"Or otherwise made it right," Stevan insisted. "But only those few who really needed it."

"Who needed what?" Brigit was back, sweeping into the living room with a grace that made her seem more as if she were wearing a ballgown than a gray lounge suit. The coldness didn't return with her, and already I was wondering if maybe their air-conditioning had malfunctioned.

"Nothing important." Stevan strode to her side, holding out his hand. "Were they hard to find?"

"No, I just cleaned up a bit." And she had. She wore makeup now, subtly applied. She held out a hand with a prescription bottle on it. "But you're wrong if you think Peter took the pills himself or that we took them to him. They're all there. It's recently filled, and there's only one missing for every day, except when he was in the hospital. I counted them."

Shannon stood and let her drop the bottle into an evidence bag. "Thank you. As I said, we're covering all the bases. We'll get them back to you after they go to the lab."

"I don't want them back," she said, sinking to the couch. "I never want to see them again."

Quincy began asking her the same questions they'd put to Stevan, with no new answers except to the will.

"I get the house," she said, "our savings, and his life insurance. He made sure he had good life insurance so I would always be taken care of."

"Is there a suicide clause?" Quincy asked.

For a moment, her jaw clenched and her nostrils flared. "Yes, there is. But only in the first two years. The policy is three years old."

"What about the business?" Shannon asked.

"His shares go equally to me and Stevan, but Stevan retains the voting rights for both. Peter had a will to that effect drawn up three years ago when he realized Futura was not only viable but destined to be enormously successful. That was the same time he took out the life insurance."

Stevan gasped and stared at his mother. "What?"

She nodded. "He was so proud of you. He was hoping to give the other half to Niklas eventually, instead of me, but he didn't yet." She shrugged. "You know how things have been between them."

"I can't believe . . . I never expected . . ." Stevan murmured.

No one spoke for a long moment, so I filled the gap. "You said before that Peter loved himself too much to have committed suicide," I said to Brigit. "What does that mean?"

Brigit's gaze shifted to me where I still stood by the bookcase. "Just what I said. Peter loved himself, he loved working, and he loved his family. He would never choose to kill himself, and certainly not on the verge of Futura's launch."

It was a good save, but usually saying that someone loved themselves wasn't exactly a compliment. "I see," I said. "May I use your bathroom?"

She blinked at the request. "Uh, well, yes, of course. It's out there, to your left, then take a right. If you end up in the kitchen, you've gone too far."

In my line of business—the imprint business, not the antiques business—I often asked to use the bathroom in an attempt to find good imprints. So far, I'd come up empty in this room, and that meant I had to go elsewhere to find what I needed. I leveled a stare at Shannon, hoping he'd get the hint to keep Stevan and his mother here while I did a little investigating on my own. I'd miss the rest of the interview, but Shannon would fill me in if they found out anything more important, and I'd already learned that sometimes what you can't see meant so much more than what came out of people's mouths. Of course, somewhere in the house, likely upstairs by now, was a woman with two young children that I'd also have to avoid.

I checked the paintings in the entry on the way to the bathroom. Nothing except faint imprints that were months old. Likewise in the bathroom. The kitchen and dining room held more imprints, details of daily life and some disagreements, but I learned nothing new about the family. I could tell two people lived here, but one—Peter—was rarely home, and Brigit, who didn't have an outside job, didn't leave nearly as many imprints around as I'd expect. The cleaning lady, who apparently came every day, Monday through Friday for two hours, to clean and make dinner, left more imprints than anyone, and those were all about her family or her annoyance that the Griffins didn't seem to know how to unload the dishwasher.

In the family room adjoining the large kitchen, I learned the Griffins had moved to the house five years ago, and that it had been new then, and not Brigit's choice. She'd resented the money Peter had lost on the first business that had forced them to downgrade.

Downgrade? Three apartments the size of mine could fit in their main floor alone.

Stevan and his wife were regular visitors, especially on Sundays, the day Brigit made dinner for the family. Niklas came less often, and on those days, Brigit worried about a confrontation with his father.

Opposite the kitchen and family room was a large sewing

room. Everything there was immaculate and in place, except right around the machine where pieces of a princess costume sat awaiting construction. I touched the machine.

I was pleased with the way the baby's costume had turned out. This one would be even better.

The sewing room was Brigit's real domain—I recognized that at once. She had drawers full of various materials and patterns, and closets of custom clothing, mostly children's, but also a woman's half-finished sequined gown. Brigit loved sewing, craved the satisfaction of making something that was unique in all the world. But even her satisfaction was muted, as if she constantly worked at keeping her feelings to a manageable size.

It was in a drawer next to the sewing machine that I found my first real piece of information. A prescription bottle of five milligrams of Valium for Brigit Griffin to be taken up to every four hours as needed.

Valium. That explained why Brigit's emotions felt only half involved in the imprints here. I touched the bottle gingerly with the knuckle of my forefinger. Immediately, I was gripped by an imprint from a month earlier.

I took a deep breath, staring at the bottle in my hand, wishing I didn't need its contents. Longing filled me. So much longing, but the loneliness was far worse. He didn't want to be with me, that was clear. He didn't care to make room in his schedule. He never touched me anymore. Never kissed me unless I initiated it, and then his response was only perfunctory.

Could he be having an affair? I almost wished he were because then it would be an answer. But I knew that wasn't true. He couldn't perform any more in the bedroom, and an affair wouldn't fix that. He had refused to go to the doctor for help and chose instead to avoid anything that would lead to intimacy and failure.

Which left me alone. No caresses, no stroking my hair. No cuddling at night in the darkness. Together, but not together. Like a roommate he was fond of, and maybe proud of, but didn't really love. Not as much as he loved himself. Not as much as he loved work, or even Stevan.

But I had to be strong. Somehow, I would find joy in my life, even if it was separate from his.

That meant I couldn't let myself cry when he didn't come home for dinner again. So what if he cared more about his job or the gym or sleep than he did about me? I had my life and the boys. Maybe I'd go back to school. Maybe I'd even find love again.

Still . . . I remembered—like a cancer that ate at my resolve— the old days when he couldn't wait to be with me. Me and only me. When his eyes lit up every time I entered a room. When I couldn't pass by without him reaching for me, if only to give me a little kiss. Or those passionate nights when he couldn't wait to unzip my dress and fall with me to our bed. I'd lost all that to the crafty mistress called work and ambition.

No. I had to be strong. I would stand tall. I'd love me first. I'd find a way to stop the yearning, to stop needing him as he no longer needed me. Until then, I'd silence the anxiety of knowing what I'd lost. The doctor's little yellow pills would help.

It was all I could do to pull away from the bottle. Tears were coming fast, and I wiped them away. I'd felt a similar loneliness after my father's death, but I'd had Jake by my side, and Tawnia had appeared in my life soon after. Brigit's loneliness was different. It was hopeless and unending. While Peter Griffin had built his business, he'd somehow lost touch with his wife, who loved and needed him more than she ever had.

Could he have realized what he'd done? Maybe that's why he'd bought the tickets to Venice.

I felt like a voyeur into their lives, a spying witness to a problem they hadn't been able to repair and now would never have the chance. Yet even as I experienced Brigit's loneliness and mourned with her, I wondered if there was more to the situation. While reading imprints, I saw only the viewpoint of the imprinter, which meant her feelings and her interpretation of what happened. There could be more she didn't understand or wasn't willing to consider.

I also had to wonder if she'd found a solution. Maybe she'd followed through on her promise to love herself. She might have found someone else. If so, maybe she knew more about her husband's death than her imprints implied.

I emerged from the sewing room, debating on whether I'd been gone too long already to check upstairs when low, tense voices came from the family room and kitchen area, as if the participants were furious but trying not to let their voices carry.

I glided to the family room entry and peeked cautiously inside.

Chapter 6

Stevan Griffin was standing where the carpet of the family room met with the rock floor of the kitchen. With him was a man who looked so much like him, he had to be Niklas Griffin, despite being two inches shorter than his younger brother.

Niklas was the better looking of the two men, though, or he worked harder at it. His arm muscles bulged like a weightlifter's, and the deep V on his T-shirt showed that his chest had been waxed or lasered clean of hair. Light blond streaks wove generously through his brown hair, and an earring gleamed in each ear. I pulled back before either of them noticed me.

"You shouldn't have hired an attorney without discussing it with mother and me," Stevan said, his voice hard and sharp. "You had no right."

"I have every right," Niklas answered in a tone that was equally unbending. "He was my father too, and that hospital is responsible. They killed him, and they'll pay."

"It'll drag on for months, and Mom will have to relive this day over and over. We all will. Is that what you want?"

"I'll keep her out of it."

"Right. That attorney will milk her tears for all he's worth. And the publicity might hurt the launch. Did you ever think of that? Dad's worked five years on Futura. Everything he owns is wrapped up in the company. We can't get sucked into a lawsuit."

"Don't worry about your precious company. I'm not asking for money. The attorney is taking the case on speculation, which means he only gets paid if we do."

"If *you* do, you mean."

"So?" Niklas sneered. "You get his company. I deserve something."

"For doing what? Drinking away the money Mom gives you? For refusing every chance Dad gave you to make something of yourself?"

"Oh, we're back to that, I see. Good old Saint Stevan, the righteous son."

"I had to be!" Stevan's voice held vengeance now. "Because you broke his heart. You broke both their hearts." There was more under the surface in the accusation, hints that maybe Stevan's heart had also been broken by his big brother.

"Oh, no. It's not all on me. And I'm not the reason Mom's sad. That's because Dad abandoned her emotionally, just like he did me. And don't think he wouldn't have left you too if you hadn't done everything he asked."

"You got it all wrong." The anger in Stevan's voice abruptly died. "He was building it for us. For our family. He loves us. Things were going to be different after the launch."

I expected Niklas to scoff at that, but he didn't speak right away. He stared at his hands, his jaw clenched. "He asked me to join the company."

"I know. I told him he was wasting his time," Stevan said bitterly. "You shot him down again, didn't you?"

"Actually, I told him I'd give it a try."

"A try." Stevan snorted. "Of course. You expected him to kill the fatted calf for the return of the prodigal son. At least long enough to get a few hefty paychecks."

"You're wrong. It wasn't like that. He convinced me the company has a good future. I wanted to be a part of it."

I didn't know Niklas well enough to know if he was serious, and maybe his brother didn't either, because when Stevan spoke again, it wasn't about work.

"Please drop the suit," Stevan said. "Mom's suffered enough. Let the police find the cause before you start going around with dollar signs in your eyes."

"No. I finally had a chance for a relationship with my father, and I want whoever took that away to pay."

"Do what you must, then. But don't come to Futura. I'm running the company now, and we're not hiring alcoholics."

"Why you . . ."

Steps coming down the hall from the main entry propelled me into the family room. Better to interrupt their fight than be caught eavesdropping at the door. Both men looked up, staring at me.

"Sorry," I said. "I think I got turned around. I was using the bathroom. This is a really big house."

Stevan's laugh sounded forced. "I'll take you back to the others."

"Thank you." I moved toward them as Stevan's wife entered the kitchen from the other doorway.

The woman reached his side and put her arm around him, a question in her eyes. He gave a slight shake of his head.

Keeping hold of her husband, she gave her brother-in-law an unfriendly stare. "Niklas," she said.

His response was equally curt. "Carmen."

"So this is your brother," I said to Stevan.

They all turned to me, as if surprised that I was still there. "Yes," Niklas answered. "Guilty as charged. And who are you?"

"Autumn Rain." I extended a hand.

"She's a consultant with the police," Stevan said.

Niklas's touch was warm and strong. The edge of my finger touched his ring, sweeping me away from time and place.

"I think you'll like it at Futura," my father said, using the buttons on the side of the hospital bed to adjust the angle. "We'll get you started next week. Welcome aboard, son."

"What about Stevan?"

"He'll be fine. But don't come in until mid-week when I'm back. There are a few things I have to take care of first."

"Okay." Maybe this time it would work. Maybe I could finally make the old man proud of me. I just had to make sure Arthur kept his mouth shut about—

Niklas released me, and it was all I could do not to grab his hand back to see the rest. The imprint had been from late Sunday morning, and Peter Griffin had died before Niklas had a chance to prove anything to his father.

"Should we join the others?" Stevan said.

I nodded. "I'm sure the detectives will want to interview Niklas."

We followed Stevan back to the living room, where Shannon gave me an uneasy look as we entered. He was likely waiting for someone to say they'd caught me snooping.

"Detective, I'd like to introduce my brother, Niklas," Stevan said as I slipped over to Shannon. "My older and much more fashionable brother." Stevan gave us a smile that didn't reflect in his eyes. "You might be interested to know that he's hired a wrongful death attorney, who I'm sure will be contacting you for information."

"Niklas?" Brigit gasped. "Is that true?"

Niklas sat next to his mother and put his arm around her. "Yes, Mom. We need to know the truth. And having an attorney on our side will get us to it faster. He's already pressing for the autopsy results."

"Your father's dead," she said dully. "Nothing you do will change that." She stood in an awkward motion. "Please excuse me. If you have more questions, they'll have to wait for another day. I need to take some medicine and lie down. Stevan will see you out."

Without waiting for a response, she swept from the room.

"Well, we have a few questions for Niklas," Quincy said. To Stevan, he added. "And if you could get the bag of things you brought from the hospital, we'll need to take that into evidence. We'll get it back to you as soon as possible."

"That's cold," Quincy said sometime later when we were back outside near our three cars, having learned little more from Niklas. "Hiring an attorney before your dad's autopsy is finished."

"I think a deeper peek into Niklas Griffin's finances might be in order," Shannon agreed.

"Or his reaction might be a natural result of a suspicious death," I said. "Because Peter Griffin shouldn't have died. What worries me more is why Stevan and Mrs. Griffin seemed opposed to it."

Shannon arched a brow. "What did you find out?"

I told them about Brigit's pills, the brothers' argument, Niklas's pending job with Futura, and the glimpse from his ring.

"To tell the truth, any one of them could have done it," I said. "Brigit could have gotten tired of waiting for him to notice her. Niklas is obviously money-hungry, so maybe he saw a malpractice suit as preferable to punching a time clock. And Stevan is harboring a lot of hurt and anger toward his brother—and maybe his father as well."

"If Peter Griffin was going to let Niklas into the company, he might have been only a step away from changing his will." Shannon rubbed his chin in thought. "Depending on the ways the shares would have gone, either Stevan or Brigit might not have liked that idea."

"He still could have killed himself, too," Quincy added. "If maybe the business isn't all that it's supposed to be."

"Since Peter bought tickets to Venice last week, and all his medicine seems to be accounted for, I'm betting he didn't kill himself," I said.

"Probably not," Shannon agreed. "But we need to visit Futura and get an idea of what's happening there."

Quincy checked his watch. "I have time now."

Shannon nodded. "I can go too, if we hurry."

I raised a hand. "Count me out, boys. I have it on good authority that they're closed today because of Peter Griffin's death. Plus, I already have an appointment with them in the morning at nine-thirty, to which neither of you are invited."

"You do?" Shannon's eyes shot daggers at me.

"Apparently, he's hired Elliot and me to make sure no one at Futura is responsible," I explained, "and that the company doesn't get mixed up in anything that's going to hurt their launch."

Quincy gave a guttural laugh. "As if that doesn't sound suspicious."

"I don't know," Shannon said. "Billions of dollars is enough to make anyone paranoid."

"Whatever is going on," I said, "Elliot and I can't take police detectives to the meeting, but of course I'll share everything we learn. As long as you two do the same. And, yes, I'll be careful." This last part was for Shannon, who would be worrying about dangerous imprints, even with Elliot watching my back.

"Text us when you're finished then," Shannon said, making the wise decision to let me do my thing.

"In the meantime, I'd like to see what imprints are on Peter Griffin's belongings." I pointed first to the transparent sack in Quincy's hands and then to the black duffel Stevan had placed in Shannon's care. "Because even if this stuff contains evidence, your chief won't give you permission to have it examined until the autopsy comes in."

"Right." Quincy motioned us over to his car, where he opened the trunk. With a glance in the direction of the trees that hid the house, he opened the transparent bag and dumped out the contents.

I held my hands over the mixture of cards, hygiene supplies, and the clothes Griffin had worn when he checked in at the hospital. Nothing radiated from the clothing, but there were faint tingles from a tiny bottle of lotion. I touched it with a knuckle to find a hint of frustration. There were only three cards, and all of them tingled a bit.

"Give me a pair of your plastic gloves," I said to Quincy, who tossed them to me.

I opened each of the cards, finding a serious one from Stevan Griffin, an off-colored one from Niklas Griffin, and a humorous one from someone named Robby. I touched each card to a bare spot on my wrist. Faint worry emitted from Stevan's card, annoyance was imprinted on Niklas's, along with a glimpse of a hospital gift shop. Agitation was strong on the final card, but there were no accompanying images.

"This Robby may be the same Robby whose imprint I found on the hospital chair," I said. "The guy who had something to hide. But he didn't leave anything obvious on this. Only agitation."

Shannon removed the prescription bottle of nitroglycerin from his pocket, still in the evidence bag. He worked it out far enough to touch on my wrist.

I stared at the bottle in my hand. The pills were like a noose around my neck, reminding me of my mortality and all I hadn't accomplished. Now that the launch was close, I'd expected to feel I'd finally achieved something—and I did to some extent. But seeing the indifference growing in my wife's expression and the way Stevan swallowed any objection before it could escape his throat, maybe Futura's success didn't make up for my other failures. Especially where Niklas was concerned. I needed to change that. I'd blown him off yesterday, but maybe it was time to try again.

The imprint had taken place two weeks earlier on a Saturday. The imprints that followed were similar to the first without the reference to Niklas or Peter's family. Mostly, it was Peter's dissatisfaction with his dependence on the medication. It was sad, and I didn't feel the need to explain the very private emotions to Shannon or Quincy.

"Two weeks ago, he blew Niklas off about something. I

think Niklas went to see him at work. Peter planned to reach out again."

"Maybe that's when he offered Niklas the job," Shannon said, unzipping the duffle he balanced on the bumper between the car and his legs. "Guess this is all we have left."

I pulled out the items one by one and placed them in the trunk. Then I removed one plastic glove and tested them. I found no imprints on the clothing, but there were plenty on the iPad. Glimpses of conversations, business dealings, and more, but nothing seemed related. I watched the past unroll to a year before I gave up and moved to the phone. An imprint from the previous day swept me away instantly.

A nurse came inside the room, probably with my next meds, but I pointed to the phone and held up a finger. She nodded and retreated. I couldn't wait to get out of here. The way she moved reminded me of Brigit, who I'd finally convinced to go home. She needed to rest.

"Don't worry, Titus," I said into the phone pressed to my ear. "I really am okay." I laughed, and it only slightly hurt my stomach. "But even if I weren't, everything's under control. Production is well ahead of schedule, and the orders are pouring in. I'm sorry the new password caused you concern. I'll stop by on my way home from the hospital tomorrow to help you forward the file."

"I can't help but worry," Titus's voice said in my ear. "It's been a long five years."

"It has at that. But we're almost at the end."

"Well, there's version two . . ."

Good old Titus was always looking for the next improvement. "That can wait. For me too. I'm going to take your advice and go on that trip with Brigit. You ought to find someone and settle down yourself. It's time, old friend."

"I don't think so. I work too hard. No woman wants to share her husband with such a needy mistress."

Titus had that right. I'd learned the hard way. I hoped it wasn't too late.

"About the new password," I said. "I'd like to keep it in place, even after we send the file. Just in case."

"Fine by me. Take care of yourself."

"See you tomorrow."

The scene ended. Like I'd found with the iPad, there were more conversations imprinted on the phone, mostly about business, but they didn't seem related to Peter's death. There was nothing about making an appointment with his son, so maybe that duty had fallen to his secretary, if he had one. Or he'd used another phone.

I shook my head. "Nothing that seems important. Just business stuff."

Quincy began stuffing the items back inside their respective containers. "Well, that's it then. For now."

"Wait, there's no wedding ring," I said. "If he'd been wearing it, that would have been a good thing to read."

"I'll call and ask the wife about it." Quincy slammed his trunk shut.

I looked at Shannon. "I'm going back to my antiques shop. I need to make sure Jazzy comes in to help Thera."

"I thought she was reliable these days."

"She is, but her head is still immersed in online sales. I need to make sure. And there's stuff I need to do." My voice lowered so Quincy couldn't hear. "You see, there's this certain guy I want to marry in three weeks."

Shannon gave a soft chuckle. "Less than that, now. I'll bring dinner to your place tonight. We'll talk budget."

I grinned. "You had me at 'I'll bring dinner.' I'm starving."

"Yeah, I know that look." He smoothed my forehead with a roughened fingertip.

I leaned into him. "Don't get me wrong. A budget is good too, especially if you have secret plans to impress your parents." His parents had retired to run a bed and breakfast in Jacksonville, Florida, and I hadn't met them yet, except once briefly online.

He raised both hands in a protective gesture. "No plans here. Well, not related to impressing anyone but you."

"Good. I'll see you tonight."

I waited until both men drove away before calling Elliot. "Look," I said, settling into my car. "I need you to search for a man named Arthur who's somehow connected to Peter Griffin."

"Arthur what?"

"I don't know."

"The plot thickens," Elliot said. "Maybe this Arthur is a former disgruntled employee or a cohort of the son."

"And did you ever find anything about the guy named Robby? I've been thinking he might work in the accounting department at Futura."

"Nothing on him yet. Why's he so important anyway?"

I gave him a complete rundown of the imprints at the hospital and my visit to the Griffins, only feeling slightly guilty about the nondisclosure document I signed with the Portland Police Bureau. Elliot was my partner for this case, and both Shannon and Quincy had seemed okay with his help.

"I'll check out the wife too," Elliot said when I was finished. "See if she's got someone on the side."

"Anything else your programs discovered?"

"Nothing since we talked before, but I'm nearly done with the list of girls named Opal from the nearby schools. I'll be emailing it as soon as I'm finished."

"What about the boy?"

"His mother still hasn't found Pax. She's worried."

"She have any other kids?"

"Another son. He's twelve or something."

Somehow that relieved me. I didn't want Luna Medina to be sitting home worrying alone. "I'm heading back to my shop. Let me know if you find him. Otherwise, I'll see you tomorrow morning at our meeting with Futura."

"Our meeting?" An odd note crept into his voice. "Uh, no. It's your meeting."

"You're not coming?"

He hesitated a heartbeat before saying, "I'm afraid I've had my people limit for a while."

"People limit? What do you mean by that?"

Only faint breathing told me Elliot was still on the phone. "Since I'm trying to convince you to work with me, it's probably not a good idea to tell you I have an anxiety disorder. But in the interest of full disclosure, I do have one."

"What anxiety disorder?"

"I'm agoraphobic. Don't worry. It's under control. I know my limits, though, and with the school, the Medina's, and talking to Griffin's partner, I've already stretched enough for the next twenty-four hours."

"I see."

I really didn't see anything. I knew he usually met his clients at the same food court in the Lloyd Center near the Subway restaurant where Luna Medina worked, and then did most of his investigations online. But how could a full-time private investigator limit his physical interactions with the outside world because of panic? There would be things he had to check out in person, and he'd have to tail people occasionally. Did that mean his car was a safe place for him? At least his anxiety explained why he'd acted uncomfortable at the school and so abrupt during our interview with Pax.

"You're in the wrong profession, you know?" I said, trying to keep my voice mild.

"Yeah. I know." Elliot's voice was subdued. "But it beats trying to clock in at an office, especially when people are always stopping by with a problem for me to fix."

That, I understood. "Okay, I'll do the meeting. Send me a text or call when you have something else."

"Will do." He hung up.

So it appeared my would-be partner needed someone to conduct in-person interviews every bit as much as he needed a person to read imprints. Well, we all had issues, and Elliot hadn't for a moment teased me about my bare feet or doubted my ability. With that in mind, I wouldn't let his phobia affect my decision whether or not to work with him.

I stopped at Smokey's, my favorite organic restaurant that happened to be located across the street from Autumn's Antiques, and was heading into the store when Elliot's text came in.

I've sent the pictures. If you can identify the girl, I'll work on getting an address.

The text came too late. Inside my store, on an antique bench that I'd refinished, sat Pax and the girl, Opal. They were sitting close together, lips locked, oblivious to the two other customers Thera was helping in the next aisle. If I'd had any doubts about the girl's feelings for him, those were gone now. His certainly were. Between the last imprint I'd read on his arrowhead and this moment, they'd obviously overcome their personal space barrier. Maybe my assurance that Opal cared about him had finally pushed Pax to make a move. I wasn't sure that was a good thing.

They tore their lips from each other long enough for Pax to bounce up from the bench. He stepped in front of Opal, his lean arm out, hand in a stopping motion. "Please don't call my mother," he said. "I just talked to her. She's the one who gave me this address and made me promise to come. We're here to tell you what we know."

Opal stood beside him, clutching his arm. Her blue eyes were wide and frightened. "But you can't tell my parents. They'll *kill* me."

I weighed the information they might have against the liability of keeping a secret from her parents. I'd never kept anything from Winter or Summer, but they'd had no rules to break, so it hadn't seemed necessary.

"Tell you what," I said. "You explain what you were doing with the paint, and we'll figure out together what to do about Opal's parents. I'm just trying to make sure you don't lose your future. Both of you."

The teens exchanged a glance, and then Opal nodded. "Okay," she said. "We'll tell you everything."

Chapter 7

"I just wanted to fix the pointers," Opal said as she leaned back in the ratty easy chair that was the crowning glory of my back room. She didn't know it yet, but getting out of the chair was always more of a challenge than sinking into its comforting depth.

I sat on top of the worktable with my legs crossed under my colorful skirt. I alternated between shoveling in forkfuls of Smokey's delicious organic potpie and asking questions, while Pax paced like a caged lion.

"Let me get this straight," I said, setting down my fork. "The teen janitors at the elementary school near Opal's house spray-painted crude pointers showing where the sprinkler heads go during watering."

"Right," Pax said. "They manually screw in those big sprinkler heads before turning on the water, and they take them out after so no one gets hurt or damages them. They spray a lot of water really far, and the pointers make it easy to find where to put them in."

"One of the images was a finger flipping the bird!" Opal

exclaimed. "It was terrible. Little kids play there, and there's a park right next to the school, so a lot of other kids are also there every day. And that wasn't the worst picture, either. When I reported it to the head janitor, he just laughed." Her chin lifted. "So I did something about it." She glanced at Pax. "Or we did."

Pax stopped pacing. "Opal went to buy the paint while I cut templates from a cardboard box. One big rectangle opening to blot out the old pointer with black paint, and then a thinner arrow we sprayed white."

"They look amazing," Opal said. "And there's no way those guys will paint them again because they're too lazy to do it on their own time, and the head janitor won't pay them twice." She smiled before trying briefly—and maybe halfheartedly—to rise from my chair.

"How did the paint end up in your car?" I asked Pax.

He shrugged. "Mom and I need paint sometimes. There was enough left that I thought it could come in handy."

"It was my fault," Opal said. "I didn't want my parents to ask questions. My dad does all my car maintenance, and my Mom comes in my room all the time. They'd notice the paint, even if I tossed them in the garbage."

"So that was Thursday night?" I asked, taking another bite.

They both nodded. "We got a lot of paint on us," Pax said. "I thought I got it all off, but there was a spot near my elbow and another under my wrist that I must have missed, even after showering twice. That's what the cops found."

I swallowed my mouthful of food. "The police believe the vandalism could have taken place on Friday night instead of Thursday."

"We were together on Friday night too," Opal said hurriedly. "After Pax got off work, we met at the Lloyd Center to see a movie. We were late getting tickets, so we walked around the mall for a couple hours. It was our first real date." She grinned. "Our only date really. Until today."

"Why don't you tell all that to the police?" I asked. "I'm sure the mall has video. As far as I'm concerned, you did a good deed, and I'm sure they'll think so too. At the very least, you should tell the principal at Franklin."

Opal's shoulders wilted. "Because they'll want to check out the story, and my brother was one of the boys who painted the pointers in the first place. I think it was to get back at my dad for making him work there this summer. My brother told me if I got him into trouble, he'd tell dad about me and Pax."

Ah, now we were getting somewhere. "Your dad doesn't want you two to date?"

Opal shook her head. "My dad's the head of Portland Public School District. That's how Pax and I first met. Dad stopped off at the school to talk to Principal Tillmon one day when he picked me up from dance class, and I heard Pax playing. I went looking for the music, and we sort of hit it off." She shrugged, blushing a little. "Anyway, when my dad saw us later, talking in front of the school, he yelled at me all the way home. He said that he'd moved us to Lincoln so I wouldn't be around boys like Pax, so I'd have better kids to meet and date. He said no way had he made sacrifices so I could attach myself to a janitor."

Her gaze strayed to Pax, softening as he stopped pacing to meet her stare. "I tried to tell my dad that Pax isn't like those boys he was talking about, that he is smart and thoughtful and talented. But he wouldn't listen. If he knew I was still sneaking over here to listen to Pax play, he'd ground me for months and separate us for sure." Opal's gaze shifted to me. "And he'd make sure Pax was fired, or probably worse. He knows everyone in the school district."

"And how does your brother know about you two?" I set down my fork.

Opal sighed, crossing her arms over her chest. "Because we share a car. He's a year younger, so I usually get the car, but there were a few times when he had to use it, and I asked him to drop me off at Franklin High so I could meet Pax. My brother is right to be afraid of my dad finding out about the pointers, but I have every bit as much reason to hide what we did to fix them because I was with Pax when I did it."

It was sad to see her so afraid of her father, because if the pointer incident was any indication, she seemed to have her head on straight. "Look, I don't think you should be sneaking around your dad's back, but my primary concern here is making sure Pax doesn't get charged for the vandalism. That means I will need to tell the principal something."

"Couldn't you find out who really did it?" Pax asked. "Then after I graduate and get a music scholarship, maybe Opal's dad won't mind when he finds out we're together." He said this with a questioning look at Opal, who blushed becomingly.

"Well, it would take suspicion off you if we did find the real culprits," I said. "Do you have any idea who might be involved? What are people saying?"

The teens exchanged a puzzled look. "No one's saying much of anything," Pax said. "I don't think anyone really knows. The coach is out of town, and none of the players have been in. Maybe we're the only ones who know, except the Franklin head janitor and the principal. And maybe the secretary and a few others. But it hasn't been in the papers or on the school website."

Opal frowned. "My dad probably knows. He's been to Franklin a lot in the past few weeks."

"Don't forget the police," I reminded them.

Pax blew out a sigh and finally sank to the hard chair next to my worktable. "I'm going to jail, aren't I?"

"No," I said, my mind mulling over the problem. "I think it being summer and the vandalism not widely known about will actually work to our advantage."

"You mean because if someone does know, it's because they're involved?" Pax's splayed fingers tapped on his thighs as if he were silently playing a piano.

"Something like that." But another idea was occurring to me. "Opal, does anyone else besides you two know that you repainted the pointers?"

She shook her head. "No one except my brother. I didn't tell him we fixed them, but he must have seen us fixing them because that's when he threatened to tell my dad about me and Pax. If anyone else saw us out there, they didn't stop us or say anything."

"That's good to know," I said. "It's interesting that the kids who vandalized the equipment room also chose black and white paint. I wonder why they didn't use other colors." It was almost as though someone wanted to incriminate Pax.

The kids had nothing to say in response to my comment about the colors, so I unfolded my legs and slid off the table. "Look, you two go home and call all your friends, go on social media, or do whatever you do to connect with others. Don't bring up the vandalism or the equipment room. Just listen and see if there are any rumors going around."

"I don't even go to Franklin." With great effort, Opal tried to push herself out of the easy chair. Pax popped to his feet and grabbed her arm to help. "Neither do most of my friends," Opal added.

"No," I said. "But we don't know if the vandals are even from Franklin, and I'm sure your friends will know others from both schools. Now give me your phone numbers, and I'll text you mine so we can stay in touch."

The teens left, holding hands and staring into each other's eyes. They'd probably forgotten me the second they walked out of my back room.

I inhaled more food while I texted Elliot with the details of my conversation with the teens. *Do you have a contact in that precinct?* I wrote. *I'm pretty sure Franklin is in the East Precinct.* Shannon had plenty of contacts there, including Quincy, but they both had their hands full. *We need to know if they found out who bought the paint.*

Already have a call out, he texted back.

I had to admit, it was pretty nice having a partner who wasn't dealing with a half-dozen other cases like Shannon and Paige always were at the Central Precinct.

There was only one more thing I needed to do at the moment and that was to call the principal of Franklin High School. He picked up on the second ring.

"Hi, Mr. Tillmon?" I said. "This is Autumn Rain. I'm the woman working the vandalism case for Luna Medina. We met this morning."

"I know who you are. Any news?"

"Yes. Pax does have a solid alibi for both Thursday and Friday nights, and a very good reason for the paint." I quickly outlined the pointer issue.

"Sounds like something he would do." Baird Tillmon sounded admiring. "I take it he wasn't doing it alone?"

"No. With a girl they believe is going to get into a lot of trouble if her parents find out about their relationship, so he won't give her up."

"But you know who she is."

"Yes, and I talked to her personally. I know you can't go by my word only, but I'm going to find out who's responsible, so hopefully you won't need her corroboration," I told him. "But I'm not working for the Medinas, because Pax isn't guilty. I'm working for you now. Or for the school district, depending on who really did this. Don't worry. My rates are reasonable. But you know Luna Medina's situation, and it's not fair that she has to pay for something her son obviously didn't do, and if the police or anyone had tried to look further than Pax, they would have already made a lot more progress on the case." I let that sink in a few seconds before rushing on. "As a deposit and a measure of good faith, I'm asking you to reinstate Pax immediately at his job. I think you'll agree that's best, because once I do find out who's behind the damage, you're leaving the school open for a wrongful dismissal suit."

Silence on the other end of the phone made me wonder if I'd gone too far. But nothing made me more upset than people in power settling for the first convenient, naïve kid who was willing to take the fall.

"Okay," Tillmon said finally. "I do want to get to the bottom of this. And you're right about Pax. He shouldn't be suffering if there's no proof he did this. I'll give the boy a call now."

"Thank you." My respect for the principal increased, especially when I suspected the police still planned on arresting Pax. "Oh, and I'd like to know who has keys to the equipment room, or access to them."

"Besides me, it's just the assistant principal, the head janitor, and, of course, the coach."

"No students?"

"Not unless someone with a key loaned it to them."

"Or they took it without asking."

He sighed deeply. "Right. Is there anything else I can help with?"

"There is. I'd like you to call a meeting of the football team for tomorrow at one. I need to question them all. You can be present, of course, and their parents, if you want to explain it to them."

"What are you going to say?"

"That depends. I take it you haven't told them what happened in the equipment room?"

"No, but they might have heard."

"Who does know for sure?"

"The janitorial staff is aware that there was damage, but we've asked them not to say anything until we complete the investigation. A few members of the team were interviewed by the police, so they might suspect. Luna Medina was told by the police when her son became a suspect, and her son knows, of course. There might be a few others who know. I was waiting until the coach gets back to make an official announcement to the team."

"What about the media?"

"I haven't alerted them, and I don't intend to. I don't want anyone taking stabs at our students."

"That was a good call, and I'd still rather keep the media out of it. But telling the students where we can watch their reactions could be helpful. Before that, though, I'd like to pull each of the kids off to the side and play a little game I like to call imprints. It may not point to who did it, but it should at least eliminate some of the players."

He sighed. "All right. I can get on board with that. It's going to come out eventually, and we need to get something done before practice starts next month. But I'll have to make a call to the district to clear it."

"Okay. Let me know if they don't approve the meeting. Otherwise, I'll be at Franklin tomorrow at one."

I said goodbye and hung up, aware that the electronic bells above my door were going off like crazy. Either I was having a rush of customers, or thieves were hauling all my antiques away.

With regret, I abandoned the remaining fourth of my potpie and hurried from the back room. In the shop, I found my entry door blocked by two chairs and half a dozen large boxes. Blue-haired Jazzy was pushing her way through the door with another box, a big smile on her face.

"Sorry I'm late," she called. "But look at all this stuff! I finally convinced Claire to let me clean out her attic. The stuff that was from her grandmother. I was at it all day. These are the things I thought you'd be most interested in for the shop, but there might be more if you can go over to the house with me this weekend to look. I probably included a few throwaway items, though. I'm still not quite sure what makes an antique valuable." The teenager shrugged.

Jazzy Storm, aka Jessica Sandstorm, had come a long way since her days on the street. Living with successful attorneys

Claire and Bridger Philpot had done wonders for the former runaway.

I stared at the chairs, my heart beating hard in my chest. "Um, these are Nineteenth Century Chippendale armchairs." My words felt breathy.

"Chippendale?"

I nodded. And they were worth two thousand each, at least. "Let's put them in the back on the worktable. I need to do a little research to determine their worth before tagging them. Is Claire wanting to put them on consignment?" My normal charge was ten to fifteen percent, depending on the item, and I only did commission on large ticket items that I couldn't afford to buy before I resold them. Of course, it was much better for me to buy something at a steal and sell it on my own because I had a list of people who were always looking for interesting high-ticket items. If I had found the chairs at auction for five hundred, I could sell them for less than their true value while making more profit. But even at ten percent, I'd make a tidy little sum on the chairs once I matched them with the right buyer.

"She said she'd call you, but maybe you can make her an offer for the lot, and you can't do that until you see the rest." Jazzy grinned, obviously pleased with herself. "I did good, didn't I?"

I hugged her. "Yes. You did great. Let's carry it all to the back, and I'll give Claire a call."

Before we'd finished moving the boxes, traffic picked up and there ended up being no time to make the call or give more than a cursory glance into the boxes. Thera, Jazzy, and I spent the next few hours helping customers from my store and from Jake's Herb Shoppe that was also having a good rush of business because of a week-long BOGO—buy-one-get-one free—tea sale he'd advertised. Jake and I had networked computers, and sharing a database and employees helped a lot during both slow and busy times, though Jazzy now worked exclusively for me.

"Jazzy," I said when I finally turned over the closed sign at six, "can you come in tomorrow morning for a few hours? I have an appointment, and Jake needs Thera tomorrow morning for his promotion. She'll check in on you, in case you need help."

Jazzy's eyes, rimmed in thick black mascara, widened. She met me in the middle aisle in front of the counter. "Does this mean you have another case?" When I nodded, she said, "I'll be glad to come in, as long as you promise to tell me everything." But her smile almost faded at once.

"What's wrong?" I asked, glancing at Thera, who was cleaning fingerprints from the music box case on my right. She stopped rubbing to listen. I knew she also felt responsible for the teenager we'd trained together and helped grow from a kid we needed to make sure wasn't stealing me blind to a contributing member of society who was helping more and more each day.

For a while, Jazzy didn't answer, and I began dreading her response. Had her parents returned to the picture, the ones who hadn't bothered reporting that she'd run away?

"It's school," she said, her bottom lip protruding.

"What about it?" I knew she was doing online classes to catch up and had been since January, a month after I'd found her.

"I'm almost caught up, and Claire says I have to go to high school next month. Tenth grade."

"But that's wonderful!" I hugged her. "That's always been the goal, right? You've been working hard to make it happen, even though it's been boring and isolating doing school online." She'd complained enough that everyone knew how much she wanted to return to normal school.

"I know, but . . ." She sagged in my embrace. "But I won't be able to come in here whenever you need me, and I'll have to cut back on the online sales. And I love making all those commissions."

I laughed. "I'll schedule you after school, and I'm betting you can finish most of your homework in school anyway. There might also be a class or two you can take that will give you credits for work experience. You can use that time to come here or to keep up on the online stuff and still get commissions."

Even with this, her frown didn't go away, and I looked helplessly at Thera, who moved closer. "It's the classes, isn't it?" she said gently. "And the kids?"

A tear dripped from Jazzy's eyes as she nodded. "I feel . . . well, I'm not like all the other sophomores. They don't . . ." She heaved a sigh. "I remember what they're like. They don't know anything. Or at least not about what's really important. They're like little children. They get mad at their parents for not giving them enough money, they worry about designer jeans, or who to go to the dance with. Girls are mean just because they think you looked at them weird or might steal their boyfriends. It's all so stupid. They don't know how life works if you don't have parents standing over you making sure you don't do something dumb that could affect your whole future. They have no idea what's out there. They can't imagine what it's like to live on the street, to eat from a garbage can, or to have people try to sell you to some rich guy in a foreign country." Her shoulders started shaking, and I held her tighter.

"That's all true," I said softly, "and I'm not sure what to

tell you. I'm the last one to say high school is going to be fun. Remember, I was the weird hippie girl who didn't wear shoes or go to school half the time because Winter needed me in the Herb Shoppe. I'm not even sure how I graduated."

Jazzy laughed at that. "I wish you went to my school."

Thera put her hand on Jazzy's thin shoulder, drawing her slightly away from me. "I'm sure there are other options for graduation, but maybe . . . hmm, how do I say this?" She smiled and wiped Jazzy's tear from her cheek. "I know you feel older than the other girls, but maybe it's time you did get to be a child. You've come so far, and we're all so proud of you, but sometimes I feel like you're skipping your childhood altogether."

This truth resonated inside me. We'd all been so busy trying to make Jazzy become responsible, that maybe we'd forgotten how very young she was.

"Thera's right," I said. "It's okay if you worry about your clothes for a change, or about going to a dance. What if you give it a try? Go for a term and see what happens. If you hate it, I'll help you talk to Claire about an alternative. But you know how much you've hated online school. Think about it. It might actually be fun to meet other kids. Maybe even boys."

Jazzy thought about that for a few minutes. "But what about my hair?"

I looked at the flyaway blue locks that went a few inches past her shoulders. "What about it?" Her guardian had nixed the nose ring until her eighteenth birthday but hadn't felt hair color was something she should fight about. Jazzy dyed it herself, so it was a splotchy job that revealed sections of darker hair beneath.

"You think it's okay?" Jazzy asked.

"As long as you're comfortable and the school allows blue hair." I touched the hair on the top of my head. "But if you change your mind, Tawnia has a great hairdresser she's been threatening me with."

Jazzy laughed. "Okay. I'll give school a try. Do you think Tawnia will go school shopping with me? I have a bunch of money saved up."

"Tawnia? Not Claire?" I grinned. "Or me?"

"Claire looks like an attorney, and you . . ." Jazzy squeezed her lips together. "You're a little retro."

"You should get Randa to help you," Thera said.

Jake's younger sister had graduated high school in May and was soon heading to college, and the girls had worked together in the Herb Shoppe up until last month when Jazzy started online sales. She was the perfect choice.

Jazzy seemed to think so too. "I'll ask her. Thank you for the idea." She hugged Thera and me both.

Crisis averted, I collected my things, and the three of us headed to the door together.

"I have one more question," Jazzy said as we stepped out into the still-bright evening light. She held up one finger at someone in a car who was waiting to drive her home. "Now that you're getting married, do I get to be a bridesmaid? I mean, I know you're my employer, and we're not exactly hanging-out buddies, but who else would you have?"

I hadn't even thought about bridesmaids. "I'm not sure yet."

"But you've got to have bridesmaids," Jazzy said. "Your sister should be the maid of honor, of course. And you have to pick a color."

Thera nodded vigorously, her white hair threatening to fall

from its secure bun. "That's right. You should have a few people stand up with you. At least your sister and a best friend. With the wedding less than three weeks away, you need to hurry and ask them so they can get a dress. And I've always thought blue was a nice color for a wedding."

Jazzy squealed excitedly as if her mini-breakdown had never happened. "I think so too. Oh, this is so exciting!"

Jake was my best friend, after Tawnia, but I was pretty sure that wasn't something they'd want to hear. Both of them clearly hoped to be in the wedding party.

"I'll look at my parents' wedding pictures and figure it out," I promised. "I'm trying to recreate their event."

"That's perfect!" Jazzy did a little dance. "And Shannon, if you don't mind me saying so, is hot, hot, hot, despite his dumb girly name. And you'll have all that land at his place for parking a trailer so we can bid on abandoned storage units. I'm so happy for you!"

I was feeling hot, hot, hot myself. Why did planning a wedding seem like a worse idea than flushing out a possible killer?

"We'll talk about this all later," I said, waving at them both.

I hadn't yet reached my car when Shannon called. I thought it would be about dinner, but it wasn't.

"The Griffin attorney has apparently pushed the autopsy through," he said. "Initial results are already back. Autumn, it's worse than we thought. Can you meet me at Matthew's? I'd better tell him and Paige the news before they hear it from someone else."

Chapter 8

Shannon texted me the address to Matthew's high-rise, luxury condo in the Pearl District, which was good, since I'd never been there, although I'd heard about the place from Paige. Matthew had made decent money during his medical residency and cardiology fellowship, and even more money this past year as a full cardiologist, but even knowing that, I hadn't expected the luxury that soon confronted me. The apartment building was only ten minutes from my shop via the Broadway bridge, twenty minutes with traffic, but it was like entering another world.

The lobby interior reminded me of a five-star hotel with far more windows and lights. A security guard greeted me with a smile before calling Matthew's apartment and showing me to the elevator. The marble floor felt marvelously cool on my bare feet.

Upstairs on the fifth floor, someone had left the door to Matthew's apartment slightly ajar, and I let myself into a spacious living room, leaving the door partially open in case Shannon hadn't beaten me here. For the size of the living area, the furniture was sparse: two couches, an enormous flat-screen television, a throw rug on the polished wood floor, and a few end tables. It looked like the typical upscale bachelor pad, though there were two antique paintings I recognized that Paige had bought from my shop. Overshadowing everything, however, was a panoramic view of Portland visible through the floor-to-ceiling windows that ran along one wall and half of another. That view was definitely not standard fare.

I tore my stare from the windows to give Paige a hug. She was back to her normal self, with not a single iron-straight blond hair out of place. Instead of her customary navy work suit, she wore black dress pants and a blue blouse that she could have worn to work as a detective had she been more willing to dress down a bit.

"Thanks for coming," she said.

"Did Shannon call you?" I asked, because he didn't appear to be here yet. It wasn't like him to be slow about meeting me, especially when we were working a case.

She nodded. "He said it was about the autopsy, but we already know. Matthew's on the phone with the hospital's attorney right now."

As if on cue, Matthew came into the room from a hallway, a phone pressed to his ear. He looked as haggard as he had at the hospital that morning, and I guessed he still hadn't slept. "I know what it looks like," he said, his voice tight to the breaking point, "but he wasn't on tadalafil or anything like it. Of course I didn't take his word for it. I looked at the blood tests."

He dropped down onto a brown leather couch, as if in defeat. He listened for a long time, and then said, "I understand. But, look, I heard the police might have a few leads. There might be more to it." He listened for a moment longer. "Yeah, okay. Thanks." He hung up and stared at the blank face of the television screen.

"He's been like this all day," Paige said in a low voice. "Distracted, worried. He can't sleep. I'm about ready to put sleeping pills in his coffee."

"Don't," I advised. "With the luck we're having . . ." I didn't need to finish.

"Right." Paige motioned to a loveseat that was kitty-corner to the couch. As I headed toward it, she went to Matthew and sat close to him. "What did he say?"

Matthew started suddenly, as if he'd been unaware of her presence. He twisted his head in her direction. "The attorney for the Griffins is saying he's going to sue for negligent homicide."

"But I thought they said the level of nitrates wasn't responsible," Paige said.

"Not alone, it wasn't." Matthew raked a hand through his dark hair.

"What else then?" Paige began kneading his shoulder.

For a moment, Matthew didn't speak, and then he leaned in Paige's direction. "They found an extremely high level of tadalafil in his system, and since there was none in his earlier blood test, he would have had to take a huge dose after the blood draw to get it anywhere near that high. Yet there were no partially dissolved pills in his stomach, so that means either it was administered intravenously or the pills were crushed, neither of which they'd do at the hospital for a man as well as he was, even if I ordered the dose, which I didn't."

"What's tadalafil?" I'd never heard of the drug, at least not by that name.

"It's a drug some men take for impotence," Matthew said. "Adcirca and Cialis are some of the brand names. But that's not the issue exactly. The Griffins' attorney is claiming the nitroglycerine I ordered interacted with the tadalafil, and that's what first incapacitated and then killed Griffin when his blood pressure got too low. Mostly because his reaction was so swift and severe that he apparently didn't have the mental capacity to call the nurse."

"Is that even possible?" Paige asked. I leaned forward, as eager as she was to hear the answer.

"Technically, yes. The two drugs do interact, but Peter Griffin should never have gotten enough of them in the hospital, which is why they're claiming negligence." Matthew shook his head morosely. "Because we would have had to ignore the huge amount of tadalafil in his system and still give him an overdose of nitroglycerin."

"But you had blood tests, right?" Paige took his hand between both of hers. "So there's proof backing you up."

"We did, but whoever recorded the amounts didn't put in zero. They left it blank, which is typical, but the hospital says the Griffin attorney will use the blank line to suggest that I should have run another verifying test before giving him the nitroglycerin. He feels it'll be enough to get the jury to go their way." Matthew's swallow sounded dry and painful. "And they might be right."

Paige rubbed his hand. "But didn't you say that even if you'd given him both, he wouldn't have died at the hospital?"

Matthew nodded. "Exactly. Not at the normal dosage levels, and we would have caught the reactions to normal dosages in time—even if there had been an accident. Unless . . . unless someone really was trying to kill him."

"I read an imprint from his wife today that took place a month ago," I said. "They were having intimacy problems, but he wasn't taking anything for it, at least not then. We'll have to ask."

"They already did," Matthew said. "She said he wasn't taking tadalafil. Just the daily nitroglycerin."

"The nitroglycerin that just happened to also be much higher than normal in his system," Paige said, her voice clipped now, as if reverting to detective mode.

"Right." Matthew rubbed a bloodshot eye with a finger. "And he likely had a lot more tadalafil in his body just before death than they found in the autopsy. The body metabolizes the drug rather quickly if it's broken down. Which is why the quick-acting kind can work so well."

That made me ask, "Who would know that the two drugs taken together would cause a negative reaction?"

Matthew snorted, ticking off those possible on his fingers. "Anyone working in the hospital. Anyone taking either drug who looked up interactions. Anyone who knows someone using the drug or who read about them. Pretty much anyone."

I stood and paced to the wall of windows. The sun was still bright, but low in the horizon, and it sent a glittering of gold across the city. "There's something we're missing here," I said. "We need time to find out what."

Matthew stared at me for a long moment without responding, as if not quite comprehending. "If we don't find a reason—if you and Shannon and Quincy don't, I mean—then I won't be able to practice medicine again. Not at Providence. Maybe nowhere." He heaved a sigh.

"So let's take out the accidental dose option," I said, turning from the window and coming back to the couch. "How could he possibly get that much of either drug in his system between the blood tests, enough that it would kill him so quickly?"

Matthew shook his head. "Unless he had a death wish and crushed a bunch of pills when the nurse was out of the room and downed them, or someone snuck in, maybe injecting him with something they prepared, it's not possible."

"Yes, it is," Paige said firmly, "because it did happen."

Matthew was silent a moment, his brow furrowed in thought. "Well, the three o'clock blood test later showed Griffin already had too many nitrates in his system. The nurse had given him medicine for a headache, remember, because he wanted to sleep, so the phlebotomist who came for the blood had probably been told to keep conversation down to a minimum. He might not have noticed if Griffin was acting strange."

"The headache was probably caused by the overdose of nitrates." I sank back onto the loveseat.

"Yes," Matthew agreed, "and if he ingested the tadalafil after the blood draw or right around that time, he would have quickly become incoherent and unable to call for help, especially if he fell asleep."

I thought about the small white box and the chocolate liners we'd found. "Could either of the drugs be disguised in food?"

"I'm sure both could." Matthew's anxiety was apparent in his words, and I didn't blame him. "If they had enough sugar or other sweetener to disguise them."

"Wouldn't that get kind of bulky?" Paige asked. "For that much of the drug? In conjunction with the food, I mean. He'd just had surgery."

"Both drugs are highly concentrated," Matthew said, "and come in very small pills, and there are sweeteners that are far sweeter than sugar. You wouldn't need much of those to mask any bad taste. For the nitroglycerin, there's also an under-the-tongue version that doesn't even taste bad. The drugs could have also been injected or dissolved in something he drank."

"Injections would mean Peter Griffin's consent or hospital personnel," I said. "And for now we're ruling out hospital negligence, and we don't have any evidence of suicide. I think our next step is to match visitors to his room to our suspect list."

"I've been trying to work on that." Paige looked past me at the door, and I followed her gaze to see Shannon coming into the apartment. He shut the door firmly behind him with his backside because both hands were filled with takeout bags. My stomach growled. I loved that man, and not only because he knew that food was the fastest way to my heart. Even if he made me eat entirely too much pasta.

Paige and I set up two large folding trays, one each in front of the couch and loveseat. We rehashed the tadalafil and nitroglycerin issue as we went about eating pasta and Chinese food, from two entirely separate take-out places. I had the Chinese while Shannon, of course, went for the pasta.

"You need to stay out of sight and don't talk to anyone," Shannon counseled Matthew when the talk wound down. "Give us time to figure out another scenario."

"That's what the hospital attorney said." Matthew had taken only a few bites with his chopsticks, which he now put down. "He said Peter Griffin's death will likely be in the news, and the more I'm recognized, the worse it'll be for the hospital and my career." He paused, and then added, "Who am I kidding? It's over for me."

Paige scooted closer to him. "Autumn and Shannon will find something. And you know Quincy won't give up. If there's something to prove, they'll find it."

"What if there isn't any proof left to find?" His voice broke on the last word.

She scowled at him. "Matthew Kellogg, this isn't like you.

Now you go get in the shower and then go to bed. I'm going to check on you in a little while. You're no good to anyone without sleep. And we still have a bunch of surveillance footage to go through."

Matthew made an agonized face. "I'm being a colossal jerk, aren't I?"

"No," Paige said. "But you will be if you don't go take a pill or whatever and sleep."

He nodded. "Okay." He put his forehead against hers for a moment, as if drinking in her strength. "Thank you."

When Matthew left, Paige turned on the television and navigated to the online surveillance footage. "I know I'm getting ahead of myself since I don't have a complete list of suspects, but I've watched all of Sunday morning so far," she said, "and I don't see anything unusual. I only recognize the family getting off the elevator and heading into that hallway, and we already know they were there to see him. I looked at the security list Quincy sent me, but no one came to see Griffin after ten o'clock when the sign-in time began." She shrugged. "I'm capturing images of anyone entering that elevator who got off on Peter Griffin's floor. They have cameras in front of the elevators and in the waiting rooms, and one of those shows part of the hallway leading to Griffin's room. We can compare my images to all the suspects once we have pictures of them."

Shannon nodded. "We can also run the images you've made of the visitors through facial recognition."

"Yeah, that's what I was thinking." Paige went back to watching the feed while Shannon and I cleaned up dinner. When I took Matthew's nearly untouched food to the kitchen to put away in his fridge, Shannon followed me.

"So," he said, "about the budget for the wedding . . ."

I paused near the refrigerator. "Are your parents expecting something big?"

"I don't think so. My dad did ask me if I needed help, but I told them we were doing something simple and were okay." He made a face. "I know they aren't in all that much of a position to help anyway. He has his department retirement, but they've had to roll all their income back into the bed and breakfast. They're doing all right, but not as well as I am, since I got my grandpa's house and it's paid for. I think between you and me, we'll have plenty."

To my way of thinking, I'd only have plenty once my mortgage was paid. We were competent adults, though, and I didn't want money from Shannon's parents any more than I wanted it from Cody, but not accepting their help meant I'd probably have to make concessions for the wedding. I knew it was silly, that a thirty-four-year-old, independent woman would suddenly become all dreamy about a wedding like a starstruck, eighteen-year-old girl. In my mind, I knew that menus and colors and dresses and guests weren't important to the overall promises we'd be making, but somehow I found myself wanting that day to be perfect—wanting it all. At the same time, another very scoffing part of me was annoyed that I couldn't settle for a quick trip to city hall.

"Depends on what we want," I told Shannon. "After I talk to Tawnia, I'll have a better idea of what we're looking at." I put the cartons of Chinese food into Matthew's pristine, black stainless steel refrigerator. He had more food inside than I imagined a bachelor would, until I remembered Paige said Matthew enjoyed cooking. I'd have to find out if he knew any good recipes.

"Okay, just let me know, and if you want me to take care

of planning anything, I will." Shannon reached for me, pulling me into his arms. I leaned against him, letting his warmth seep into me. "I already have an idea for the honeymoon," he said, kissing the skin beneath my right ear and making me shudder. "How does an isolated cabin in the mountains sound?"

"No cell phone service?" If the Portland Police Bureau could call him, they would.

"No cell service and no internet."

"That sounds promising." I arched toward him as I enjoyed the feel of his lips trailing their way to mine. My mouth parted as he finally reached it, and for a long moment, I knew nothing but the heat of his mouth and the press of his body against mine.

"There is one thing I need to tell you," Shannon said, reluctantly drawing away. "My parents are coming this weekend to meet you in person."

It took me a moment to switch from romance mode to worry. "With the wedding so close?"

"Apparently, they have frequent flyer miles, and they want to get to know you before the wedding."

"In case they don't like me, you mean."

He actually laughed.

"What's so funny?" I demanded.

He placed a kiss on my nose, which was a little bit condescending and not in the least satisfying. "It's not like you to care what anyone thinks of you."

He had a point. "Well, these are your parents," I said. "Not just anyone."

"They live in Florida on the other side of the country." His arms tightened around me. "It's not like they'll be stopping in to borrow sugar."

"I don't use sugar."

"Or raw honey or monk fruit," he amended. "Whatever. The point is, they haven't interfered in our relationship before now, and I don't think they intend to. I think they're just happy I'm finally getting married. I'm their only child, and I suspect they'd about given up on me."

He kissed my mouth again, and I let myself be convinced. "When are they getting in?" I asked. "Because I have my black-belt testing Friday night, remember?"

I'd be testing for my second Dan, or second-degree black-belt in taekwondo, to be exact, and I was paying for a private test because I didn't like the idea of testing in front of a bunch of gawkers. Private meant only my instructor and two other high-ranking blackbelts would be in attendance.

"Right, I remember," he said. "But I'm not sure of the details. They'll get a car rental from the airport anyway, so I assume they'll let me know. Or they'll show up at the house when they can."

Which meant I was making sure I'd be nowhere near his house when the time came. At least not alone. We spent most of our time off watching movies at my apartment anyway because of its proximity to my store—and because I normally had groceries and knew how to cook. But weekends now usually found me in the herb garden I'd planted in Shannon's back yard.

All of which reminded me that the wedding was fast approaching, and we'd have to talk about what our future looked like. I loved his acre of land and his quaint house, but adding fifteen minutes of travel to every single workday, both ways, was a little daunting. Yet keeping my apartment didn't make much sense either.

How would I give it up? My apartment was the only home I'd ever known. My parents' lives had unfolded there, and so had Summer's illness and death. We'd laughed and loved in that little apartment—and it was there I'd said a final goodbye at both their home funerals, twenty years apart. Could I give it up? I didn't have to, but my practical side was giving me trouble with that idea. Shannon and I were only two people, and keeping the apartment didn't make sense. Selling would put me close to paying off my store mortgage, which would ease my financial pressure considerably.

But I'd lose one more piece of my parents.

"Hey," Shannon said. "What's wrong?"

"Nothing." Because it was *my* problem, and I needed to decide what to do about it before letting him weigh into the equation. I loved Shannon, but he was as strong-headed as I was, and I wanted to know how I felt about the future before I asked for input.

"Good." He kissed me again for a long while until Paige came into the kitchen and broke up the fun.

"You guys still here?" she said. "I thought you'd left when I was checking on Matthew."

"Actually, we're discussing the wedding." Shannon stepped back and shoved his hands in his pockets.

Paige stared at him. "Did you say wedding? Have you guys set a date? When?"

"Three weeks from last Saturday," Shannon said.

"No!" Her face flushed. "I mean, yes! But when did you decide, and why am I only hearing about it now? Couldn't you have called or texted or posted on Facebook?"

Shannon threw me an uneasy glance, as if he hadn't expected this kind of reaction. "We only decided this weekend, and we've been a little busy today. You know we don't go on Facebook except to like pictures of Destiny."

"I barely told my sister this afternoon," I put in. "I was going to tell you this morning, but it didn't seem like the right time at the hospital. Anyway, we want you and Matthew there."

Paige threw herself at me, hugging me tightly. "Of course, I'll be there! Both Matthew and I. Well, unless . . ."

"He won't be in jail," I said. "It'll all be over by then."

She drew back, blinking back tears. "Even if it's not, you go through with it. I mean it. You never know what tomorrow will bring."

It was that kind of thinking that had put me into the three-week rush in the first place, but I wasn't going to second-guess myself now. I loved Shannon, and I wanted to marry him now.

"Yeah, okay." I tried smiling, sure it looked more like a grimace.

Paige nodded a little too vigorously. "Shannon mentioned you're going to Futura tomorrow to hopefully find some of your suspects who might work there. When's that?"

"Nine-thirty," Shannon and I said together.

"They've hired me," I continued. "Or rather, Eli Stone and me." I used Elliot's professional name rather than his full name because she'd be more familiar with it.

"Oh, the PI. So are you going for the professional license?"

"I'm trying it out for now."

The commitment for the private investigator license involved fifteen hundred hours of investigative research, which was discouraging. As an experienced PI, Elliot could sign off on those hours for me, and he'd said he'd count my old cases and the time I spent consulting for the police. But even after nearly two years of solving missing person and murder cases,

I had nowhere near that much time. I also didn't like the idea of being required to work as an assistant, even if it was only on paper, but someone had to vouch for my hours. Maybe if I got Elliot to agree to count some of the research I'd done for my antiques over the years, I could make it work.

"It's a big commitment," Paige said.

"Right." Truth was, even with the daunting time requirement, it didn't seem like all that much of a commitment. It wasn't anything like, say, getting married. That would be a lot more than fifteen hundred hours.

"Look," I said. "I have to get home. I have a few things I have to do before I get to bed." I still hadn't found the time to research the chairs Jazzy had brought in, which I needed to do to add them to my insurance. Lower cost things were automatically covered, but the high-end items had to be claimed individually. I also had to let Jake know that Shannon and I had set a date. After the way Paige had reacted, the last thing I wanted was to alienate him.

"But Eli is still working the case," I added, "so if he finds more information, I'll send it over immediately."

Shannon's arm dropped from my back. "Good. Meanwhile, I'll stay here for a bit to help Paige with the hospital surveillance tapes. I know we don't have all the suspects yet, or pictures of all the suspects we do have, but we might as well get a jump on the footage. There's nothing else we can do tonight, and the angles we have should give us a good idea of who had access. We might see someone who stands out."

"Unless they were trying to hide from the cameras," I said.

Paige nodded. "We have to ask if they have any footage of the stairwells and the nurses' desks."

"We already have everything." Shannon frowned and

looked thoughtful. "At least I think we do. I'll have Quincy ask again because I know hospitals are concerned about their drug cabinets, and the quick look I took so far didn't show those. Maybe they didn't share all of the footage because it didn't appear to be related to Peter Griffin's room."

"It's worth a try." I moved toward the door, and Shannon came with me. He rode down with me to the lobby and would have walked me out to my car if I didn't stop him.

"Go help Paige," I told him.

"Okay. But look, I have to go to the precinct tomorrow morning and spend a little time on my other cases. I may end up taking a comp day if they let me, because there's no way I'm using my vacation days. I've already gotten the two weeks off approved for the wedding."

"Good," I said, kissing him.

He kissed me back, and heat rushed through both of us. Only the concierge's clearing of his throat pulled us apart.

"Right." Shannon held the door open for me.

Out in my car, I thought for a moment before calling Jake. I hoped my marrying Shannon wouldn't change things between us. The two men had finally developed a tentative friendship, but I wasn't confident that I could make both relationships work. I'd chosen Shannon, and I'd choose him again, but I loved Jake too.

Chapter 9

The next morning, I pushed my Victorian couch and the coffee table closer to the fireplace so I had more room between them and the outer door to run through my taekwondo *poomsae*, or forms. The living room was the hub of my apartment, with the bathroom, two bedrooms, and kitchen connecting to the space. No hallways here. With the couch moved, the room looked vastly different, and for a moment, I imagined it without the crush of antiques that filled the apartment. The way it might look if I decided to sell.

Pushing the thought away, I concentrated on my *poomsae*, making each movement count in a perfectly choreographed fighting dance. I could do it in my sleep, but still I pushed, practicing it a total of ten times, until I felt it was perfect. Sweat dripped down the back of my neck.

After my shower and full glass of grass-fed cow milk, I wandered into Winter's room. It was still filled with his stuff, even two years after his death, and many of the objects held his or Summer's imprints. Like the photograph of their wedding and the afghan she'd made, and which I would never in a million years wash or dry.

Their bed was a double, not a queen, and it filled most of the small room. Winter had given away Summer's clothing, except for her wedding dress and matching sandals, and a few other pieces that had meaning to him. Only the wedding dress contained imprints. Summer hadn't owned much even before he gave her things away, but my favorite was the small jewelry box that held cheap, vintage, dangly pearl earrings, a simple chain with a single pearl, and her wedding band made of two thin bands of yellow gold twisted together. With the exception of the ring, the jewelry was ruined and falling apart.

The ring itself I was careful to avoid touching because the most recent imprint had occurred on the day she'd learned the cancer treatments hadn't worked and that she'd have to say goodbye to both me and Winter. I'd discovered the heartbreaking imprints after Winter's death and hadn't touched the ring since, despite the imprints that followed, both good and bad. I'd put Winter's ring in the box too, and it held similar memories, but they were faded to a feeling rather than vivid scenes. He'd had twenty-one more years to imprint on it, and most of those imprints had been happy ones.

I'd secretly hoped the cheap pearls would have magically changed from junk jewelry that should be thrown away to beautiful keepsakes I could wear on my wedding day, but one peek into the box told me a miracle hadn't taken place. I'd have to figure something else out. I sold vintage jewelry at the store, and maybe there was a similar set. If not, there was always the Internet.

I stared at Summer's wedding ring for several long minutes before going to the bathroom for the blow dryer. Maybe I could at least wear the ring.

I was well into heating the gold with the blow dryer when

a hand fell over mine. I looked up to see Jake, his dark face framed by locs, or dreadlocks as some people not in the know still called them. His were finger width, and only a bit longer. His huge brown eyes stared kindly out from his handsome face.

He took the blow dryer from my hands and turned it off. "I knocked, but no one answered. I guess you couldn't hear me."

"That's why you have a key."

"What's wrong?" He pulled me up from the bed where I sat next to my mother's ring. With his forefinger, he wiped a tear from underneath my left eye, near the scar I still had from the bridge bombing that had stolen Winter from me.

"Nothing's wrong. Shannon and I have set a date for the wedding. That's why I called you last night and asked you to stop by before work."

His grin returned. "That's great! When?"

"Three weeks from last Saturday."

"Good for you. I bet Shannon's happy about that." He studied me for a minute. "Big step, though. Are you really okay with it? Because you don't look okay."

I nodded through tears that had decided to come without my permission. "I'm fine—Shannon and I are fine. It's just . . . I don't know if I'm ready to sell the apartment. If I lose it, it's like I lose more of—"

"Your parents." He hugged me close, his strong arms and chest making the perfect cradle for my hurting heart. For a long moment, we stood there, not saying anything. Then Jake asked, "What does Shannon say?"

"I haven't told him." I tilted my head to look up at Jake. "He'd say keep the apartment if I wanted, but for how many years? I mean, Winter wouldn't want me to hold onto something that wasn't useful."

Jake chuckled. "You got that right. But think of it this way. You don't have to decide today or next month, or even in a year."

"I could use the funds to pay down my store mortgage." I surveyed the room. "But if I sold it, where would I put all this stuff?"

"You could also rent it out until you're ready to make a decision. I really think you should talk to Shannon." Jake looked down at the ring on the bed, reaching to pick it up. "Ow, this is still hot." He tossed it up in the air, catching it and then tossing it once again.

"It was my mother's. I'm trying to get rid of the imprints. The most recent ones on it are tough. If I could get rid of them or fade them, I might be able to wear it for the wedding."

"Right. I'd forgotten about the heat thing. But do you really think you should get rid of the imprints?" he asked, bouncing the ring again. "You don't have all that much from your mom."

"I have enough good imprints. Hold it steady for a minute."

He held the ring out on the palm of his hand, and I touched it, the yellow gold still warm on my skin. Emotions rushed out at me. I experienced sadness first, but the once-vivid scene of the doctor telling Summer she was dying was gone, leaving only a sense of sorrow. Less than a heartbeat later, the sadness was covered by love—so much love.

"It worked," I said, barely breathing. "Love is stronger." Other imprints rushed out at me, also simple emotions now. The clear scenes were no longer there, but I could still feel Summer. I grabbed the ring and held it tightly in my hand.

"Now if only the dress fit a little better," I said. "Summer was so thin. It'll need to be let out."

Jake raised both hands, stepping back. "I know nothing about sewing."

I laughed. "I'm not asking you. And thanks for being happy for me about the wedding."

He grinned. "Hey, you getting married isn't going to change anything between us. I still love you, Autumn. I will always love you. I know marrying Shannon is what you want, and I'm happy for you."

"And you want Melinda." I needed to know he really was okay that I'd dumped him for Shannon.

He nodded. "You're going to love her. And speaking of that, when should we go on our double date?"

I'd been giving them space with the hopes that Melinda wouldn't take a dislike to Jake having a former girlfriend for a best friend. And maybe I secretly didn't want to see them together, but it was time.

I slid my mother's ring onto the ring finger of my right hand and led Jake out of Winter's bedroom, suddenly feeling a little claustrophobic. "Maybe this Friday? I'm helping Paige right now with something that can't wait."

I explained about Matthew, downplaying my role and leaving out the fact that in less than a half hour, I'd need to leave for my meeting at Futura.

"But aren't you testing for your second-degree black belt on Friday?" Jake asked.

I nodded. "It'll only take an hour. Oh, wait, I forgot." I made a face. "Shannon's parents are coming to visit this weekend. To check me out, I think."

"Probably."

"We don't know when they're arriving, so Friday night might not work after all."

"Let's play it by ear then," Jake said. "But speaking of your taekwondo test, can I come watch?"

"No, sorry. There's a reason I'm paying for a *private* test."

He chuckled. "Fine, I get it. I'd better get to work. Call me if you need my help with this case." He strode to the door, where he paused. "Oh, and I wanted to say that I'm sorry about the BOGO. I know I've been using more of Thera's hours than I should."

"That's fine. I'm going to need Thera full time for two weeks after the wedding. Tawnia will fill in for the rest, and Jazzy can come in for the busy times. I can't really have her there alone long since she's so young."

"I'll schedule Randa instead of Thera while you're gone. And I can always look out for the place too."

He always did. "Thanks." As he reached for the doorknob, I said, "One more thing before you go. Will you be my best man at the wedding?"

He turned back to face me, his hand dropping from the door. "I thought it was the groom who had a best man."

"He will, but I'm having one too. You."

"What about Tawnia?"

"She won't mind. Her dress will be prettier than yours. And you can bring Melinda, of course."

"Okay, okay. Sure."

"Wait a minute. I'll walk out with you." I grabbed a pair of gloves, this time black ones that matched the gray, black, and red peasant blouse I wore over my gray pencil skirt. The skirt was a hand-me-down from Tawnia, and I liked it precisely because it was stretchy and almost reached the ground. It was this or holey jeans, since everything else I owned was currently in the dirty laundry basket. I'd also put on a pair of beaded barefoot sandals that wrapped around my ankles and looped down around my second toe. At a casual glance, they looked like sandal tops, and that helped with the questions.

"You going to the store this early?" Jake said, only a little mockingly.

"Actually," I replied airily, "I'm going to see the future."

When Jake learned where I was going, he wanted to come along to learn more about the smart glasses, but his BOGO sale couldn't wait. We parted ways outside my apartment. With Google as my guide, I made only a few wrong turns while finding Taylor Street, where the two-story, red-stucco Futura building was located next to what appeared to be a small furniture manufacturer. I was twenty minutes early, a record for me.

Elliot had been remarkably silent since our last conversation yesterday, so after parking in the nearly full parking lot next to the building, I decided to check in.

"Where've you been?" I asked when he answered.

"Sorry, I actually fell asleep last night."

"That's probably a good thing." I didn't want his anxiety acting up. "I take it that means you don't have anything new for me?"

"I have two things," he said, sounding slightly offended. "My programs don't need baby-sitting. It took some digging, but I think I've found the Robby you've been looking for, and he might be our man. He's Robby Hartford, and it *is* Robby, not Robert. As you suspected, he's an accountant for Futura. But that's not all. He also worked for Armed."

"Griffin's failed business?" I pulled up one knee and rested it against the steering wheel.

"Yes, and he refinanced his house at that time, taking out some of the equity. I suspect he invested the money in Armed."

"That could have given him a very big bone to pick with Peter Griffin."

"It could, but then why go work for the guy at another company? It might not be as straightforward as it looks."

"Okay. I'll do some snooping around at Futura. But did you get a photo of him? We'll want to verify what time or times he was at the hospital. The imprint said around nine-thirty at night."

"I have a photo. Sending it now."

"What about our guy Arthur?"

"No one by that name seems to be connected to Armed, and I haven't found a link between Niklas Griffin and anyone named Arthur. I have become friends with Niklas on Facebook under a fake account, though, so I might be able to learn more there."

"I thought you were strictly white hat," I said. "Isn't that against Facebook policies?"

He laughed. "They aren't the police, and it's not against the law. Plus, I don't give any social media platform my real information. That would be plain stupid."

Either he was paranoid, or I was too open. "I don't have anything to hide," I protested.

"You say that now, but if you were stalked, or if you were trolled . . . Anyway, I'll look back through all Niklas's posts. He was quite active a few years ago, a real partier. It would help if we had Arthur's last name. Keep in mind that he might work for Futura. If you could get a complete employee list, that would be helpful. I couldn't find one online or through my contacts. I only found Hartford because he was quoted online in an article written about both companies. And in researching Robby Hartfords in the Portland area, there is only one whose first name isn't Robert. I learned he recently took out a second mortgage on his house."

"Well, it's a start." I looked up at the red Futura building. It wasn't upscale in the least, but the location showed some measure of wisdom in the use of investment dollars. "What was the other thing you found?"

"It's about the school vandalism case. I called an officer I know in the East Precinct, and he said he's checked out a few local paint and hardware stores. In the days leading up to the attack, they didn't notice an uptick of paint being sold, or at least not anything more than a few cans. So either the vandal purchased from a bunch of different stores or he bought the cans over time."

"Or more than one kid is involved. Can't the police go through the surveillance footage and see if anyone connected to the case bought spray paint?"

"They could, but they aren't going to. Too much time and manpower. It's much easier to pin it on Pax since he already looks guilty."

"Did you tell the cop about Pax's alibi?"

"He says it won't prove anything because Pax had access at other times, even during the night."

"Well, that's not true. He doesn't have access to keys when he's not working."

"They're thinking he had illegal copies made, but unless they can prove it, none of it would hold up in court. Frankly, I think the officer is overworked."

"We could go through the surveillance tapes ourselves."

"I asked, and that was resounding no. Too many people shop at those stores, and it would violate their privacy if they gave it to someone who wasn't working for the police."

I sighed. "I might have to get Quincy involved then. He got us access to the hospital surveillance."

"If it comes to that." He hesitated a minute before saying, "Please tell me you're on your way to Futura."

"I'm sitting in the parking lot now. I have plenty of time to check out the lobby before my appointment. Do you have any questions you want me to ask?"

"Besides touching everything you can, we need information on all their employees. And ask about any personal relationships Griffin might have had outside of his family."

"You mean girlfriends? That hardly seems likely with his medical issues."

Elliot snorted. "Maybe or maybe not. He wouldn't be the first husband to ignore his wife after straying. Most of my business is made up of cheating husbands."

I hated those kinds of cases. "You're not doing much to convince me to work with you long term."

"What I'm saying is that we can't overlook anything. Especially his personal relationships. And that goes for how he and his partner and employees got along."

"Okay, I'll see what I can find out."

"I'll let you go then." He hung up without a farewell.

I sighed and shoved my phone into my pocket. Time to find out what Robby Hartford had wanted to hide from Peter Griffin—and if it was a motive for murder.

Chapter 10

The Futura lobby was every bit as unimpressive as the outside. It had all the amenities: a long reception desk—currently vacant—a waiting area, and pictures on the wall. But it looked more like a waiting room at an auto shop than a future billion-dollar company. Was this more frugality, or were the smart glasses a scam? Behind the receptionist desk, a banner pronounced in bold letters: The Future is here with Futura!

I went to work, ignoring the camera that glared blatantly at me from the corner of the room. I checked the couch, chairs, coffee table, magazines, and the top of the reception desk. There were no imprints—or at least no important ones. If investors came here, I doubted they'd waited long.

As I contemplated going behind the desk and checking for imprints, a woman emerged from a door next to the desk. She was middle-aged, with brown hair, blue eyes, and a ready smile. "I'm sorry for making you wait," she said. "May I help you?"

"I'm here to see Titus Grey. I have an appointment at nine-thirty."

"Oh, right. You must be from Eli Stone Investigations.

Titus is in a meeting at the moment, but I'm sure it's almost over. He's not one for idle chat. I'll let him know you're here."

"It's still a bit early," I said.

"I'll just leave him a message." She flashed me a smile. "That's one thing about working at a tech firm. They have all the gadgets."

I looked doubtfully around the lobby, but if she noticed my skepticism, she didn't let on. "Thanks."

Sitting at her computer, she typed something and then smiled up at me. "All done. It'll flash on his phone and computer."

"Thank you." I let only a heartbeat go by before asking, "Have you worked here long?" If she had, she could be a valuable resource.

"Since the beginning. I'm the receptionist, but not many people come here, so I'm mostly Peter's secretary. Or was."

"I'm sorry about Mr. Griffin."

Her smile wavered. "It's such a shock. He was so vital and alive. Always said good morning and apologized when he was in a bad mood." She shook her head. "I can't believe he's not coming back."

"Is his son Stevan in today?" I asked. "I was with him and his mother yesterday. They were having a difficult time, so I wondered if he came in." Giving her that information would put me in the inner circle, I hoped, and make her speak more freely.

"He was here earlier, but he had to leave for an emergency investor meeting." Her lips pursed. "If you ask me, he should take a few days off, even before reassuring the investors, but he always did try to please his dad, and I guess death doesn't change things like that."

"I guess not." I still wondered far too often if Winter would be proud of what I was doing. Most of the time, I thought he would. "It's a sad situation, especially since Niklas Griffin was going to be working here."

Her eyes widened. "Really? I didn't know that. I didn't think he got along with his father or brother." She let out a little rush of air. "It's odd timing, with the release so close. Makes me wonder a little."

"You mean with the potential profits coming into the picture."

She nodded but instantly looked contrite. "Not that I know anything about it. I'm sorry. I shouldn't have said anything."

"It's okay. I'm here to look at every angle of the case." I didn't add that Niklas Griffin was high on my list of suspects, though with him not inheriting his destined share of his father's business, the motivation wasn't strong. Unless his mother gave him the shares, which was a possibility I couldn't rule out.

Robby Hartford and the mysterious Arthur were next on my list of questions for the nameless receptionist, but a man came through the door before I could ask.

"Welcome," he said, glancing at me with a smile before averting his gaze awkwardly. "I'm Titus Grey."

He wasn't at all what I expected. Instead of a chubby, balding, poorly-dressed tech nerd, he was thin and had a full head of wavy, perfectly combed, black hair and ice-blue eyes that looked sleepy as if he'd come from his bed and still needed a few more hours of rest. His stylish loafers, snug black pants, and fitted, multi-colored shirt looked as if someone up-to-date on current styles had chosen his perfectly tailored wardrobe.

"Autumn Rain," I said, extending a hand.

He stepped forward nervously and shook it. Unfortunately,

he wasn't wearing rings, and the bracelet he did wear was up too high on his wrist for me to casually touch.

"Thank you for coming." His eyes briefly met mine again.

He was about my height, which made him short for a man, and he looked overwhelmingly familiar somehow. The one thing I had pegged about him was his social awkwardness. He seemed to have that down pat.

"If you'll come with me," he said, "I'll give you a quick tour before we get started."

As I moved with him toward the door, still staring at the hair that waved back from his face, probably held in place with some kind of oil or gel, the receptionist laughed. "You see it, don't you?" she said.

I glanced toward her. "See what?"

"He looks like Elvis Presley. At least we all think so."

Now that she mentioned it, despite his thinness and height, he did look like a slightly older version of the long-dead music king.

Titus waved her comment aside, a slight flush on his cheeks. "It's a joke," he said. "Don't listen to her." He turned and hurried back through the door. He didn't move gracefully or with confidence, but rather like someone in a perpetual hurry.

I followed him down a long hallway to a door with a coded lock, where he quickly typed in a password. We stepped into a large, brightly illuminated lab whose structure was nothing but bare bones. Thick-looking concrete made up walls, huge lighting fixtures with bare bulbs hung on long metal rods, and scarred wooden tables were scattered everywhere. Three small groups of people sat at separate tables, their heads bent over their work. The soft hum of a fan was broken only by the occasional tidbit of conversation or the beep of a machine. A few of the employees eyed us curiously.

"This is the heart of Futura," Titus said. "Well, or it was when we were working on the prototype, and it's still important because this is where we're working on version two. I know it doesn't look like much at first, but once you take a closer look, it's all there."

I scanned the room, trying to see what he saw. Then I had it. Computers, gadgets, and electronic equipment graced every table, some bolted to the surfaces. They came in all shapes and sizes, some with robotic arms and long spiraling tubes. I recognized none of the devices except for the huge 3D printer that was familiar because of a past case. None of the equipment was haphazard but placed for perfect access and usability. If I was guessing, I'd say this equipment was top-of-the-line and likely represented a heavy percentage of the Futura investment dollars.

"It looks ready for business," I said.

He gestured to a tall door across from us, meeting my gaze for only the second time. He looked less nervous now, and I could tell he felt comfortable here. "There's a smaller area beyond that door with electrostatic discharge protection where we work on the microchips, but I won't make you get all dressed up to see that." He shrugged. "Unless you think it's important to the investigation."

"I'll let you know. I'm taking it Peter didn't go in there much?"

Titus shook his head. "Or in here for that matter. Peter's a smart man"—he grimaced—"*was* a smart man. But he didn't know much about this side of the business." He motioned me to follow him from the room.

The hallway was eerily silent after the ever-present humming of the lab. "So I take it that Futura is your idea?"

He nodded with a shy smile and an embarrassed duck of his head. "Yep, from the beginning idea to every single component inside it. Futura's my baby, you might say."

"When did you get the idea?"

"Twenty years ago, but it took me fifteen to get it to the point where I could get anyone else to take me seriously."

We were silent as we walked to the end of the hallway, where he started up a flight of stairs.

"You're a major shareholder in the company?" I asked.

"I own twenty percent."

"And Peter owned thirty-one?" I remembered the number from Elliot's information.

"I see you've done your research. Peter owned thirty-one, and that kept us with a majority. The rest we divvied out to different investors or reserved for key employees once we launch."

On the second floor, we were met with another long, tiled hallway, this one lined with doors, some open and others shut. Titus paused at the first door on the right—a closed door—and typed in a code to open a lock. The interior of the office was larger than I'd expected by the intervals of the doors in the hallway—until I spotted another door farther down the wall. Apparently, Titus had used two smaller rooms for his workplace. A thick, tan carpet spread over the floor, and the excellent quality of the mahogany furniture was obvious to my antique-trained eyes. A large window glowed at us from the far wall, but there were bars over it, visible through the beige curtains. As we entered, two separate rows of receded lights turned on, making the entire office seem airy and light despite the barred window.

"Nice," I commented, moving to a painting on the wall by the door we'd entered. Art wasn't my specialty, but I knew enough to suspect it was an antique. I ran my finger along the frame of the picture to check for imprints and found nothing.

"This was Peter's office." Titus sat in one of the three armchairs in front of the desk, which reminded me of the Chippendale chairs Jazzy had brought into the store yesterday, though these were only replicas. "My workstation's down in the lab, but I think it'll be more comfortable and private here."

I crossed the room and sat in the chair next to his, first pulling it back and slightly around so we were facing each other. "Eli Stone said you were interested in hiring us."

He nodded. "On a conditional basis. He said his partner—you—had a unique connection with the case, and I thought it would be a chance to make sure nothing here is . . . amiss."

Amiss seemed to be a word from another era, but it was the one I'd choose in his place, so I went with it. "Did he tell you what kind of connection I have?" I hoped Elliot hadn't spilled too much of my connection with Shannon, or it might get back to the attorney for Niklas Griffin, who could claim the police were biased, which wouldn't be far from the truth. We were all on Matthew's side, and we weren't going to let his life be destroyed if someone else was responsible for Griffin's death.

"He said you're friends with the cardiologist's girlfriend and that you have inside information from the police." He crossed his legs and then uncrossed them, his gaze dropping to his hands. "I thought that would most likely mean your company could find out what happened."

"I do consult with the police," I said by way of agreement. "I've only been called in unofficially, though, for this case, and that connection needs to be kept between us if I'm going to look into this for you."

"Of course," he agreed readily.

"Good. Because I believe I've already discovered information that connects at least one person here to Peter's death. To what extent, I don't know."

"Your partner said as much. That's why I agreed to have you come. I want to make sure no one here was responsible."

"Because of Futura's release."

"Yes." He looked at me. "If something happened now to delay things, it could destroy us." His gaze went to the large monitor on the desk and back to me. I had the distinct feeling there was more, a deeper reason for me to be here, but he didn't seem ready to share. Or maybe he wasn't aware of it himself. "If you can clear my employees definitively, or catch whoever did it, I'll pay your fees."

"When I talked to Stevan Griffin yesterday, he said there were hundreds of millions of dollars invested in Futura. How many hundreds are we talking about?"

"Three hundred thousand, or thereabouts. That was all Peter's doing. But we did it on a shoestring. Peter and I haven't wasted a blessed dime." He motioned to the room. "He paid for this carpet himself and brought in his own furnishings. He needed a place to talk with investors who came to check out our operation, but he didn't want to take away from my operating budget." A tiny smile graced his well-molded lips. "Peter was accustomed to good things, and he worked better here than in our first building. Now, that place was a dive."

"That explains our conditional hiring," I said dryly.

"Sorry about that." Titus was back to not looking at me directly. "We won't have any profits for months, and I can't justify a private investigator expense to our investors without it meaning something, especially without Peter here." He raked a hand through his hair, destroying the perfect combed-back style. He looked better that way. Younger than the fifty-five I knew he claimed.

"Peter's death was not a hospital mistake," I said.

He nodded. "That's my feeling. It would be too coincidental. But I have to confess, you probably should be talking to Stevan. I really only know the tech part of our business. Peter was over everything else, from manufacturing to marketing. My job was to create a working prototype, and I did that. Mostly from scratch. Every part of Futura is proprietary. Which means we don't use anyone else's tech for any of it."

"I'm interested in the tech side as well. I'll need to have a clear understanding of everything, so I know where to look for information." Money and passion were the two primary motivations I was searching for, but that still left a lot of possibilities: love, hate, revenge, power, wealth, and so many more. I needed to narrow the field.

"Well then, let's start with the tech." He popped up from his chair and went to another painting on the inside wall behind the desk and opened it like a door. Behind the painting was a safe. He put in the code, opened it, and brought out what looked like a small virtual reality headset and a pair of even smaller black glasses.

He brought the objects back to the chairs, handing me the headset. "Meet the original Futura," he said. "This was my prototype, the one that got Peter on board."

An imprint raced through me, coming from five years earlier.

This was it. I could tell Peter Griffin was impressed. I'd

finally done it. Futura would have a chance to meet the world.
"You won't regret this, Mr. Griffin," I said.

He extended a hand. "Call me Peter. I have a feeling we're going to become great friends."

More imprints followed, extending from six to eight years back.

It's almost small enough. I need more money.

Yes! That worked at least. But the laser was still a problem.

If only I could figure out how to make the laser smaller. And the microchips. I wish I could work on this full time.

Another failure. I wouldn't give up.

I lowered the headset to my lap in what I hoped looked like a natural gesture, and the imprints ceased.

Titus didn't seem to notice anything odd. He held up the glasses. "This is Futura now. You can check email, watch a movie, read a recipe, follow a map, and even answer a phone call. And much more. Plus, we have a dozen people working on other programs that will enhance the Futura experience. Go ahead. Try them on." He extended the black glasses.

I traded him the headset for the glasses and was amazed at the light weight of the current prototype. Except for a thickening at the temples, they felt like normal glasses. Wait, that emotion was an imprint and not my feelings. And more amazed imprints were coming fast.

"I can call someone on this?" I put on the glasses, but the imprints didn't quit. Investors had sat in this office and tried these very glasses on. They'd been impressed—and greedy—enough to imprint on them.

"You can," Titus said, his voice coming to me above the imprints. "But that takes a cell phone carrier and a lot of battery power, which means you can't do it for long, so right now it's more feasible to connect to wi-fi or through a phone. But I'm working on that. Someday we might be able to include all the phone abilities in a pair of glasses, but as yet the technology is still out of reach unless you want them larger and heavier. But this Futura was impossible ten years ago, so maybe it'll be here soon. Would you like a demonstration?"

"Sure."

"Just turn it on. Right temple. Pressure switch. Then look down. Do you see a display?"

But I was already reliving the same instructions someone else had imprinted on the glasses: *You use the pressure switch here. That's right. Now look down.*

I did—and it was miraculous.

When I looked back up, the display disappeared.

As the imprint ended, I forced myself to turn on the display in real life. It was every bit as amazing the second time around. Another imprint was beginning, but it was fainter than the first, and I could tune it out somewhat by focusing hard on Titus. He directed me to focus and hold my gaze on a file of recipes and then choose one to show up on the inside of the glasses.

"The display is not really on the lenses," he said, all his awkwardness having disappeared. "The image is actually going right into your eye."

That sounded worrisome, but it was still miraculous. "It's so clear," I murmured.

"Exactly. Now imagine cooking with it. Or using it to follow Google Maps."

"While you drive? That doesn't sound very safe."

"I've been using it for years," he countered. "It's actually easier. The enhanced reality never covers the important part of your vision. Unless you're trying to watch a movie or whatever."

Another imprint on the glasses began, this time a stronger one I couldn't ignore.

"What's that blinking thing in the corner?" I asked. It wasn't very noticeable, but it might bother me long term.

"That's the notification simulation," said Peter Griffin. "That's what it looks like if a text message or other notification comes in—or if you've set a reminder. You choose what, if anything, to appear there. It's all up to you."

With effort, I removed the glasses and laid them on my lap. I didn't know what upset me more, trying to carry on a conversation when I was reading an imprint or seeing the dead Peter Griffin looking so alive and well.

"I researched smart glasses last night on the Internet," I said, "and none of them look like this. At least nothing that actually does this much."

Titus chuckled. "That's what makes them so valuable. They'll come in four colors—black, red, tan, and navy blue. I expect there will be more later. The plastic shells are all made in our factory in China, along with a few of the components. The rest is made in our US factory." He held his hand out for the glasses, and I passed them to him, experiencing again part of the first imprint.

"I see," I said, taking a breath before plunging into the question that was burning inside me. "So about you and Peter. Were you friends? Because it might seem to some that you'd be resentful of him owning thirty-one percent of an idea that was all yours."

Titus walked over to the safe and returned the glasses, putting the picture back in place. When he turned to me, his face was grave. "Without Peter, I'd still be at a job I hated.

I'd still be working in my spare room every night and every weekend on Futura and pouring every single spare penny I have into the project. So the answer is no. I was not resentful of Peter. He's the only reason Futura is finally getting out there. I owe him everything. I was willing to settle for ten percent or even less. He was the one who insisted on twenty because of the million-plus dollars and fifteen years I'd put into it. Then he invested enough of his own money, much of it borrowed, to get us to a point where investors were willing to look at us." He paused, pursing his lips and trying to contain his emotions. "Peter was a good friend. You might say that Peter and Brigit were my only friends. And that's the real reason I agreed to talk with you. I want to make this company work for Peter's family. For Brigit and Stevan. If not, they'll lose the future he worked so hard to build for them."

I studied him for a long moment. "Did you know that his family will receive two million dollars from a life insurance policy?"

"Yes." He sighed and sat back down. "That was at my insistence. When he started taking those heart pills, I convinced him it was a good idea. Just in case. Too many men who work as hard as we do drop dead from a heart attack, and I thought he needed to protect his family. He agreed, so we added it to our current policies because it was less expensive that way. But he paid the additional premium himself."

"Policies?" I'd only heard about the one.

"We have key man insurance on both of us." Titus was holding eye contact more now, so maybe he was growing accustomed to my presence. "Most big investors require the insurance under the assumption that it'll pay the bills while the company recovers from the loss of a key employee."

"How much are we talking about? Will you be able to pay off your investors?"

He made a face. "Not a chance. Not without the release of Futura. The business will get ten million dollars, which I admit will come in very handy right now, especially since Peter's not going to be able to close with the new investors he was working with. But that's a drop in the bucket compared to what we owe our current investors. We're barely going to make it to the launch, even with the ten million—if nothing else goes wrong."

Ten million dollars seemed like an enormous amount of money, but when compared with three hundred million, I guess Titus had a point.

He fixed his blue eyes on me. "I'm hoping Stevan will be able to step into his father's shoes. He knows the ins and outs better than anyone. We can more easily hire someone else to manage marketing."

So his father's death meant a huge step up for Stevan, both in his job and because he now owned half of his father's thirty-one percent of the company, not to mention retaining the voting shares on his mother's portion of the business. Though Stevan seemed genuinely surprised about the will, he could have faked his reaction. Which ultimately meant that either of Peter's sons might be involved.

Another idea occurred to me. What if the company didn't have enough money to make it to the release even though it was only two months away? What if there were no new potential investors? Would saving the business be enough to make Peter take his own life for the insurance money? Or for someone here to murder him?

I had to admit that it was a possibility. Just about anyone at Futura could be involved. Including Titus Grey.

Chapter 11

"Okay," I said, pushing aside my unease. "You knew Peter well. Did you notice anything strange about him lately? Was there anyone who might have issues with him? Did he have close personal relationships that you know of outside work or his family?"

Titus blinked at me. "Are you asking me if he was cheating on his wife?"

"I'm asking if you noticed anything out of the ordinary about Peter. But, yes, that too."

"He wasn't unfaithful." Titus frowned and sighed. "Not this time anyway."

"He was unfaithful before?"

"I'm not really sure, but maybe. Four years ago, he started spending a lot of time with one of the women in marketing." Worry creased his brow. "Of course we'd had a lot of disagreements and compromises as we hammered out our business, but when I confronted him, it was bad. It almost derailed us."

"Because his relationship was affecting the business?"

"No, because of Brigit." Titus's face became rigid as he stared at me. "Peter loved his wife, and she trusted him. I told him if he was the kind of man who'd betray his wife, then I couldn't trust him to be fair in business. If he wanted to fool around, he had to separate from his wife first. It was a matter of respect."

"You risked all that because of an affair?" I admired his loyalty to the Griffin family, but such a thing was rare in this day and age.

"It wasn't a risk. I was giving him a wake-up call. Brigit is the best thing that ever happened to Peter, and he knew that. The next week, the woman in question found another job somewhere else, and we all went on."

I wondered if Brigit knew she had such a friend in Titus. "I'll need her name," I said.

Titus grimaced. "All right."

"So back to my question. Did anything out of the ordinary happen in the past few days?"

"Nothing that stands out."

"I know you called Peter on Sunday night when he was in the hospital. What did you talk about? Did you also go see him?"

Titus rubbed the thumb of his left hand along the palm of his right, as if trying to rub out a spot. "No, I didn't go to the hospital. We see each other every day, and this was supposed to be routine surgery, so there was no need for me to go. We did talk on Sunday like you said, but also on Saturday after his surgery as well. Both times he said how good he felt and that he was sure he could finish up his remaining projects this week while he was supposed to be resting at home." His hands stopped moving, and his gaze once more strayed to the monitor on the desk. "But now that you mention it, the phone call on Sunday was a little strange."

"Why's that?"

He yanked his hand through his hair again, freeing more of it from the oil holding the strands in place. "Because I discovered that the final production file, the only one we haven't released to our US factory where we're building the microchips, was recently protected with an extra password that isn't protocol. The chip is the last step besides snapping it all together, and the files are due to be transferred at the end of this week so they can put the final touches on the thousands of Futuras we have nearly ready for shipping. But since we completed the file a week early, I wanted to get the specs to the factory as soon as possible. When I couldn't get to the file, I called Peter to ask why."

"And what did he say?"

"That it was an added precaution he'd put in on Friday and had forgotten to tell me. He was already experiencing pain, I guess, from the kidney stones by then and didn't want to make me come up from the lab. Of course, when I called him at the hospital, he wasn't about to give me the password over the phone. Our plan was for him to stop by on his way home from the hospital and help me transfer the file."

"Is it odd that he put in a new password?"

Titus gave a shake of his head. "Not exactly. We change passwords all the time, but usually we do it together. So it was unusual, but not enough for me to worry about it. Especially with his sudden surgery. I wasn't sure I was even going to mention all this because it isn't exactly why I hired you. But if you do discover anything regarding the reason for the password, I'd be grateful to know about it."

I might be able to help him with a reason and with the password itself, but I'd have to find the right imprints. "Will you be able to access the file now without Peter?"

"Eventually. Stevan didn't know the password either, so we've tasked one of our programmers to hack into our own system. He'll be able to do it by Friday, but it won't be easy."

"I'm glad you told me," I said. "The password could be a very important reason for what happened to Peter." Standing, I wiped my hands on my pants. "I'll need to look around this office, and I'll need a complete past and present employee list and access to current employees, preferably in their own work environment."

Titus also came to his feet. "That can all be arranged, but didn't you say you already have a suspect?"

I shook my head. "Just a person to ask some questions. How well do you know your employees?"

"All the tech guys and programmers here meet with me on a regular basis, so I know them fairly well. And I know everyone in this building, except for a few of the new hires in marketing. I don't know many of the employees in our US factory, and even fewer in our factory in China, except for the managers, of course." He moved around the desk and reached for the landline next to the monitor that was three times the size of mine.

"I am particularly interested in two names," I said. "One is Robby, and I think his last name is Hartford."

His hand hesitated over the phone. "Robby Hartford's our accountant. Good man. Very dedicated."

"And Robby is his first name, not Robert?"

"Yes, it was kind of a joke here in the early days."

"I believe he worked for Peter at his last business?"

Titus nodded slowly, drawing back his hand. "Yeah. I think that's why Peter hired him. Robby apparently invested in the business, and Peter felt guilty when it went bankrupt."

"I heard Peter paid some people back with his own money."

Titus shrugged. "I don't know. It was before I met him. But Peter was on good terms with Robby, if that's what you're asking."

"Robby went to see Peter at the hospital. I need to talk to him about that."

"Okay, sure. When you're finished here, I'll take you to his office. Peter was very good at keeping records, so everything should be in his filing cabinet or in his desk. Unless it's top secret, and then it's either in his safe or on the computer protected by passwords. I can let you look at the safe when you're ready."

"Thank you." I moved around to the other side of the desk and sat in the huge chair that had been Peter Griffin's. I hadn't realized he'd been tall. It's sometimes hard to tell from imprints because the imprinter might not feel another person was tall or think at all about his size.

Imprints from the chair assailed me, but they were from long ago and didn't seem relative. Whatever time Peter had sat at this desk recently, he hadn't wasted time relaxing or gripping the armrests. I moved on to the desk, opening one of the drawers, looking for a pen, which were normally good carriers of imprints.

"You mentioned there were two names you were looking into," Titus said. "What's the second?"

I paused in my search and looked up at him. "Arthur. I don't have a last name. Do you have an employee by that name?"

"Yes, Arthur Dean. He's worked here over two years."

"What does he do?"

"He's a programmer. We hired him to write programs to go with Futura. Like all hardware, Futura needs good software to really shine. We also released specs months ago online to free-lance programmers who are interested in designing programs for our glasses, but we needed to release Futura with some built-in apps. Arthur refined our recipe app and a couple of others. It's good work."

"He wouldn't be the programmer you've tasked with breaking into Peter's file, would he?"

Titus froze, and for a long moment we stared at each other. "He is. Why do you know his name? Does he somehow figure into Peter's death?"

"I don't know yet, but until I clear everyone, you might want to hold off on getting into the file."

"I'll think about that." Titus picked up the phone. "Penelope, can you print a complete employee list, past and present? And any contractors we've hired. Send them up here to Peter's printer. Also, I need the investor list. You'll need a password to access the file." He rattled off a chain of letters and symbols. "Thank you." To me, he added, "We keep our list of investors safe. I'll give you a copy as long as you promise to shred it when you're finished. We need to protect them."

I could imagine why. If someone got wind of people investing millions of dollars in smart glasses, the investors might become targets for anyone else looking for money. Or maybe a smart glasses competitor could use the list to stir up trouble. With that possibility in play, if we didn't have a break in the case soon, I'd have to call every single investor to make sure there hadn't been any odd communications to them.

No, I thought. *If it becomes necessary, Elliot can call them.* I smiled to myself. Calling was something he could do from the very safe confines of his own chair, even with his agoraphobia.

I found a pen with imprints, but they either weren't

important, or I didn't understand the context well enough. Peter had used that pen to sign various contracts with investors, and everyone who imprinted on it had been excited and confident.

Also in the desk were papers, copies of invoices, and the usual office essentials. No important imprints on any of it. I touched the photograph of his family, recent by the looks of it, and that did have strong emotions of longing and sadness.

I'll give him one more chance, I thought. For Brigit. Maybe I've been too harsh on the boy. Maybe now he's finally ready to grow up.

That had been two weeks earlier, around the time of the imprint I'd read on the nitroglycerin pills. Another imprint followed from four years earlier, which told me this frame had likely held an older picture before this one.

Titus was right. I wasn't willing to abandon my family. The distance between Brigit and me was my making, not hers. She wanted me home more. She wanted me to try more with Niklas. She wanted her family to be happy with each other. I couldn't give her all that, but I could keep our lives intact. And maybe things would change. Maybe after we finished Futura.

Things apparently hadn't changed between Peter and Brigit, or had only been slowly changing, because the loneliness on Bridgit's Valium had been starkly clear. But Peter hadn't been without his own sadness, and I felt his emotion as if it were my own. How utterly sad that he'd waited too long.

The printer, sitting atop a beautiful, waist-high mahogany filing cabinet against the wall on the right, began spitting out pages faster than my ancient printer ever dreamed of doing.

"Is everything okay?" Titus walked over to the printer and picked up a few sheets.

It must seem strange, me sitting there at the desk touching the picture frame when I had that filing cabinet full of important documents to go over.

"Yes." I reached for the tray under the desk that held Peter's keyboard.

I let my fingers touch the keyboard, hoping to experience an imprint that would tell me what the password was. But there was nothing imprinted since last Thursday—excitement that he'd found a potential new investor, one whose funds would easily get them past the release date and provide enough capital to start version two in earnest.

Once I closed things with the new investor and signed the contract, I'd take a little time off to spend with Brigit. And maybe see a doctor for the odd twinges I'd been having lately in my back.

I paused in my typing as I looked over at the picture of my family. Brigit was still so beautiful, and every bit as unaware of her beauty as she had been on the first day we'd met in college. Of course, her beauty was something I couldn't forget—not with Titus always breathing down my throat about her. If I didn't know better, I'd think he was in love with her.

The chuckle that rose in my throat sounded strangled. If something ever happened to me, Brigit could do a lot worse than Titus. He'd never think to betray her.

I pushed the thought away to the past where it belonged. By next week, both my boys would be here, and with them holding down the fort, it would definitely be time for a vacation.

In fact, now that I'd found the investor and Futura was safe, I'd buy those tickets to Venice today. For once, I'd make Brigit happy.

The irony of his timing didn't escape me.

My gaze went to Titus, who watched me with curiosity.

"Does he have another computer he uses regularly?" I asked. "A laptop maybe?" If Peter hadn't imprinted on this device since Thursday, it was possible the password changes hadn't been done on this computer at all.

"Yeah, a laptop." His gaze swung around the room. "Looks like he must have taken it home. He works a lot, even on the weekends. He keeps most of his important files on our network, so it didn't matter what machine he accessed. We don't need the laptop. I can get you into most of his files on our network. Unless he changed the passwords on those too."

"It's not his files." I rose from the desk and crossed to where he stood. "It's tracing his steps on his last days here."

"I can ask his family if it's at his house."

"Do that, please."

Titus gave a mirthless chuckle. "He probably took it to the hospital with him."

"It wasn't in his things from the hospital. I was with the police when they picked those up from the family." I'd have asked about a laptop if I had known it would become important.

Titus's shoulders stooped a little. "How was Brigit doing when you saw her?"

"She's holding up." On a hunch, I reached out and touched the leather bracelet on his arm. "Interesting piece," I managed to say, as a vivid imprint rushed out at me.

The phone felt like a rock in my tight grip. No! Peter couldn't be dead! The knowledge was like a gaping hole in my stomach.

"How?" I forced myself to ask.

"They say it might be an overdose of medication, but they don't really know." Brigit's voice was soft and controlled. Too controlled. I wondered if they'd given her that mind-numbing Valium. "I'm on my way home now. The boys are with me."

I thanked God silently that she wasn't alone. The urge to go to her was overwhelming. I wanted to hold her and shield her from the pain I knew she was feeling. But if I did that, I might never let go.

"Please let me know if there is anything I can do," I said. My voice sounded like gravel grinding under my boots.

"I will. Maybe you can tell everyone there?"

"Of course. And don't worry. Stevan and I will take care of everything at Futura."

"I know." Her tone said she couldn't care less about Futura now—and maybe never again. I didn't blame her. Futura had stolen too much, and that was partly my fault.

"I'll let you know about the funeral," she added. "Maybe Wednesday or Thursday. You can give the employees time off to come, if they want. He'd like that."

"Okay." My heart thudded painfully in my chest. "But I meant what I said about calling. Anything you need. At any time. Just call."

"Thanks, Titus. You're a good friend."

I pulled away from the bracelet, not wanting to see more. So Titus was in love with Brigit. Maybe he didn't even know it himself, but I recognized the feeling. The imprint also put him in the clear. I didn't believe he'd killed Peter.

I met Titus's gaze. "I'm really sorry about Peter."

"I keep thinking if maybe he hadn't worked so hard . . ." Titus let the phrase dangle unfinished.

"Peter spending all his time here wasn't your fault," I said, keeping my tone light. "If it hadn't been Futura, it would have been another business."

He nodded and looked away. "You're probably right."

"So when was the last time you saw him?"

"Friday morning. We meet every morning, even if it's only for five minutes to touch base." He gave a slight chuckle. "Mostly, I think it's for me. I get worried, and talking through our plans for the day and highlighting any changes that happened or things we're anticipating helps me focus. Peter was good at helping me focus."

"You created a working prototype of Futura before you met him. I think you know how to focus."

"Maybe, but Peter showed me how to do it without a lot of anxiety. Work on one thing at a time. Take the first step and worry about the next after you complete the first. Focus on what you can change. That's what helped me figure out how to get Futura as compact as it is with only losing some of my originally-intended functions. Now I'm working on those for the next release."

It was sound advice, which I could probably use in my own life. "So what did you and Peter talk about on Friday?"

"About whether or not we should start the last part of the production sooner than we intended. Since I'm in constant contact with the manager at our factory, we agreed that I should email him to see if it would be useful to have the final microchip production file early. The manager got back to me on Sunday morning with an emphatic yes. He said he'd put a couple of people on making the new adjustments to the equipment and then free up more employees to begin production mid-week. Which would put us ahead on our orders. That means more end product to sell—and sooner. With how tight our budget is, that means a lot. We'd have to pay the employees regardless."

"Peter didn't mention the possibility of a new password in your Friday meeting?"

"Nothing. But he told me about a new investor he was hoping to sign this week."

Something must have happened later on Friday to make Peter want to protect the files. I needed to find out why. "Did Stevan know about the new investor?" I asked, changing directions a little. If he hadn't, it might be a motive for murder if he wanted to lay hands on the key man insurance.

"I'm sure he did. Stevan was literally Peter's right-hand man. He did all the work too important to give to the secretary. And he's over marketing as well. He works as much as I do." Titus shook his head. "I hope the launch changes that. He's got two little kids he shouldn't miss out on."

Nodding, I moved over to the many books and few knick-knacks on the nearest bookcase, running my hands over them to check for strong imprints. There weren't any. The papers in the filing cabinet and the safe were more of the same. The small refrigerator contained a bottle of wine and a case of cinnamon Coke—Peter's favorite soft drink, Titus informed me—but no interesting imprints. If someone had killed Peter Griffin, they hadn't been in this office thinking about murder.

During my search, I'd pretended to look at documents and contracts and invoices as much as possible, even jotting a few notes under Titus's interested gaze, but any more time in here would be a waste. Besides, I had a business to run and a meeting at the school with the football team I couldn't miss.

"Okay," I said, "I have enough here."

"Any clues?"

I nodded. "I think so, but I'll need to do more research before I can tell you anything definitive." I held out a hand for the papers he'd had the receptionist print for me, pleased to see color photographs of the employees next to their information. "Does the list seem to be complete?"

"Yes." He took a pen and made a mark by one of the names before handing it over to me. "This is the woman I told you Peter was interested in."

I scanned the pages. There were far more people than I'd expected, but I guess three hundred million did pay for a few employees. "If I could see Robby Hartford now," I said, my finger finding his name on the list, "that would be perfect."

I had a feeling neither Titus nor Robby was going to like what would happen next.

obby Hartford's office was minuscule, and his chair bumped into the wall as he stood up to greet us. He was an average looking man with close-cropped blond hair, light blue eyes, a nice smile, and a firm handshake. His hawkish nose was the only thing that stood out about him. He was taller than Titus by a foot, and the paunch on his thin frame looked out of place, as if he were one of those people who usually never gained weight, but constant snacking on junk food at his desk had taken its toll.

"This is Autumn Rain," Titus said. "She's looking into Peter's death."

Was that panic crossing over Robby's face? I didn't know him well enough to tell.

"Nice to meet you." Robby didn't extend his hand to shake, and since he wasn't wearing a ring, I didn't force the issue.

"I'm here to ask you a few questions," I told him.

"Do you need me here?" Titus asked with an anxious glance toward the open door. "I can stay, if you'd rather, but I would like to talk to the programmer regarding that file we talked about. I can come back for you when you're finished, or Robby can show you to the next person on your list."

I considered that for a moment. Robby was hiding something, but he didn't seem the violent type. "We can talk alone." The man would probably be more open without one of his bosses hovering over him.

"Okay, here's my direct line, if you need it." Titus took a card from his pocket. I still didn't know who dressed Titus, but the style gap between the two men was glaringly obvious. Robby's pale blue shirt and black dress pants could have been from a past decade while Titus's attire was on today's cutting edge. My curiosity about Titus's wardrobe wouldn't let that go.

"Please have a seat." Robby gestured to the only other chair in the room, shoved against the wall in front of the desk. He reseated himself behind the desk.

Instead of accepting his invitation, I crossed to the small window that was the saving grace of this broom-closet office. The parking lot below wasn't pretty, but light was everything. "I understand that you've known Peter a long time," I said, turning to face him.

"Uh, yeah. We worked together before."

"At Armed."

"Yes," he said with a slight hesitation.

"How much did you invest in Armed?"

His eyes widened slightly. "A few thousand."

"How much is a few?"

"Forty thousand." He sighed, shoulders slumping. "I really believed in it. The concept was miraculous. But not even with a billion dollars could we have done it."

"You lost everything?"

"Not everything. I have this job, which pays better than most in my field."

"I heard Peter reimbursed some of the investors."

He nodded. "Yes, mostly those who were going to lose their houses."

"Not you?"

His eyes dropped to his lap. "He got me this job. It was what I wanted."

"You went to see him at the hospital Sunday night?"

"Yes." His gaze lifted again, his eyes almost colorless in the light from the window. "I consider him a friend."

He'd used the word consider and not considered. Was that important?

I moved closer to the desk. A picture of him with a woman and two preteen girls stared out at me, yet he wasn't wearing a wedding ring. "Your wife?" I asked, gesturing to the picture.

He nodded without smiling. "Yes. And my twins. They're ten now."

"Ten going on sixteen by the looks of it," I said. He was so tightly wound, I hoped the comment would lighten the mood.

"Yeah," he said, almost painfully. "That's true. They need a lot of guidance."

I reached out to touch the picture, turning it slightly more toward me, pretending to look at it more closely but in reality checking for imprints.

Sadness, so much sadness. Anger and betrayal.

Not a scene, but vivid emotions all the same. I snatched back my hand before I drowned in it.

Furrows appeared in Robby's brow as he studied me. I calculated that my chances of touching things here in his office without interference were close to nil. Instead, I'd use what I already had. I pulled the chair to one side and sat where the monitor on his desk didn't obscure my view of his face.

"Look, Robby, I'm going to be honest with you." Usually I hated it when people said that because it was likely they'd lie right after. And maybe I was lying a little. "I know you've been cooking the books."

He drew in a quick breath that told me I was on the right track.

"I also know Peter suspected and that you were worried about him finding out." I let the words hang for a bit. "How much did you take?"

He blinked a few times before saying softly, "Forty thousand."

"Because he owed you?"

A long silence followed, one I let continue until he felt compelled to break it. "It's not like that. Peter wasn't the reason I invested in Armed. In fact, he warned me not to invest. He told me he was beginning to doubt the tech behind it. I was the one who thought my paltry contribution would do something to sway the odds." He snorted in apparent self-loathing. "And make me a millionaire."

"The tech looks solid this time," I said, thinking of the second mortgage Elliot had discovered. "Did you invest again in Futura?"

"No. I have shares, though. All top full-time employees do."

"You're two months away from launch. Why would you jeopardize your position here? Why would you risk your shares, especially when you, of all people, know that Futura is hurting for operating funds?" He didn't answer, and I waved a hand to show it didn't matter. "None of that concerns me. What concerns me is if you decided to do something about it. If you decided to hurt Peter."

"Of course not!" The words shot from him like a bullet.

He seemed sincere, but so far, it looked like he had the most to gain by Peter's death. Forty thousand secreted away now might lead to millions of pilfered funds after Futura's release.

Again, silence compelled him to speak. "Peter was going to find out," he said. "I knew I probably didn't have time to put it back before he reviewed my books."

"Which pleads my point. Was killing Peter your backup plan?"

He shook his head emphatically. "You think I'd kill Peter to cover up what I did? That I would risk life imprisonment or even death penalty? No way. Forty thousand isn't enough to send me to jail for a year. I'd probably get a commuted sentence with payback and community service. I have two daughters and a wife who depend on me. I wouldn't risk murder."

"Maybe you thought you wouldn't get caught."

"I wouldn't hurt anyone like that, especially not Peter."

"Then why did you take the money? I also know you took out a second mortgage. What did you need it for? Drugs? Gambling?" Those were my bets.

"No." His tone was agonized. "Why I needed it is personal. And my backup plan was a computer glitch to buy more time. If that didn't work, I'd go to my parents. What can I do to convince you I had nothing to do with what happened to Peter?"

I thought about that. "First, you can tell me if you or anyone you know takes tadalafil."

"Tadalafil?"

"I think one of the brand names is Cialis."

He flushed, the color standing out again the pale blue of his collar. "Oh, right. I've seen the commercials." He shook his head. "I don't take it, but my father does, and so do a couple of the guys around here. They talk about it sometimes in the break room. I guess they like to take their daily pills after lunch."

Which meant he had access here at work and maybe at his father's. Not good for him.

"What else?" he asked, looking almost hopeful.

"You can let me search your desk."

He stared at me in disbelief. "Are you kidding? There's nothing here. The books are on the database."

"I told you I don't care about your embezzling. I'm looking into Peter Griffin's death."

"It wasn't embezzling. It was just a loan."

When I didn't respond, he added, "So, you're looking for the tada—whatever it is. Does that mean you won't tell them about me?"

"Of course I'm going to tell them. It'll be in my report."

He closed his eyes and gave a moan, which made me feel sorry for him and also gave me an idea. "The report could take a day or two. Which means if you let me look around your desk, I'll give you time to talk to Titus yourself."

He grimaced and closed his eyes as if in pain. I'm sure he was. If he had a secret gambling or drug problem, it meant facing the consequences of that and probably losing his job.

After what must have been an entire minute, with nothing but the fan of his computer softly buzzing, he stood and moved toward the window. "Go ahead," he said. "I have nothing to hide."

I arched a brow as I went around the other side of the desk. "Nothing?"

"I mean about Peter's death. Which I thought was an accident anyway." He turned his back to me and looked out the window.

Which meant if Robby had poisoned Peter, he hadn't left the tadalafil in his desk. Well, of course not. He would have used it all and disposed of the evidence. But I'd already guessed that much.

I ran my fingertips over his keyboard. Strong imprints emanated from them, going back several months. But they were all about the money he'd taken.

If they find out, they'll fire me. But I'd had no choice.

Twenty thousand more should be enough until the profits from Futura began to come in. And it would bring me up to the forty thousand I'd lost. Not that Peter had been responsible.

But he had blamed Peter, after all. I could tell from the justification in the imprints.

I have to protect Elaine and most of all the girls. It was only twenty thousand, total. I could pay that back, and no one would know.

What was I going to do? I couldn't let the girls down. Or Elaine, though she'd brought this upon herself. The money was there in the account, and we had more investors on the horizon. They might never know. Ten thousand would be enough.

Robby felt terrible about what he'd done, even from the beginning, and there'd been nothing in any of the imprints that wished ill for Peter. Leaving the keyboard, I checked his drawers, knickknacks, pens, stapler, printer, and other pictures. He'd imprinted on some of it, but nothing was out of the ordinary except the occasional piercing guilt about the embezzling and sadness over an argument with his wife about separation. This last had resulted in him removing his wedding ring, though he still hoped to make the relationship work.

"Okay," I said, moving around the desk but not taking the chair again. "I'm finished."

He turned from the window and stared at me. "Did you find what you're looking for?"

I didn't answer. "You went to see Peter at the hospital. Did you see anyone else there that you know?"

"Just his wife, and she left when I arrived. It was nine, and she was tired. She and their sons had been in and out all day."

"You know his wife well?"

He shook his head. "Not really, but she seems nice. Kind of quiet compared to Peter." He paused before adding, "Sometimes when I've talked to her at company events, she seems"—he waved a hand in dismissal—"not all there. Distracted."

Valium does that to a person, I thought.

"Is there anyone you know who might want to kill Peter? Who might have something to gain?"

He snorted. "Besides me, you mean?"

"Yeah, something like that."

He considered for a long moment. "No one."

"Not even former investors of Armed?"

"It was only a drop in the pan to the major investors. They'll get it all back and more."

"Get it back? Does that mean some of them are investing in Futura?"

He nodded. "Absolutely."

I pulled the papers Titus had given me from my purse where I'd stashed them. "Show me." I handed him the sheet of investors. He marked seven names and handed the sheet back.

"So no one else comes to mind? Especially here at the office?"

"No. Everyone worships Peter. He's one of those people who can make you excited about daily reports and cleaning our own offices to save money." He shrugged. "The only person I've ever heard him raise his voice at was his son."

"Stevan?"

"Definitely not. Stevan's his golden boy, heir to the throne." The words were good-natured despite their content. "Stevan doesn't have the courage to stand up to Peter. But his older son does. They had an argument out there in the hallway a couple of weeks ago."

"About what?"

He shook his head. "I don't know. But they must have made up because the son was back on Friday."

Friday, the day Peter had put in the new password. "No yelling that day?"

"Not that I'm aware of."

"Do you know what they talked about?" Surely the accountant would have been told about Niklas working for the company. Or did they have a different department for that?

"Not a clue. They went into his office to talk."

"Do you know a man named Arthur?" I asked. "He's a programmer here, and I'll be interviewing him next."

"Arthur Dean, yeah. Great guy. We sometimes play racquetball together. His workstation is in the programming bullpen across the hallway. But he might not be there. In this morning's meeting, I heard Titus asking him to do something to Peter's files, and he'd have to do that on the servers inside the lab."

In the meantime, those orders might have changed. "I'll take a chance. Thank you for your time."

He arose. "I'll show you where Arthur works."

"That's okay. I can find my way." As I moved toward the door, cold air waved over me, as if blocking my passage. I reached out, but nothing was there. Goose bumps rippled up my arm and across my shoulders.

As I started to walk through it, my gaze fell to the trash can by the side of Robby's desk. I'd passed it earlier in my search, but now something white inside caught my eye. I bent over and removed a tiny, unmarked bakery box that looked similar to the one I'd seen in Peter's hospital room. There were no imprints on this one either, but inside were the same four chocolate wrappers that resembled small cupcake liners and flecks of chocolate.

"What's this?" I asked, holding the box out on my palm.

"Oh, it held some chocolates. Mrs. Griffin brought everyone some last week. They're homemade. She gives them out a few times a year. They're delicious."

"What day was that?"

He shrugged. "At least a week ago. I'd eaten a big lunch that day, so I only ate a couple. I put them in my bottom drawer and forgot them until this morning." He flushed as if newly remembering that the woman's husband was dead.

If Brigit Griffin had made the chocolates, that would explain why a similar box had been in her husband's hospital room. I felt a little disappointed at the thought because last night I'd started thinking the box might have been how the murderer administered both the nitrates and the tadalafil.

Unless . . . had Brigit perhaps dosed a batch of chocolate for her husband with tadalafil in an effort to save their marriage? It was entirely possible, and it might mean perhaps his death had been an accident.

Of course, after a surgery hardly seemed the time for

romance, and that didn't explain the higher level of nitrates in Peter Griffin's system.

Or that odd coldness I kept feeling. I needed to ask my biological father if he'd heard of anything like that before.

"Can I take this with me?" I said to Robby. It was a long-shot, but Quincy might want to have the remaining bits of chocolate tested.

He shrugged and said uneasily, "Sure, I guess."

I pushed through the cold air and opened the door.

"Please," Robby said, making me turn back to face him. "Can you not . . . uh, let what I did become public knowledge? Bad publicity could really hurt the launch."

"Then maybe it's best for everyone if you talk to Titus or Stevan sooner rather than later." I could tell Quincy and Shannon to hold back on the information during their official visit today, but they wouldn't let it ride forever.

Without waiting for a reply, I slipped the box into my purse and went across the hallway to an open door. The invisible cold seemed to come with me. The programming bullpen was even larger than Peter Griffin's office, and inside were a dozen small cubicle workspaces, eight men and two women sat at desks in front of large monitors that took up nearly all the space. The two cubicles closest to the door were empty.

A petite Asian woman looked up from the nearest occupied cubicle. "May I help you?"

"I'm looking for Arthur Dean." I rubbed my arms for warmth. Maybe they kept it cool in here so the computers wouldn't overheat. That would explain the temperature drop.

She motioned to the cubicle in the far corner near a window. "Over there."

A few people looked up as I moved down the aisle, but

most didn't take their eyes from the monitors. As I approached, I heard Arthur talking on the phone.

"Don't worry," he said. "I won't say anything. Why don't we meet and play racquetball? I promise to let you beat me at least once." He paused. "Oh, right. Well, that seems a little hypocritical after what you said to me, but yeah, I understand. Good luck with everything. I'm sure it'll work out."

My first thought was that Robby Hartford had called to warn him about me, but then I remembered the imprint from Niklas that hoped Arthur would keep his mouth shut. *About what?* I wondered.

Arthur hung up as I came around to the opening, his dark eyes lighting up at the sight of me. "Hello," he drawled, with more than a little suggestion. "Are you one of the new programmers?"

I shook my head and lifted my arms to rest on top of the padded cubicle wall, studying him. He was tall and dark and handsome, typically so, though the somewhat pointed, clean-shaven chin might be a turn-off to some women. His figure was trim and strong-looking—no belly here—and his snug black pants and dark gray shirt put me more in mind of Titus Grey than Robby Hartford. A few of Arthur's shirt buttons were open to reveal a gold necklace. I wasn't surprised to see he didn't wear a wedding band.

"I'm Autumn Rain," I said. "I've come to ask you a few questions about Peter Griffin. I've been hired by Mr. Grey."

"Yeah, he told me you'd be in when he sent me back upstairs." He reclined in his chair and put his feet up on his desk. "Peter was a great guy. I'm really sorry about his death."

I took out the papers Titus had given me. "I see you've worked here for over two years."

"That's right. It's been great. You know, getting to see it all from the beginning. Or mostly." He waved an arm at nothing in particular. "Of course, a few of these people have been here from the very beginning."

"Well, only Titus is actually from the beginning." I allowed myself a friendly smile. It never hurt to be sociable, especially to a flirt. "When was the last time you saw Peter?"

"Ah, let's see." He stared up at the ceiling. "Last Friday, I believe."

"Where?"

"The hallway. Just in passing. We didn't talk." Had there been a hesitation in his response?

"How well do you know his family?"

"I know Stevan pretty well," he said with a smile. "I have to give him weekly reports about my work so he can pass it on to the higher-ups. I've also seen his mother at a few company parties."

"You don't know Peter's oldest son?"

His shrug was casual. "I might have seen him around. The rumor mill says he's going to work here. But you know how that goes."

Strange that a programmer would have heard that particular rumor but not the accountant who had an actual office and a longer working relationship with Peter Griffin. "You mean nepotism?" His statement could be interpreted as resentful.

"No. I meant you know how rumor mills are. And I don't care what the bosses do as long as I get paid."

"So you didn't go see Peter Griffin while he was in the hospital?"

"Only a suck-up would do that." He laughed. "Besides, I didn't know he was there. So, no, I didn't go see him."

I thought for a moment, my eyes roving over his desk to find something I could touch, but aside from his keyboard in a drawer that he'd pushed under the desk when he put up his feet, there wasn't much more than a wireless mouse. No pictures or books or anything. That was odd.

"Do you know anyone who might want to hurt Peter Griffin?" I asked.

"Probably there are dozens," he said. "I mean, he's pushed and prodded and organized everything so Futura can be successful. He was a powerful man, and I'm sure a lot of people would have loved to squash him." He held my gaze for a moment with eyes some women might call dreamy. "But why all these questions? We were told the hospital was at fault. That it was some freak accident."

"Maybe," I said. "We're just covering all the bases."

"Well, if I think of anything, I can let you know."

Normally, I'd give him one of the cards I carried with my shop name and my cell phone number, but his flirtatious manner stopped me. The last thing I needed was him showing up at the antiques shop. Elliot had mentioned making up cards for me with his business name and my phone number, but I hadn't yet agreed to our working relationship, so he hadn't made the cards.

"You have a pen and paper? I'll give you my cell number."

He awarded me with a slow, seductive smile. "And I didn't even have to ask." He opened a drawer and pulled out a pad of sticky notes and a green and black pen, handing them to me. No imprints registered on the notes, but the pen was the type of expensive one you bought new ink cartridges for instead of throwing out, and a strong imprint swept me away.

Charmaine, Charmaine, Charmaine. Her name echoed in

my head. I couldn't believe she'd dumped me. What had I done wrong? I'd thought I'd finally found my soulmate, but it was definitely over. She'd made that clear.

My eyes lifted to the cubicle near the door where she stood now, talking to Titus Grey about her new block game app for the Futura. Her black hair was cut to perfectly frame her face, and her dark eyes would be earnest as she spoke.

I wished I could sink through the floor. I might have to quit working here. It was too hard seeing her every day.

The imprint from last Friday afternoon faded enough for me to place the pad on top of the cubicle and begin writing my number, slowly, because I was still cold. I waited until more images came—this time of flirting with the woman named Charmaine at this very cubicle. There were also moments of him staring at the pen itself. It had been his father's, and he valued it greatly.

There was nothing about Niklas or Peter. No thoughts of evil or duplicity. Whatever Arthur was supposed to keep quiet about didn't seem to involve murder. Maybe he wasn't the Arthur in Niklas Griffin's imprint.

When I'd finished writing the number and my name, the imprints were still going—and probably would continue for decades. I practically shoved it back at Arthur. He thought himself in love with Charmaine, and she no longer cared about him that way. I felt sorry for him.

"Let me know if you think of anything," I said.

He stood and stepped close to me—a little too close. I could smell his spicy aftershave as I looked up into his face. He was taller than I'd estimated. "Actually, I'd love to ask you out," he said. "If that's okay with you."

He was probably trying to make his former girlfriend

jealous. "Sorry, I'm engaged." Remembering his heartbreak, I kept my tone light.

His eyes went to my fingers. "No ring?"

"I forgot to put it on." I made an apologetic face. "But it's nice to meet you." I took a step back. "I'd better continue my interviews."

I went to the next cubicle and introduced myself. After two more brief interviews, I was beginning to wish I'd come after hours to read imprints without anyone around. It didn't help that I was hyperaware of Arthur occasionally watching me. I was relieved when I escaped the room and headed to the marketing room, which had only four employees in half the space. The interviews there were as fruitless as with the programmers. At some point, I was no longer cold, but I couldn't recall when the temperature changed, or if I'd simply become accustomed to it.

Stevan's office next to the marketing room was locked, and there was no response when I knocked. It was now approaching noon, and I was both ravenous and exhausted from reading imprints and making up creative excuses to touch things. I'd learned nothing new since my interview with Robby, except that one of the women in marketing had a crush on Arthur Dean, and some of the employees were using Brigit's little chocolate boxes to hold office supplies at their workspaces.

Back on the main floor hallway, Titus Grey met me in response to my text. "I'm going to do a little off-site investigation to confirm a few leads," I told him. "I may need to come back here and talk to the rest of the employees." Or at least touch everything in the lab and upstairs in the offices. I also still had questions for Stevan about how much he knew regarding the terms of his father's will and if it had been possible for the company to survive until the launch without the proceeds from the key man insurance.

"Thank you for coming," Titus said. "I hope we've been helpful."

"You have. Thank you. Eli or I will contact you soon." We shook hands firmly before he opened the door leading into the lobby.

The receptionist turned and smiled as I emerged, every bit as friendly as she had been earlier. "I bet you're exhausted," she said as the door shut behind me.

She wasn't far from the truth. Ignoring my rumbling stomach, I paused to talk with her. "You said you weren't aware of Niklas Griffin coming to work here, but did you see him last Friday?"

She nodded and pointed to the door I'd just come through. "This is the only way in, so I see everyone, even the employees. No one not working here gets in without someone to accompany them."

"Even Niklas Griffin?"

She gave a light snort. "With the way things were between him and Peter, especially him. But there weren't any fireworks last Friday during his visit, thank heaven."

"Does Niklas know anyone here besides his father and brother?"

"No idea. If he does, no one has said anything." She smiled. "He's cute though, and the boss's son, so if he really is going to work here, he'll probably be popular with the women in marketing."

I smiled and couldn't think of anything more to ask. My mind felt sluggish. The best thing I could do now was to find something to eat.

I'd turned to go when the Asian woman, Charmaine, from the programming bull pen opened the door by the desk. She smiled at me in recognition before turning to the secretary.

"Hey, Penelope," she said, "has Mateo picked up his stuff yet?" She held up a suspiciously familiar green and black pen. "Arthur took over his desk the second I had it cleared this morning—you know how they fight over the window cubicles—but apparently I missed this. Arthur found it in his desk."

"Not yet," the receptionist answered. "I'll put it in with the other stuff. Titus said to make sure he handed over the last of his program updates before we release his paycheck. I still can't believe he quit yesterday—and over voice-mail, no less."

Charmaine frowned and adjusted the purse strap over her shoulder. "Me either. When we broke up last week, I thought he took it okay. Besides, once the launch is here, and we move to a new building, we wouldn't be running into each other every day. We were both hoping to be hired as full-time employees instead of temporary contractors. He shouldn't have left."

"Wait," I said, leaning forward in my eagerness. "Mateo was your boyfriend? I thought you were dating Arthur." That was the worst problem with imprints. It was easy to confuse who had imprinted a scene or emotions unless that person happened to be looking in a mirror, or someone in the scene addressed them by name. Obviously, Arthur Dean hadn't owned the pen he'd lent me, which meant he was back on my suspect list.

Charmaine did a doubletake. "Arthur? Not in this world. No, not in this universe. He's a brilliant programmer but too much of a partier in my book. And a big flirt. I'm surprised he didn't get your phone number."

I flushed slightly at that, though the reason Arthur had my number was not for dating purposes. "And Mateo quit yesterday? On the day Peter died?" The timing was suspicious. "Do you still have the voice-mail?"

Charmaine bristled. "Mateo would never hurt anyone. Why are you investigating this anyway? We were told something went wrong at the hospital. Wasn't it with Mr. Griffin's surgery?"

Both women stared at me intently. I lifted my shoulders and said, "I'm sorry. I'm not at liberty to discuss the case."

Penelope nodded. "I can play the message." She pushed a few buttons, and a male voice came from the phone on her desk, flavored with an accent that made him seem both sensual and aloof.

"This is Mateo. I'm sorry, but I'm not coming into work today. Or ever again. Please tell Mr. Griffin that I'm sorry. I know he took a chance on me, and I'll get him my finished program when I come back to get my things. It's personal, not anything about Futura. I have loved working there. I wish you all the best with the launch."

Despite his bad timing for quitting, the pen imprints had indicated Mateo's innocence. And after quitting, he really had nothing to gain by Peter's death.

Charmaine looked ready to cry. "This is all my fault. I'm going to see him." Without giving the receptionist the pen, she passed me and hurried toward the door.

"They'll get back together," Penelope predicted with a smile. "She only broke up with him because her grandmother was causing turmoil in the family because he isn't Chinese."

Other employees were coming through the inner door now, probably heading for lunch. With a nod at the receptionist, I beat them to the door.

I needed food—and fast.

Chapter 13

The Futura building was only six minutes from Sayler's Old Country Kitchen, which was a favorite of mine because of the delicious steaks. Often when people discovered I was into herbs, healthy food, and alternate medicines, they were surprised when they learned I wasn't a vegetarian. Maybe it was the no-shoes, flower-child image that gave them a certain idea of me. But I loved steak and just about every other meat as well.

I ordered an eighteen-ounce New York steak with the full meal. It set me back nearly forty bucks and was a luxury I could ill afford, but I was drooping. If I was to get through the meeting with the football players at the school, I had to be alert. That meant I was keeping my gloves on for now, so I didn't have to read any imprints, casual or otherwise.

As I waited for the food, I removed one glove long enough to write an email on my phone to Elliot, highlighting everything I'd learned and what information I needed him to research. I also snapped pictures of the employee and investor records and sent them as well. I sent a copy of the email to Shannon, Quincy, and Paige, asking for any updates. I hoped someone had new information because I hadn't made much progress, except maybe clearing Titus Grey and learning more about Robby Hartford.

As I ate, I considered what I'd learned and what I still needed to find out. Would Futura have had enough money to launch without Peter's death? With the new investors, I thought it likely. So that meant Stevan and Titus wouldn't have motive. But how much had Stevan known about his father's will? He had the largest number of voting shares now, and that could be important.

Or had Robby Hartford stolen more than he admitted to? And why did he need the money?

Was there a connection between Arthur and Niklas? Since Niklas hadn't inherited any part of Futura, he seemed the least likely at the moment to have wanted his father dead. Except the imprint on his ring said he had something to hide. But if he'd killed his father, why bring in the attorney, who would put a spotlight on the death?

There was also Brigit Griffin and her chocolate making. Did she have access to tadalafil? Could she have put it in the chocolate she'd made for her husband? If she had, how had the nitroglycerin ended up in his system? That made me wonder if two people were involved, with two separate agendas that might or might not have included plans for murder. I didn't believe Brigit's imprints at the hospital had been those of a woman trying to kill her husband.

After inhaling all of my rather large meal in less than ten minutes, to the utter shock of the waitress, I started on my way to Franklin High School. If traffic didn't hold me up, I'd get there by one, which would give me time to observe the kids as they arrived.

I'd resisted technology, but I was grateful now for how easy it made finding the school again. All I had to do was resist the seemingly ingrained temptation to turn left when my phone said to go right. I might have been born using more of my mind than most of the world, but my imprint ability seemed to have taken up some of the space meant for directional instinct.

As I walked from the parking lot into the school, I called my store. "Hi, Thera, how's it going?"

"Been pretty steady since Jazzy left at noon," she said. "I think it might actually have to do with all her posts on the Facebook Marketplace. Well, that and Jake's BOGO. There is a definite trickle over from his shop, and they aren't just buying his herbs. We actually sold out of those little metal cars."

"That's great. Do you think I need to call in someone else?" We both knew I meant Tawnia because there was no one else.

"No, I've got it. I won't be able to do the cleaning, but the customers are okay."

"I'll take care of that tonight. I should be in soon. I'm at the high school to meet with some kids."

"Everything's fine here," Thera assured me. "But I hope they're paying you for all this legwork you're putting in."

I hoped so too. "Well, we have a few clients, not including Matthew and Paige, so I'll probably get something," I said. "But thank you for worrying."

"I'm not the only one. Jake's been in here three times asking if you were back yet. I think he knows you're reading imprints."

That was Jake for you. "I'll send him a text." Which I did as soon as I hung up. I didn't want him to worry.

The doors to the school were open, and Principal Baird Tillmon was standing in the lobby with Pax and two other boys, one of whom looked like a linebacker. Tillmon came to meet me. "The boys will likely straggle in. You know how that is."

"I expected as much." I pulled off my gloves and tucked them into my purse. "So I'll talk to each of the boys for a moment as they gather. Then I'm thinking you might say you have something important to show them, and we can take them to see the equipment room. You'll have to explain what happened, but we'll be able to watch their reactions. Would that be okay?"

He inclined his graying head, giving me another glimpse of his bald circle on the back. "Okay. But just so you know, the head of the district, Cyrus Anderson, is on his way. He's worried about the students' rights since we haven't exactly laid out why we're having the meeting. We shouldn't start without him."

"Okay." It didn't bother me that Opal's father had decided to attend. I was accustomed to bureaucracy, especially in protecting the rights of children—which didn't always turn out to be in the child's best interest.

I headed toward Pax. "Can I talk to you for a moment?" I gave the other boys a smile. "You guys are next. I'll be talking with everyone." They blinked in confusion, which was a good thing. Keeping them off balance would make them tell me more in the end. And someone knew what had happened—I just needed to find an imprint that would tell me who.

Pax walked with me to one of the staircases on either side of the lobby that led to the second floor of the building. He turned his back to the others and whispered urgently, "Opal says her dad is coming, and she's tagging along, so don't let on that you know her, or that we're . . . you know."

"Got it," I said. "But have you two been asking around? What are people saying?"

He twisted his head to look at the other players. Four more teens had joined the others. "We tried, but no one's saying anything. Except this one guy from her brother's football team posted a meme of some kid doing a faceplant into a football. He said he predicts a lousy year for Franklin football. She's going to ask him about it."

It could be simple rivalry, or something else altogether. "You think another football team might be involved?"

Again, he glanced behind him—probably looking for Opal and her father. "Yeah, because I can't imagine anyone from our team doing it. Most of the guys would take a bullet for Coach Valdez." His voice lowered further so I could barely hear. "I think I'm the only one who doesn't want to play. I only play because Coach Valdez arranges it so I can play basketball without paying."

"Who else knows that?" I looked past him to the gathering boys.

"No one except my mom. And Opal. The coach asked me not to tell anyone." He hesitated before adding, "But sometimes I think they know. I know I don't work as hard as some of them do at it, and they're mad I get to start when they don't." He leaned forward earnestly. "I can't help that. I play my best when I'm out there. That's all I can do. But my heart isn't in it. I'd rather be playing the piano."

He shouldn't have to play football at all if he didn't want to. I wondered if I could somehow help him.

He must have read something of my thoughts in my expression because he shook his head. "Don't get me wrong. I'm not quitting. I want to help them make it to the state playoffs. It's only one more year. Only half a year really, and then it'll be over. Staying on the team won't make a difference to me in the long run, but it seems to make a lot of difference to everyone else. I don't want to let the coach down."

I stared at him, thinking hard. He didn't care about football, but what if he was taking the space of someone who did? Someone who wasn't put on the field because there was no more room and the best players—regardless of their feelings toward the sport—were given first shot.

"If you weren't playing," I said, "who would be in your spot?"

He shrugged. "It's a toss-up. Could be Armando or Memphis."

"Okay. I'll talk to them next. Send one of them over, okay?" I took out a small notebook from my purse. I used it mostly to record a list of things I was looking for at estate sales and the most I would pay, but this would make me look official.

A handsome kid with pale skin, blond hair, and heavy eyelashes approached me. "Pax sent me over?" He wore a heavy-looking football ring, which I hoped most of the other boys would be wearing as well.

"What's your name?" My pen poised over my notebook.

"Memphis Tillmon."

"Tillmon?" I glanced toward the principal, remembering the imprint in the equipment room where Principal Tillmon had been asking the coach to put a boy on the team. Had he pulled strings for his own son?

"Yeah, he's my dad." The boy sounded aggrieved, but almost immediately he smiled engagingly. "Guess you weren't expecting anyone with those genes to be athletically inclined. But I love football. I plan to play it in college."

I laughed with him. "I like your dad. But tell me, what were you doing two weeks ago on Thursday and Friday nights?"

"You mean when the vandalism happened in the equipment room?"

"You know about it?"

"I heard my dad talking on the phone."

"Who have you told about it?"

"No one." He snorted. "I learned my lesson long ago that nothing I hear him say about school is repeatable. One time in tenth grade, I let it out that a student was going to be suspended, and my dad grounded me for a month. A month!"

"So, what were you doing on those nights?"

"Hanging with my friends."

"They can vouch for you?"

He nodded. "Absolutely."

"Who are they?" I looked over at the knot of boys. Beyond them, a man was entering the front doors, his figure silhouetted by the brighter light outside so I couldn't quite make out his face.

"Not those guys," Memphis said, following my gaze. "My friends aren't on the team. I can give you names if you want."

The shadowy figure came into view—a dark-haired man I assumed was Cyrus Anderson, head of the school district, because Opal was at his side.

I dragged my gaze back to Memphis. "Okay, give me two names of people who can vouch for you." I jotted down the names and numbers, then held out my hand to shake his. The boy hesitated, but he finally offered me his hand. The strong imprint that came from his ring was less than a few seconds old.

She was here! And looking better than ever. Maybe today I'd ask her out. Now that she'd soon know what a loser Pax was, she wouldn't look at him again.

But she was looking at him, though I could see she was trying hard not to. Jealousy's cold fingers gripped my heart. She'd said they were only friends. Maybe it wasn't true.

Our clasp broke before I could see more. I was disappointed, but I couldn't exactly keep hold of a kid's hands until all the imprints played out. At any rate, it seemed Memphis had a crush on Opal. I didn't find it unusual that the two would have had interactions. Their fathers both worked for the school district, and they could have run into each other on a fairly regular basis. However, along with the boy's on-the-bench status, it seemed like motive for him to trash the equipment room. Maybe he'd even hoped Pax would be accused. But unless he'd somehow known about the black and white spray paint Pax and Opal had used to fix the sprinkler pointers, and Opal said she hadn't told anyone, the theory was farfetched. Still, Memphis was a definite suspect.

I called the other on-the-bencher next, with no new findings, and then the other boys, one at a time. In each interview, my question about where they'd been on the nights in question was met with surprise. The imprints from the boys with school rings showed only snatches of things that interested them. The quarterback had a goal to gain twenty pounds and bench press a hundred so he could be a better football player. Another boy was worried about his parents' divorce and hoped it wasn't his fault. A short, stalky boy had imprinted a motto about endurance. Nothing screamed, or even hinted, that they'd been involved in the destruction of the equipment room. On it went, until I'd seen all the boys except one.

Principal Tillmon came up to me. "That was pretty fast," he said. "I think you've seen all of them. What now?"

"I still have to talk to that boy." I pointed to a teen near Memphis and Opal, who were talking.

"Oh, no. That's Otto Anderson. He's not on the team—at least not Franklin's team. He goes to Lincoln. Mr. Anderson is a great believer of including his children in his work when he can."

So that's Opal's brother, I thought, considering the new information. From what I remembered of my talk with Opal, he was a member of the Lincoln football team, and it had been his friend who had posted online about Franklin facing a tough year. As an opposing team member, he had something to gain if Pax wasn't playing, and he'd known about the black and white paint. Maybe he'd suspected some of it could be found in Pax's car. That made him a suspect. Things were clicking into place, but I needed to talk to the kid.

Tillmon's voice lowered as we watched the teens. "You know, I think my son might be a little sweet on Opal."

"That's what it looks like," I agreed. "I think you can go ahead and explain to the boys that we need to show them something, and then take them to the equipment room. Let's watch to see who doesn't seem surprised." I waited for him to nod before I added, "By the way. Your son knows about the equipment room. He said he heard you talking on the phone."

Baird Tillmon's expression changed to one of thoughtfulness. "I did have several conversations from my home office with Mr. Anderson about it." He shook his head. "Anyway, Memphis was with friends Thursday and Friday nights. In fact, they were at my house on Thursday."

He moved away and began talking to the boys, gesturing for them to follow. I angled toward Opal, who was darting glances at Pax when she thought no one was looking. Her brother, standing next to her, wasn't wearing a ring or any jewelry, which meant I'd have to get creative.

Cyrus Anderson intercepted me. He was tall, good-looking, and a little bulky. He had dark hair like his daughter. His build was that of a former football player, and I suspected that with a little height, his son Otto might mirror his looks in thirty years.

"Do you have any leads?" he said, his voice low. "Principal Tillmon tells me you've cleared our main suspect."

"Yes. And I should have more information for you soon." So far, my only certainty was that Pax wasn't to blame for the vandalism. Whoever was responsible likely carried a grudge against the Franklin team, or someone on it, and had access to the keys. I wondered if the school district kept copies of all master keys. If so, that would be one more strike against Opal's brother.

Cyrus nodded. "I'm glad to hear it. The sooner we find out who's responsible, the sooner they can start fixing the damage."

I'd lost my chance to talk with Otto for now, so I followed the group as they wove their way through the school, ending up outside the equipment room. Principal Tillmon unlocked the door but didn't open it.

"I know you've all been wondering why we're here today, and why we hired a private investigator. This is why." He flung open the door.

Gasps filled the hallway, uttered by the boys toward the front of the group. Others strained to see over and around the forerunners.

"No!" a boy shouted.

"Who did this?" demanded another.

Several of the boys, including the quarterback, had tears in their eyes. I paid close attention to Memphis, who was shaking his head like most of the others, and Otto, who stared at the floor. Neither boy looked at the other, and I wondered about that. A few of the boys pressed into the room, and the principal let them. More boys became emotional. One kicked half-heartedly at a destroyed pad.

"It's all ruined," the quarterback moaned.

Boys uttered more angry groans and a few curses, followed by heartfelt vows of vengeance.

"I bet it was the Lincoln team," someone said, casting a dark glare at me. No, not at me but at Otto and Opal, who stood near me.

"Now, now," Baird Tillmon said. "The whole point of bringing you all here is to have you help us find out who did this. As you know from the questions you were asked today, we believe it happened two weeks ago on Thursday or Friday night. Now we need you all to ask around. Together, we can figure this out. Meanwhile, when Coach Valdez gets back from Spain, he and I will put our heads together with Mr. Anderson here from the district and figure out how we can start the practice season next month."

More dark murmurs and protest. Someone growled something more about revenge.

I took the opportunity to step in front of Otto. "So, where were *you* Thursday and Friday nights?" I asked, quiet enough that only he and maybe Opal could hear.

His gaze snapped from the floor to my face. "I didn't do it. I don't need this to beat Franklin. We're better than them any day."

"Where were you?" I repeated.

His shoulders sagged, and he leaned back against the wall in the corridor, one foot bracing his body. "With my buddies."

"Was Memphis one of them?"

His eyes went past me to where Memphis was now inside the equipment room with his teammates. He nodded. "Yeah. And a couple of others from my team. They'll vouch for me."

"I'll need their names," I said. "And let me see your phone."

He made a face and pushed off the wall. "I don't know what you're trying to prove, lady, but I don't have to listen to this. I'm out of here." He turned and strode down the hallway.

I turned to find Opal staring at me. "You don't really think it was him, do you?" She looked ready to cry.

At this point, I wasn't exactly sure who was covering for whom, or if both boys were guilty. "Did you ask Otto about the post on Instagram?"

"Yeah. He said it was just talk."

"School rivalry? In the summer?"

"I know—it's weird. That sort of thing usually doesn't happen until game season." Opal darted a glance at Pax, who stood near the door to the equipment room. He was looking at Cyrus Anderson, a hint of yearning on his face. Did he miss his father? Or was he thinking of a way to impress this man who'd already judged him unworthy?

For his part, Cyrus didn't appear to notice or recognize Pax from any other boy on the team. He probably didn't.

"Look," I said, turning back to Opal. "I need you to go into your brother's room and bring me items to look at—phone, jewelry, pens. Anything special or that he uses a lot. I won't keep them."

She stared at me. "This has to do with how you knew about me after touching Pax's arrowhead, doesn't it?"

So he'd told her. "Yes. And how I know Memphis Tillmon has a crush on you."

"Oh, that," she said dismissively. "He's been that way ever since his dad became the principal here and we started running into each other. I don't feel that way about him."

"Has he always wanted to play football?"

She shrugged. "I don't know. My brother has, though. My dad was a pretty big deal in college football, and he wants to be like him."

That didn't make Otto guilty, but his school winning a state championship might enhance his options. "Will you do it?" I pressed.

"If I bring you his things, is it going to hurt Otto?" Opal's gaze strayed once more to Pax.

"Only if he has something to hide. You can't protect him from that. But you can help me protect Pax."

She nodded. "Okay, I'll do it. I'll text you when I have the stuff."

We fell silent as boys began streaming from the equipment room.

"We can remove the paint," the quarterback was saying. "It don't matter what the practice equipment looks like, we're still the best team. This'll make us practice that much harder."

Murmurs of agreement rose from the other football players, and abruptly the mood changed.

"We can hold a fundraiser to replace what we can't fix," Memphis suggested.

"Great idea," several boys said, slapping him on the back. "Let's do it."

Memphis grinned. "I'll bring it up with Coach Valdez when he gets back on Friday."

More murmurs of approval. "Coach is the best," someone said. "He'll figure it out."

I trailed the boys as they moved down the hallway.

"I think it's going to be okay," Principal Tillmon said, dropping back to walk with me. His gaze followed his son with a proud smile. "It was a good idea, bringing the boys in. I should have done it from the start."

"This disaster can bring the team together even more," I said. "If someone guides them."

He chuckled. "I have the feeling Coach Valdez can do that. No more hiding. I'm going to email him about it tonight." We took a few more steps before he asked, "But did this do any good for your investigation? They all looked surprised to me."

Should I tell him my suspicions? No. Not yet. "Yes. I think I know who's responsible. But I'll let you know when I'm sure."

He smiled now, widely. "That's good news for Pax. I'm glad."

"I'll be in touch," I said.

Leaving him in the lobby, I started out to my car, checking my phone on the way. I'd received two calls during my interviews with the boys. One was from Cody, my biological father, and the other from Shannon. I called Shannon back.

"What's up?" I said.

He sighed heavily. "Bad news. They arrested Matthew. It's a ploy by the attorney because they don't have any solid proof yet, but he's going to have to spend the night in jail, which was the intention. I'm betting the attorney will have a news team waiting when Paige bails him out in the morning."

"Quincy needs to make sure that doesn't happen."

"My thoughts exactly. I think the attorney is looking to scare up a quick settlement."

"Matthew doesn't have that kind of money." I opened my car door with more force than I needed.

"No, but the hospital does. And the more bad publicity, the more pressure they'll feel. Quincy hasn't found any other suspicious deaths there, but the hospital will worry about people making that assumption."

"Seems underhanded to accuse Matthew now with the investigation still going on."

"I agree," Shannon said. "There's other news too. Peter Griffin's body is scheduled to be released tomorrow morning to the mortuary chosen by the family."

"That was fast."

"Well, all the tests have been completed, even if the complete results aren't in yet. It won't do any good for the medical examiner to hang onto the body. The funeral is scheduled for Thursday at ten."

A lump formed in the pit of my gut as I thought about the separate home funerals I'd attended for my parents. Friends had gathered at my apartment to write messages of love on their cardboard coffins. Whether I'd been eleven or thirty-two, it had been heartbreakingly special. Peter Griffin's upper-class funeral wouldn't be anything like that, but the grief of his loved ones would be the same.

"I'll need to know where," I said. More than once, Shannon had talked about finding a clue from a killer who attended the funeral of his victim.

"I'll text you. We'll both go."

"Any news about Peter Griffin's laptop? And what about his wedding ring?"

"I talked to his wife, and apparently his finger had grown too large for his ring, so he hasn't worn it for the past year.

It was a seed of contention between them because he thought he'd lose weight after the launch, and she wanted him to resize it. As for the laptop, she looked in his office and bedroom and texted her sons. It seems to be missing." He paused and then added, "She asked me if I'd checked in the bag she gave us, the one from the hospital."

"It definitely wasn't in there." Without the laptop, finding the passcode to the Futura files wasn't going to be easy. Unless it was a password Peter typically used. I wondered if his wife or his business partner would be more likely to guess the correct one. "We need to get a list of his usual passwords."

"She said she had no idea and would ask her sons. But I'm thinking if his sons knew it, they would have accessed the files already. Futura won't be able to finish production without them."

I pushed aside the thoughts for another day. Nothing we could do about it now. "Will I see you later?" I asked.

He groaned. "I wish, but probably not. I've been researching so much on the Griffin case that my captain is a little annoyed. I thought I could take a few personal days, but with Paige not working, we're that much more behind."

"You do what you have to do," I said.

"Did I ever tell you I love you?"

I thought of all the food he brought me, the imprint on my beautiful ring, and the belief he had in my ability. "Every day. I love you too."

Hanging up, I pulled from the parking lot, glancing in the rearview mirror at a sleek black car that seemed vaguely familiar.

I sped up and turned right, even though my phone was squawking at me to turn left. The black car did the same. A lump formed in my gut. The car didn't look cheap, and I didn't think I'd angered anyone with that kind of money, unless the Griffins suspected I was looking into them.

Or was it someone from my past? Namely one of the organized crime families I'd had the misfortune of crossing paths with. I never forgot that I still owed a very powerful man a favor. I took a few more turns and felt a little better when we became separated by several cars. Five minutes later, there was not one but three black sedans behind me on a four-lane highway, and traffic was busy enough that I no longer knew which had been the original. One took a turn and disappeared.

I drove to my antiques shop, periodically checking my rearview mirror. Still one black car there. I found a lucky parking space a short distance from my shop and was more than a little relieved when the last black car sped on past me without stopping.

Obviously not someone who wanted to talk to me. I hoped.

Chapter 14

*T*hera had everything well in hand, but she was right about the steady flow of customers. I put away my purse and went to work. During the brief lulls, I priced and put out the items Jazzy had brought in the boxes from Claire's house. Only about half were things I could actually use.

On one of the breaks, I did a search on Chippendale armchairs and set them up in a sweet spot in the shop's front window, next to a baby crib holding an antique doll. With the condition they were in, each would easily sell for two thousand dollars—and they were nice enough to bring in more foot traffic. I hadn't talked to Jazzy's foster mother about terms, but any way you looked at it, I'd come out ahead.

I sent out an alert email to my best customers to let them know about the chairs and was working on the insurance forms when a flood of customers from Jake's BOGO sale came through our adjoining double doors. Some paused to peruse antiques, but most came to the counter for us to ring them up. I didn't mind because Jake had filled in for me more than once. Still, I'd be glad when his sale ended or when he hired more help. At least Jake was supplying his own sacks for their purchases.

"Here, let me do that," a voice said in my ear. "I'll ring up everyone while you go help the guy salivating over the Fisher-Price case."

I'd been feeling the tug of my sister's presence and the connection between us thickening, so I wasn't surprised to see my sister's mismatched eyes and her bright smile. Destiny, in an outward-facing baby carrier, reached for me.

"In a minute, sweetie," I said, giving her a slew of mini kisses. To Tawnia, I added, "Thanks."

In twenty minutes, the rush was over and I was back at the counter, unhooking the baby from Tawnia's carrier. "I missed you, sweetie," I said, kissing her face again and making foolish faces. It was the best moment of my day so far.

"I'm glad I came in when I did," Tawnia said.

I laughed. "Me too. I think Jake's BOGO sale is over on Friday." I unwrapped one of the honey candies I kept near the counter for Destiny and gave it to her. "Who's your favorite aunt, huh?" Not that it was much of a contest. Her other aunt, her daddy's sister, lived in Nevada.

"I brought sketches," Tawnia continued. "For the wedding. I think you're going to love what I've come up with. I put them in the back room."

"Great." The knot in my stomach at the mention of the wedding felt the same as when I thought I'd been followed a few hours earlier. Before I could reply, Thera finished talking with a customer and approached the counter.

"Should I lock the connecting doors before I take off?"

Thera asked. "That way you won't have any more of Jake's BOGO customers."

I glanced at my wall of antique clocks, seeing that it was nearly five. "I think we can handle it now. You know how dead we usually are between five and six."

"Okay." Thera played with Destiny for few moments before collecting her purse from under the counter. "I'll see you tomorrow then. I guess I'll be over at Jake's for the morning. Will you be here?"

"I should be." Otherwise, I'd have to call in Jazzy or Tawnia. "See you tomorrow."

I rang up the lingering customers and headed to the back with my sister.

"Any news on the cases?" she asked. I gave her a brief rundown, leaving out the suspicion of being followed.

"So no idea who gave Griffin the drug, but who do you like more for the vandalism, the principal's kid or the brother?"

"Leaning toward the brother at the moment."

"I don't know," Tawnia said. "Using the black and white paints—the exact colors that Pax and Opal used—seems to indicate someone was hoping to set Pax up. I think love is a stronger motive." She gave me a wink. "Now forget about all that. Look at this."

She swept up a drawing pad, pulled out some pages, and started laying out remarkably detailed sketches. A few bits of the sketches—flowers and dresses—were filled in with bright paint. "I've looked at the pictures of your parents' wedding, and there doesn't seem to be a color scheme, but several of her friends were wearing nice, bright dresses, so it might be nice if you ask a few people to be bridesmaids. We can do similar dresses in different colors."

"What kind of dresses?" I asked, thinking of the very beautiful, dressy, floor-length sage green gown dress from her wedding that I'd probably never wear again.

She paused in setting down the drawings. "I know you hate the idea of making anyone buy a dress they don't like, so I think letting them wear whatever they want is a good idea. Within reason, of course. You might want to make sure Jazzy doesn't wear something too far out there. Speaking of that, she's called me three times already hinting about being in the wedding. I hope you're going to ask her, because if not, she's going to be devastated. It may be weird, given the age gap, but all of us here are her only friends, at least until she goes back to school."

"Of course I'll ask her," I said. "And you, Paige, Thera, and Randa." Jake's sister and I weren't as close as we had been when I'd dated him, but she was still a good friend. "And Jake. He's my best man, and you're my matron of honor."

She laughed. "As long as you clear that with Shannon."

"Short dresses," I added. "All to match the flower colors. Except for Jake, of course. He and Shannon's best man can wear a medium blue."

"I can buy a bouquet of gerberas, and the girls can all pick one flower color to copy. We'll save the light pink for Destiny. We can give one to Shannon's mother as well. Maybe the reddish wine one since that is so much different than the rest."

"She'll be here this weekend."

Something in my voice made her look at me. "That's good, right?"

I sighed, hugging Destiny a bit tighter. "I don't know. Maybe I'm not ready to share him."

"You won't have to." She continued laying out papers. "There wasn't anything in the pictures to show the setup of your parents' wedding, but how about this? I'll copy the arch they had, and that's where the priest will stand. I know it's only going to be a few moments for the ceremony, and no speeches, so chairs won't be necessary, but I'd like to elevate the arch a bit so everyone can have a good view. You can see what I mean in this sketch here." She pointed at a drawing of the arch.

"If the meadow is large enough, and it looks like it is, we'll put the refreshment tables here." She set down a sketch to the left of the archway. "And I think we should have seating for the dinner. The cake table will be here. We'll buy bulk flowers, and I'll do all the arrangements in different colored vases for the tables. We can tie ribbons around a few bunches for the girls. We'll need lighting, though. Your parents only had the bonfire for their dancing afterward, but I think a few tiny lights all around the trees would give us a little more visibility. I've also priced a few floodlights and portable bathrooms."

She smiled when I didn't respond. "I know your parents didn't have those either, but I think it's wise, and I'll bring my own camper for changing or quick mirror checks. If we started at four, the ceremony would be after the heat of the day, so it wouldn't be too hot, and yet it's not all that long until dark starts to fall. We could light the bonfire right before you cut the cake."

She'd finished laying everything out and now regarded me nervously. "Well, what do you think?"

I stared at the array of detailed sketches. She'd left nothing out, and yet, to my surprise, it wasn't too much. There were no fountains or ice sculptures, expensive dresses and tuxedos, waiters or elaborately constructed buildings. It wasn't my parents' wedding, not by a long shot—it couldn't be with bathrooms and a canopy and floodlights—but it was still simple and down-to-earth. It was me.

"I love it," I said, fighting an absurd urge to cry. My sister knew me. She really knew me. I'd thought planning the wedding all by myself would be the only way I could honor my parents, but my immense relief told me this was far better.

She laughed. "Admit it. You were worried."

"I went to your wedding," I reminded her.

"Yes, but that was mostly for my parents and all their high society friends. I know you like things simple and that we're on a budget." She paused before rushing on, "Speaking of that, Shannon transferred two thousand dollars to my account this morning."

I stared at her. "He what?"

"It's for the wedding. He asked me what I needed, and I gave him an estimate for my plans so far. But I told him I was worried you were going to nix the canopy."

"Not with the Portland weather involved." I wouldn't admit, not even to her, that Shannon being so quick to give her the money was sweet. He was dependable, of course, but with my budget being so tight, it was hard for me to talk about money with him. "What about the food?"

She bit her lip. "Even if we buy it ourselves and set it out, we can't do everything for only two thousand dollars. Especially because I think they'll charge us more for delivery of the chairs and canopy to the meadow, if they'll even agree to take them that far."

"I can cover the food then," I said.

"If I leave it to you, can you promise you won't do the cooking yourself?"

Now it was my turn to grimace. How could she know me that well in two short years?

"Okay," I relented, "we'll price out some cheap catering. We could start at Smokey's. I love their food. If they don't cater, they'll probably make an exception for me."

She grinned. "As long as they send someone to set it up. We're both going to be a little busy. We should drive up to the meadow this weekend to make sure it'll work the way we're envisioning it."

"I think it will." Winter had taken me there several times over the years and walked me through that special day. His marriage with Summer had only lasted seventeen years because of her breast cancer, but my father had remained faithful to her for two more decades after that. "I'll call his friend to make sure it's okay."

"What about the wedding dress?"

"I need to soak it in special detergent to take out some of the yellow," I said. "But there's enough material to let out. I want to do that myself." I couldn't risk anyone messing up my mother's dress. "And I'll be able to wear her ring. But her necklace and earrings won't work. I'm afraid they've completely gone the way of all cheap costume jewelry." I forced a laugh.

"We'll find something special," Tawnia said with a sympathetic smile. "I also want a guest list. And I need you to look at this." She removed another paper from her sketchbook, smaller than the rest, and handed it over.

Inside a hexagon lined with colorful flowers, romantic-looking text proclaimed, *I do, me too! Come celebrate with Autumn Rain and Shannon Martin as they tie the knot.* The date and time was there as well, with placeholder text where the address to the field would go.

"Will something like this do?" Tawnia asked. "I did the swirls by hand. Well, I mean, in Illustrator with my graphic tablet."

The wedding invitation was beautiful, and since I'd considered letting people know verbally or through email, it was more than adequate. "It's perfect." I shifted Destiny to my left hip so I could hug my sister with my right arm.

Tawnia's smile widened. "Good. We should get them out as soon as possible. And the cost of printing is my gift. No." She lifted a hand to stop me from refusing. "I'm doing it. With all the times you've babysat Destiny here while I've had to go into meetings, I owe you far more."

I laughed. "You don't owe me anything. Or I'll have to start paying you for working for me when I'm out on a case. Anyway, it's not babysitting so much as it is hanging out." I kissed the baby's head. "She gets me on my level."

It was true. Destiny loved all my vintage baby toys—those that didn't have lead paint, that is—and didn't judge when I bought yet another music box and took it home instead of pricing it for the store. Which reminded me how crammed my apartment was with antiques. If I sold the apartment, where would I put them?

"Uh-oh, I know that face," Tawnia said, looking from me to the drawings. "It's the canopy, right? You don't want it after all. At least it better be the canopy because I'm not compromising on the portable bathrooms. If we don't have bathrooms, you know what people are going to do. That might have been okay in your parents' day and age, but I doubt the guy who owns the meadow would appreciate that now. Besides, it's a biohazard. People could get waste on their shoes and track it all over the field, and what if Destiny wanders off and steps into something? And then we'll have not only land conservation people but child protections services on my case, and I'll have to go to court and—"

Laughter bubbled up inside me. "You can have the bathrooms and the canopy. In fact, have two canopies if you want."

"Then what was the face for?"

Frowning, I took a few steps backward and settled in my easy chair that cradled me like an old friend. Destiny twisted in my arms and reached for my dangly silver earrings, gurgling to herself. They were inexpensive vintage, circa 1970, with black teardrop stones and filigree set into a silver teardrop frame. I'd chosen them because I'd known she'd liked them.

With a finger, I slipped off my barefoot sandals and pulled my feet up under me, not an easy accomplishment while wearing a pencil skirt, even if it was stretchy. "I was thinking about not having space in the apartment for more antiques, and I remembered that I'll have a lot less room at Shannon's. I mean, he says he doesn't care what I bring, and he cleaned out a whole room for me to use as an office or whatever I want it for. There's also plenty of land to build an addition on." For a nursery, he'd suggested, but we could add more.

"Yeah, but your apartment isn't just full of antiques." Tawnia pulled a chair from the worktable and sat opposite me. "You've still got everything of Winter's and what he kept from your mother. I think you'll find that as you clean it out, there will be a lot you won't need."

The idea of losing any more of Winter or Summer made my heart tighten. "You're probably right."

"But you're not ready."

I shook my head. "I don't think so."

"Then keep the apartment. You can always rent out his house."

The tightness around my heart eased. "That's exactly what I think Shannon will say."

"You haven't told him?"

"Not yet. And where would I put his stuff at my place anyway? I'd still have to get rid of so much."

Tawnia tilted her head and looked at me. "I think losing the apartment might be why you didn't want to set a date."

"We've only been engaged, what, seven weeks?" I protested.

"I know, but you and Shannon were in love for months before either of you were willing to admit it. Before you even started dating Jake."

"Hey, Shannon's the one who fought it." And I'd retaliated by flirting and joking with him twice as hard to make him that much more uncomfortable, all the while walling off my heart from his charms. The wall hadn't worked, but the flirting had. In the end, we'd both caved to the inevitable.

"What I'm saying is that any waiting at all is not like you. You're either all in or you're not." She reached for Destiny, who had given up on my earring and wanted her mother.

I sighed, pulling my knees to my chest as I relinquished the baby. "If my life is with Shannon, I shouldn't keep the apartment. It's a big expense and nowhere near as nice for a family as his house. Besides, I love his house. I love the acre of land, the full-grown trees, and I love that the nearest neighbor won't be able to hear if I belt out a song in the back yard. I feel peace there, and I don't want to clutter it up with too much of the past."

"And yet . . ." Tawnia urged. Destiny was fussing, and

without looking away from me, Tawnia lifted her shirt and began nursing the baby. Destiny's soft gulps filled the quiet between us.

"My apartment is like six minutes from here," I said finally. "Driving to his house will take twenty if traffic is good. Most days it'll be okay, but still a pain."

"If you kept the apartment, even for a while, you could crash there on nights when Shannon has to work. Both of you could."

I shook my head. "For that I can crash here. I have everything I need." Indeed, I'd slept here a lot in the early days of the store, and during the time when Winter had been missing in the Willamette. "That feels like I'm not all in."

"Yeah, I can see that." She paused for a moment. "Why don't you worry about it later? It's not a pressing issue. Besides the monthly building fees and utilities, the apartment is paid off. If you had a mortgage like you do for the stores, it would be different."

By stores, she meant the Herb Shoppe and Autumn's Antiques. When Winter died, I'd inherited both his store and the mortgage on it. Jake hadn't been able to qualify for a loan when he'd purchased the Herb Shoppe from me, so he paid me monthly—and I used most of his payment for the Herb Shoppe mortgage, and the remaining to pay ahead on my own. It wasn't the best deal for me, but Jake and Winter had been close, and I knew Winter would approve. The financially smart thing for me to do now would be to sell the apartment and pay off my mortgage and what I could of the one for the Herb Shoppe. The sooner I did that, the sooner Jake's payments could help me increase my profit margin.

But Tawnia was right. There wasn't a hurry, and according to my flower-child upbringing, the universe would soon show me the way.

"There's also the fact that his parents are coming," I said.

She leaned back, crossing her legs and resting her arm against the table to help support Destiny's head. The baby had apparently been exhausted because she was already asleep, though still sucking periodically. "So you said. Are you worried about it?"

"Not really. But you saw what happened with your parents once Destiny was born." Her adoptive parents had recently announced their intention to move from Kansas to Portland to be closer to Tawnia and Destiny.

"You think Shannon's parents might decide to ditch their bed and breakfast and move back here once you have children? That would be a good thing, right?" She frowned. "Unless they move into Shannon's house and give you problems about not making the kids wear shoes, and—"

"No." I held up a hand, not in the mood for more of Tawnia's fanciful stories. "Of course it would be a good thing. I need to wrap my head around it, that's all."

"They're going to love you." With a deft finger, Tawnia broke Destiny's suction and pulled down her shirt. She stood and gingerly laid the baby in my portable crib. Destiny gave a sigh and turned over but didn't wake. "They'll love you like all the rest of us do."

"Thanks." With reluctance, I climbed from my too-comfortable chair and went to the restroom at the far end of my back room. Frowning in the mirror, I splashed cold water on my face, dried it, and dabbed on a bit of base over the black half-moon under my left eye. No one in my interviews today had said anything about my black eye, but they had to have noticed it.

When I emerged from the back room, Tawnia was ringing up a man at the counter. "Herbs only," she said with a frown after the customer left. "I'm not sure this joint database, ring-up-in-either-store is a good idea."

"It's a pain when Jake has good sales," I said with a shrug, "but those sales bring me profit too, even with paying extra hours. Besides, he covers for me way more often than I cover for him. If we didn't have the connecting doors, I'd have to close up completely when I'm called away to read imprints and no one is here."

"Okay, okay. He's a good friend." She eyed my face. "Hate to tell you, but you look worse with that makeup on. Actually, a little ghoulish."

That made me laugh. "Great. It goes with my new persona—the strange psychic lady."

"Which reminds me, how is it working with Elliot?" She hadn't met the private investigator yet, but I'd told her all about him.

"I learned he has agoraphobia."

"Is that where people don't like to leave home because they're anxious about new situations?"

"Something like that." I walked to the outside door and shut it. Jake still had customers in his store, but he'd be closing now too, so I locked the double doors joining our shops as well. Neither of us wanted to encourage a double break-in, so we always shut and locked them at night.

Tawnia helped me close the register and count the day's receipts. Most purchases were on credit cards these days, so that part was easy. With our joint database, figuring out how much of my intake actually belonged to Jake was equally simple. Anything above his monthly payment on the store, I'd transfer back to him electronically. He paid me the same way. Both of us could see all the transactions. Most days, I had enough cash purchases to make a bank run necessary, and I usually did that at lunchtime when I was working. At night, I put the remaining proceeds in the safe instead.

Today, we had more cash than customary, nearly five-hundred dollars. *Thank you, Jake,* I thought, as I gathered up the money and gave it to Tawnia.

"For the food," I said, with a smile. "Or a down payment on it. You keep it, so I don't spend it on bills, okay?"

"You sure?"

I grinned. "You only get married once. And you see those armchairs in the window? I'm getting a great commission off them. At least four hundred, which I'll also give you for the food."

"We'll make it work." She tucked the money into her purse and gave me another hug that chased away any remaining shadows. "Hey, I just remembered. Isn't it this week that you're testing for your second-degree blackbelt? Can I come watch? I've always wanted to see someone break boards."

"No. Testing is embarrassing. But I'll invite you to our next exhibition, I promise."

"Okay. See that you do." With a wink, she went to retrieve a still-sleeping Destiny.

After opening the outside door for her and locking it again, I went to work, setting misplaced antiques back where they belonged, reorganizing cases, and cleaning the glass.

Quincy Duncan called me long before I was finished. "I have news," he said. "You got a minute?"

"Sure." I held the phone with one hand as I used my rag to obliterate a complete set of fingerprints from an antique mirror. "What's up?"

"Remember that second drug they found in Griffin's blood?"

"Yeah, tadalafil."

"Well, we found a prescription bottle of it in Brigit Griffin's trash."

Chapter 15

I abandoned my rag and all pretense at cleaning. "You went through their trash?"

"Once it goes to the curb, that's our prerogative. And actually, it was Shannon's idea." Quincy laughed. "Of course, he suddenly got busy at the Central Precinct, so he couldn't dig through it with us. It was just me and Paige and a lot of stinking trash. The good news is that with the tadalafil angle, my captain has agreed I have a case."

"That is good news."

"Right. No more Dumpster diving for me, and the CI team will look at the hospital trash we collected. The prescription on the bottle was from an Internet doctor and written in the name of our victim, Peter Griffin."

"You're thinking his wife had something to do with the tadalafil overdose, aren't you?"

"Unfortunately, all the pills appear to still be in the bottle, but it could be a second prescription. I'd like you to take a look at it in the morning, see if there's an imprint."

"Okay." But I had another idea. "Who was the prescribing doctor? Have you talked to him?"

He snorted. "We've been given the cold shoulder. That happens with some of these Internet outfits that are barely legal. In the old days, you could buy tadalafil illegally but easily online. Since the crackdown, these so-called doctors have popped up. They give a consult via the Internet, and you pay them like any other doctor, but you have to fill the resulting prescription right there. We can get a warrant, but by the time we do, I bet the whole site will be gone, and it'll be up under another name and IP address."

"Maybe Eli Stone can look at them, trace them through his contacts." I tucked the cleaning rag under my arm and headed for the back room, turning off the lights behind the counter on my way.

"Sure, have him take a stab. I'll text you the images of the bottle and the website. Paige also found something interesting on one of the cameras at the hospital. She matched up a visitor to the hospital with the photos you sent of the Futura employees."

"Who?"

"I'm sending you a link to the clip."

I watched the clip while Quincy waited on the line. A man in a tan jacket stood at the hospital elevators, head bowed so I couldn't see who he was, but when he moved forward, I caught a glimpse of his face. "That's Arthur Dean," I said. Instead of the flirty programmer I'd met at Futura today, his face was serious and intent. "What was he doing there? Did he go see Peter Griffin?"

"No. At least not that we know—though we can't say for sure, since not all the hallways are covered by cameras, and it's possible he used a back staircase or service elevator we aren't aware of. He got off at the floor above Peter's room, apparently to visit a sick Facebook friend. We checked, and the friend was there, and Arthur did visit him after the guy's wife posted about it on Facebook. Apparently, Arthur was there on Saturday too for a short time. Brought the guy a magazine."

"How kind of him," I said, trying to match that up with the man I'd met. He'd been friendly, so maybe it wasn't farfetched for him to care about his friend, but the timing was suspicious. "He didn't mention being at the hospital, even though I asked him point-blank if he'd been there to see Peter. He claimed not to know about the kidney stones. What time was the Sunday visit?"

"He got there just before ten, before the night security came on, and he left around eleven-thirty."

Disappointment waved through me. "So nowhere near the time when Peter would have ingested the tadalafil."

"Not for an injection. And that's the same with the accountant. But Griffin still could have ingested it in another way."

"Like through food or chocolates." Now we were back to the wife being a suspect.

"Yes. Maybe even in that box we found at the hospital. I'm having it checked for prints. And we'll check that other box you picked up from Robby Hartford's office. But it's doubtful they would be dosed with anything."

"Yeah, it's a long shot. So Arthur Dean didn't pass the cameras at all on Peter's floor?" I knew the answer, but I had to ask.

"Not that we've found. But remember that idea of other footage? I've requested the one from the nurse's station on Griffin's floor. They're resisting, but I'll get it in the end."

"What about the embezzled money? Any luck on finding what Robby needed it for?"

"Not yet. When Shannon and I went to Futura today, the partner told us Robby was taking a few days off, but with what you learned about him, he might have been fired. Now that the captain is onboard with the investigation, I can put someone on tracking him down."

"What about Matthew?"

"He'll be cut loose in the morning. Paige and I will sneak him out the back to avoid any news crews. Oh, and that reminds me, we found the hospital bed. Unfortunately, it's in use at the moment. Since it's been thoroughly cleaned, you might be our only hope of finding anything. As soon as it's empty, we'll have access, and not before. They won't even tell me what room it's in."

I imagined myself sneaking into the hospital and bothering some octogenarian. "That's probably good for their patient. I can't blame them."

After hanging up, I stored the cleaning supplies under the counter. Hunger gnawed at my stomach, so instead of calling Elliot right away, I dug in my small fridge for sustenance. I had the remains of a Smokey's sandwich, fruit, and a hot mug of tea on my worktable when my phone rang again. With a little pang of conscience, I saw the caller was Cody Beckett, my biological father. This was twice he'd called today, and I needed to answer.

"Hey, Cody," I said, trying to sound less tired than I felt. "What's up?"

"Your sister told me you set a date for the wedding," he said in his usual direct manner. "She said I could come?" It was a definite question.

"Of course, you're invited. I was planning to call you myself about it."

"I heard you were on a case. Anyway, she said you want to keep it simple. I know you wouldn't appreciate me offering to pay for the whole thing, but isn't there some little thing I can do to help?"

I grimaced. Cody had more money than anyone I knew except the organized crime boss I hoped never to hear from again. Not only did Cody live on a hundred acres of unincorporated land outside Hayesville, where he created his famous art sculptures, but he had also built a number of rental houses. He seemed to have his fingers in more investments than I could count. If he'd been a real dad, he'd probably be paying for my wedding, but he wasn't my father, not by a long shot. He hadn't meant to have children, and I didn't expect anything from him.

Except that wasn't quite true. He was the closest thing I had left to a parent in the world, and there were expectations in that, no matter how hard I fought it. Though his actions leading to our existence had ultimately cost our birth mother's life and separated us for thirty-two years, Tawnia and I were grateful for his gift of life. Life and also the other gift he'd given each of us—the paranormal abilities that came directly from his genes.

Cody had been alone without family, until life had thrown us together. Tawnia treated him like a father and grandfather for Destiny while I was more cautious, which went completely against our separate upbringings. Maybe because she still had her adoptive parents and not as much to risk. At the end of the day, Cody was more like me than I wanted to admit, and I yearned for a relationship with him, a real one that didn't include any hint of buying my affections.

But a relationship meant I had to give him something. That was how relationships worked.

"Thank you so much for calling and offering," I said, trying to channel the hippy parents who'd raised me. "Can I think on it a bit? Tawnia and I have barely started planning. But I'm sure we can use some help. Tawnia might have some ideas." I fingered one of Tawnia's sketches which still lay spread out, as if ready for business. Maybe he could pay for a canopy rental.

"Oh, sure. Let me know." The gruffness in his voice had receded a bit. I realized he'd expected a fight, and I immediately felt guilty. If he'd been a total stranger offering me funds, I'd let him help and dance for joy about my good fortune. Winter and Summer had believed in helping everyone, even to the point of giving away their own meals, and in turn, they accepted any help freely offered. Cody had paid for his sins—why did I have to keep reminding myself of that?

"I will," I said.

He didn't hang up, and I sensed there was more. "There's some stuff of your grandmother's. I thought you girls might like to go through it sometime. If you don't want it, maybe you can sell it. It's time for me to clean out my house."

I thought of the apartment I already had full of stuff belonging to the dead. This was different, of course. It was personal history—family imprints yet undiscovered—and I wouldn't be an antiques dealer if my heart didn't beat a little faster thinking about it.

"I'd like that," I said.

We went on to discuss whether he should bring up the boxes a few at a time in his old Honda, or if I should borrow Shannon's truck. It was an ordinary conversation, one that could have taken place between any father and daughter. Idly, I gathered Tawnia's drawings and put them into the sketchbook she'd left behind. As I did, an image on one of the few sheets left in the book caught my attention.

It was a room—a teenage boy's room if the football posters on the wall were any indication. A backpack, a huge duffel bag, and football shoulder pads lay on the unmade bed. A tablet teetered atop the dresser, and one of the bottom drawers was half open. A pop can littered the floor beside an empty bag of chips. I wasn't surprised that Tawnia had sketched a bed. She'd recently finished an ad campaign for a mattress firm, so she probably had a ton of bed drawings lying around. But the tops of two cans peeking out of the bottom drawer were black and white. Were they spray paint cans? If so, whose room was this?

I turned the page, and what leapt out at me there was even more curious. The sketch was of a sleek, expensive-looking sedan that despite being drawn only in pencil, looked decidedly black. Tawnia's gift had kicked in—there was no doubt in my mind. And unless she was working on a new car add marketing campaign, that meant I had been followed tonight.

Cody's voice had gone quiet, waiting for a response to whatever he'd said. I tore my eyes away from the sketch. "I really don't mind driving down to your place and helping you load Shannon's truck. We'll both come. Tawnia and Bret too. We can barbeque. But it can't be this weekend because Shannon's parents will be in town."

"That's a great idea." His voice was gruffer again now, and I knew why. This meant more to him than he was letting on. "Tell Tawnia I'll get the steaks."

I laughed. "Right. We need to keep her away from the bargain cuts." Cody knew about meat, which was more than I could say for my sister, who considered the microwave the only kitchen appliance worth her attention. "We'll bring the rest."

I was about to say goodbye when I remembered the odd cold sensation. "Hey, Cody," I said. "Have you ever felt a weird cold sensation as part of your gift? Like you were trying to read something that wasn't exactly there?"

The silence was so loud, it felt oppressing, and I began to think he'd already hung up. Then he said quietly, "No cold, but once I felt a heat. Like a cloud around me that I couldn't see."

"When was that?"

"At my mother's grave. It was . . . this might sound stupid, but it was comforting."

"Oh." I thought of the connection I experienced with those I loved. "Was it like a rope?"

"No. That was when she was alive."

I suspected he'd felt it too, and maybe even Tawnia. She'd moved from state to state to finally come here and find me right when I'd needed her most after Winter's death.

"Stranger things happen," Cody said gruffly. "What did the cold feel like?"

I shrugged, though he couldn't see me. "Icy. Frigid."

"Angry?"

"It was probably the air conditioner."

"Or a dead guy's trying to tell you something. I'd be mad if I were him."

"I guess it's possible. Look, I have to go. We'll talk soon, okay? Thanks for calling."

The last thing I needed was contact from a ghost. One strange ability was enough to deal with.

I studied Tawnia's sketches as I finished my food. My sister's ability caused her to draw images involving high emotions that were occurring at the moment she drew them. Sometimes they were connected with my cases; often, she never discovered what they meant or if an image she was drawing for her work was a real person. She had a whole city of images to interpret, and when they got to be too much, she shut off. In fact, most days she claimed she didn't see anything, and maybe that was good. Maybe her shut-off valve saved her from the craziness that had afflicted Cody's mother and eventually claimed her life.

I picked up my phone and texted Opal Anderson. *Look in your brother's bottom drawer. Left side. Tell me if you find anything.*

Next, I put on my engagement ring and my mother's wedding ring that I'd removed earlier when I'd gone to Futura to read imprints. The positive imprints from Shannon's ring settled me, and the love that came from my mother's ring, no longer overshadowed by the fear, was every bit as comforting. I held both hands against my cheeks, drinking it in. Strength seeped into me.

When I was ready, I took a picture of the black car with my phone and called Elliot.

"Hey, Autumn," he said. "I was about to call you. Are you sure you're not psychic?"

"We agreed to talk tonight. Of course, you were thinking about me. What do you have?" Because so far, I'd gotten more from the police than from my would-be partner.

"I've researched all the former Futura employees, and the woman you suspect Peter of being involved with? Well, she's married and lives in another state. They have a child together, a surprise at her age—which is thirty-seven, by the way—but quite decidedly planned since she's expecting again. I think we can rule her out. Whatever she and Peter might have had, she seems happy where she's at. And none of the other former employees look suspicious, either."

"What about current employees?"

"I've only gone through those in the main building so far. Nothing jumps out at me, except Robby Hartford's mysterious need for cash. But I found out why he needs it: drugs."

"I knew it!" I said, jumping up from my chair.

"Not his drugs, though," Elliot hurried to say.

I picked up my dishes to take to the sink. "Whose then? His kids are only ten, so that leaves—"

"Yep, his wife. It took a lot of digging from one of my contacts because they're so secretive at these places, but apparently she became addicted to narcotic painkillers after surgery some years back. She started being a regular at the emergency room for one problem or another. Now she's checked into a drug recovery program. She's been there for three months."

"I bet that's when Robby first started taking the money."

"That's my guess too. And maybe it's working well for her, so he needed more. He's paying a sitter to watch the kids too for the summer while he's at work. Poor guy. I was almost hoping someone in his family needed a kidney or something."

"Right. Addiction is tougher on a family, I think." It was sobering to think of poor Robby Hartford dealing with this on his own. As a child, I'd seen more than my fair share of my parents' freedom-loving friends die of alcohol-induced liver failure or drug overdoses. The aftermath was ugly and heart-wrenching for those left behind. My parents hadn't judged and had even made excuses for them, but the deaths made a mark on me that I'd never forgotten.

"He might have already confessed to his boss," I said. "Quincy was told he'd taken a few days personal leave. He'll probably be fired." But something in me hoped he wouldn't be. "Wait, are you sure he hasn't skipped town?"

"I'm sure," Elliot said. "I drove by there tonight. But if he followed through on confessing, you're probably right that he's not our guy. Or anyone in his immediate family for that matter. But I did score on Niklas's Facebook page. I found pictures of him and that programmer Arthur Dean, both alone and in groups. All of the pictures seemed to be taken at bars or parties. They definitely knew each other at one point."

"Arthur lied to me then, because that's a lot more than seeing Niklas around. I need to find out why. I mean, I already suspected he was lying because the imprint from Niklas's ring told me he wanted someone named Arthur to stay quiet about something, but now we have proof. And by the way, he also failed to mention that he was at the same hospital as Peter Griffin, visiting a friend on Sunday. Paige found him on the security video."

"Definitely suspicious. Maybe Arthur has dirt on Niklas. Because they don't seem to run in the same circles now."

"When were the pictures of them posted?"

"Two years ago, at least."

"That's when Arthur started working for Futura."

"You think Niklas got him the job?" Elliot asked.

"Then why lie about knowing Niklas?" I paused as an idea came to me. "Wait, Arthur mentioned that he'd heard Niklas was going to work there, so maybe there's still some kind of connection between them. Text me the pictures. I'll definitely follow up with both of them when I see them."

"There's something else I found out," Elliot said. "I have a contact who has a friend in the law firm taking care of Peter Griffin's business and personal accounts. There was an appointment on the books for Peter to discuss his will. She wouldn't give us any more details. She might not have had any. But a change was possible."

"You think Stevan or Niklas knew about it?"

"Could be. Maybe Stevan didn't want his brother to have the money. Or maybe Niklas was being cut out even more from other areas. We don't know the whole terms of the will yet or what he might get that isn't related to the company. Plus, Niklas has a lot to gain with a malpractice suit, so even though it seems counterintuitive because he's putting himself under a microscope, it's possible he was directly involved in setting up his father's death."

"Then again, it might be that death wasn't the intention." I told Elliot about the tadalafil Quincy had found. "That makes Brigit look guilty for something, even if murder might not have been her plan."

"Yes, she might have wanted to spice up their marriage, but since Peter was recovering from surgery, that doesn't make sense," Elliot countered. "Anyone could have tampered with her garbage. The police sometimes forget that if garbage is available to them, other people also have access. Believe me, I've been through more garbage than I want to admit."

"I can check the bottle for imprints in the morning. Maybe that'll shed some light on things. But keep in mind, we did find one of Brigit's chocolate boxes at the hospital."

Elliot snorted. "If the tadalafil or nitrates were given to Peter in that box, anyone at the company could have repurposed the one they were given to use as a murder tool."

"I see." Or I was beginning to. "We need to trace the tadalafil to find out how it got in Brigit's garbage."

"Now you're talking. Did you get the doctor's name?"

"I'll text it all to you. But is it even traceable?"

"Absolutely. These guys think they fly under the radar, but

I know people who keep tabs on these things. Just give me a day or so."

"There's one more thing," I said. "Can you find out if any of our suspects drive a certain car? I'm texting you a picture now." I held the phone away from my ear and sent the picture.

"Got it. Wow, nice Jaguar, the XJ, if I'm not mistaken. But that doesn't belong to any of our suspects, at least not the family or employees."

"How can you be so sure?"

"Shannon sent us the family's information, and the employee records you sent contained car information, which tells me they have problems with people who don't work there parking in the lot. I'll double-check, but I think I'd remember if anyone owned a Jag. Plus, the drawing you sent has a dealer plate. Did you draw the car, by the way?"

I ignored the question. "You think it might be a new purchase?"

"Possibly. But until the launch, I don't think anyone at Futura except Peter Griffin could afford such a car. They run seventy-five to eighty thousand, depending on the upgrades."

"Wow."

"Why are you asking about the car anyway?"

I debated whether or not to tell him. I guess now was as good a time as any to test his reaction. "A similar car might have followed me today, but I don't remember the dealer plate." I hadn't noticed it on the drawing before he pointed it out.

"You sure it was that car?"

"No. But I think so." I hadn't been sure I'd been followed at all until I'd seen my sister's drawing.

He was quiet a moment before saying, "If someone involved

in the case suddenly bought this car, that might point to something else altogether."

Goose bumps rippled across my shoulders. "What do you mean?"

"I'm not sure yet, but it starts with money. Lots of money. And I'm not talking a measly house or a two-million-dollar life insurance. Or even the ten million Futura gets with the key man insurance. Someone had a lot to gain. I just don't know if it's one of Peter's sons, his wife, or even the accountant."

"And you think whoever it was might have bought a new car."

"There aren't many dealerships in town who sell that Jag. I'll find out who bought it. But this might not be part of the Futura case. It could be connected to the school. Parents can get quite protective of their children if they think their future is at risk."

I tried to remember if I'd seen the car when I'd left Futura or only after leaving the school. "Yeah, but I didn't get the sense that any of the kids except two were involved in the vandalism, and both their fathers were there."

"Are they solid suspects?"

I told him about the meeting and my suspicions. "I'll find out for sure maybe as soon as tomorrow. But we're not charging Luna Medina any fees. No way am I taking advantage of a single mother worried about her kid. Especially when he's innocent."

Elliot moaned. "I know how you feel, but you've got to stop working for free. I have rent to pay, and you have to pay your employees."

"Yeah, but I took your lead with the Griffin case, and I found someone else who is willing to pay—Principal Tillmon."

Elliot pretended to be grumpy about the change, but I

sensed relief behind his words. A good thing, because if we were going to be partners, he'd have to get used to working some cases for free. I was my parents' daughter at heart.

I hung up, feeling satisfied at a good day's work. Now all I needed was to finish cleaning and drive home. Or maybe I didn't. I had a change of clothes here, as well as a toothbrush, and if I moved the crib, my easy chair could lay out nearly flat. It wouldn't be the first time I'd crashed here. I even had a mattress I could pull down from the three-foot-high crawlspace between my ceiling and my roof, if the chair didn't work out. I'd need a spit bath in the morning, but it wouldn't be the first time for that either. My bathroom sink and the foot-wide floor basin between my toilet and the sink would do the job.

In fact, maybe I'd go to bed now and get up early to finish the cleaning. That sounded a lot more doable because I didn't want to pick up that rag one more time today. I shut the door in the back room before turning on the alarms and motion sensors in the main store. That would cut out any noise from the sometimes busy street. After washing my feet in the bathroom floor basin and changing into a pair of old sweats, I settled into my chair with a blanket to watch an episode of Antiques Roadshow on my phone. I was asleep before the second episode finished.

From somewhere in my dreams, I heard a loud crash. My eyes jerked open, and I listened intently. I heard nothing more except the roar of an engine far away in the street, muffled because of the closed back room door. No alarm sounded. Nothing out of the ordinary. My phone had gone dark, which meant it had hit the limit of automatic plays. I set it gently on the floor, shivering as my blanket slipped to my legs.

The back room normally tended to be too hot in the

summer unless I turned on the air conditioning, even at night, but I felt icy now. I pulled the blanket halfway over my head, tucking it tightly around me. Finally comfortable, I dozed off again.

Sometime later, a piercing sound filled my ear, jerking me awake. A cough shook my chest, and my throat stung. I was cold again—freezing, really. I needed water. I could see nothing in the dark except a tiny glow coming from the refrigerator. What was that horrid noise?

I breathed in deeply, wondering if I was coming down with something. The air rushing through my nose and into my lungs smelled like smoke.

Fire! Fear waved through me as I jumped to my feet.

Chapter 16

Even as I identified the smell, I heard fire crackling hungrily through the door. I sprang for the light switch, but when I hit it, nothing happened. The door was warm to my touch—yes, the door that was my only way out, thanks to the era my shop had been built in and the grandfather clause that hadn't required a back door.

The doorknob was hotter than the door, so with sleep-stiffened fingers, I put the edge of my blanket over the hot doorknob and eased the door open. Just beyond the counter, flame blocked my way. Where had my aisle gone? Something was in the way. Then I realized one of my shelves had fallen over as it burned. How could the fire have gotten out of hand so quickly? I felt an urge to run through the flames to the door, as if propelled by an unseen hand. But logic quickly took over. No way would I make it through without protection. I'd have to wet the blanket.

And where was the fire department? Had anyone noticed the flame and called them?

I slammed the door, doubling over and coughing. This was bad. I tried to remember where I'd put my phone. Oh, by the easy chair. On hands and knees, I scrambled for it. I dialed 911, catching a glimpse of the time. One in the morning.

"Fire!" I said when someone answered. "At Autumn's Antiques." I rattled off the address, though I was pretty sure they had the ability to trace me. "I'm caught in the back room. There's no back door. I'm going to have to try to get through the fire."

"We're sending firetrucks," the female dispatcher said. "Do you have an extinguisher? What caused the fire?"

My extinguisher was under my counter. "I have no idea, and I'm not sure I can get to the extinguisher, or if it'd do any good. I was sleeping. I barely heard the alarms, and the fire's already everywhere."

"They should be there in six minutes. Can you wait that long?"

I didn't know. "I'm going to try to get out. Please hurry. I'm hanging up now." I did without waiting for a reply. Using my flashlight app on my phone to see what I was doing, I grabbed one of Destiny's baby blankets that I'd left on the worktable and wedged it under the door to prevent more smoke from entering. Then I headed to the bathroom. Grabbing the sprayer from the floor basin, I let it run on the blanket as I texted Shannon.

Shop's on fire. I'm caught in the back room. Going to make a run for it. I love you.

The phone rang an instant later. "How bad is it?" Shannon said in my ear, his voice tense but calm. "Fire trucks are on their way."

"I know. I'm wetting a blanket to put around me. The aisle's blocked."

"Tie something around your mouth too," he said. I could

hear a siren through the phone, which meant he was also on his way. "If you can't make it out safely, stay in the room and get down. You should have enough air until they get there."

I knew the protocol, but I wasn't willing to wait in this tomb in the hope that firefighters would reach me in time. What if it wasn't safe to send anyone inside when they did arrive? No, I needed to get out now.

"I love you," he said.

"I know." I hung up.

A splintering sound reached my ears as something out in the shop exploded with the heat. Squelching the panic shooting through me, I checked on my blanket. I needed more water, faster, than the sprayer could provide. Using my hands in the sink, I dumped more water on the blanket. By the time it was soaked, my bare feet and sweats also dripped. That was good.

I found Tawnia's cast-off skirt that I'd worn earlier and wet it too, pulling it over my head and mouth so only my eyes were exposed. Who knew that a stretchy pencil skirt could come in so handy? If I survived, Tawnia would be happy to hear it.

I pulled the wet blanket over me and paused at the door of the back room. Thoughts filtered through my head about things I should save, but whatever little I might be able to grab would mean nothing if it distracted me from getting out. In the end, I left everything except what I was wearing and my phone.

Removing the wadded mound of Destiny's baby blanket shoved under the door, I used it to turn the handle. The fire in the main shop was worse now, the entire area filled with red flames and smoke. The dance of red and yellow flames was hypnotizing, as if they called me to join them. It reminded me of the bonfire parties my parents had sponsored during my childhood, before Summer's cancer. Every time we'd danced around the fire, I'd felt happy, eternal.

Cold pressed into my back, urging me forward. I couldn't tell if it was my imagination or my parents or God or the universe, or even Peter Griffin, but whatever it was shook me from my reverie. I shut the door to the back room behind me in case I had to retreat. Pulling the dripping blanket around my body, I hurried forward, pushing through the fallen shelving. It gave way easily, but there was more after that. Water dribbled down my temples. I was walking over hot rubble, and my feet should have been burning, but they felt cool. I continued forward, crouching over and using my arm inside the blanket to clear my path. When had the shop become so big?

My lungs were bursting, and I realized I wasn't breathing. I took a tentative breath, and the wet skirt seemed to do its job. I breathed more deeply, regretting it as I started to cough. I could see the door now. I wanted to sing.

That was when I remembered it was locked, and I'd left the keys in my purse somewhere in the back room. I'd have to retrace my steps. I glanced behind me to see flames stretching to the ceiling. *Great.*

Then suddenly, miraculously, a figure was outside my store, ramming the door with something heavy. It burst open. A firefighter appeared, lunging for me. Another crash came from behind me. As the man pulled me from the store, I turned my head and glimpsed the roof collapsing.

"Is anyone else inside?" the man shouted in my face.

"No. Just me." I shoved off the soggy blanket and pulled the skirt from my head. The coldness I'd felt before was utterly gone. The heat from the raging fire added to the temperate summer night, making the street feel almost tropical and reminding me once more of the bonfires.

The firefighter began barking orders as three uniformed firefighters pointed a large, gushing hose at the shop. The fire sizzled in protest. "Get the sides first," someone yelled, as another fire truck pulled up in front of the stores. "We don't want it spreading to the other buildings!"

At a casual glance, one might think the row of six stores were all one building, though the façades were made of various materials and each business rose to different heights. But as I'd found out when Winter and I had put in the connecting double doors, each building had its own exterior walls, so we'd ended up needing a very thick doorway and extra insulation before putting in the glass doors. I hoped that double protection now helped both Jake's store and the jazz music shop on my other side. The fire seemed to be doubling in size with every moment that passed.

The firefighter urged me toward the ambulance that had also appeared, along with four police cars.

"Autumn!" Shannon's voice cut through the noise. I jerked from the firefighter and ran in Shannon's direction. His arms went around me as I crashed into him. His arms gripped me hard.

"Are you okay?"

I tried to say I was fine, but the words were interrupted by a cough.

"She should get checked out by the ambulance," the firefighter told Shannon.

Shannon flashed his badge. "I'll take care of her."

"I'm fine," I insisted. And I was. But the worry on Shannon's face made me capitulate. "Okay, I'll get checked out," I said. I'd worry about how to pay for it later because I had no doubt I'd be getting a bill.

The EMT listened to my breathing as Shannon spread the blanket he gave us around my shoulders. Shannon lifted one of my bare feet. I expected to see burns, but as he gingerly brushed soot away, only my regular callused skin met our gaze. The other foot was the same.

He smiled at me in relief, but the smile was tight and anxious, and it told me how bad he thought the fire was. That's when it hit me. My hand-picked antiques, the shelving I'd made or bought second-hand, the glass cases I'd only recently installed—everything was literally going up in flames. Ten years of love and devotion. Ten years of paying a mortgage on which I still owed nearly three hundred thousand dollars. Worse, Winter's Herb Shoppe was also at risk, and everything Jake had put into it for almost two years.

Sobs shook me. I doubled over, unable to breathe—my distress having nothing to do with smoke inhalation. Shannon pulled me up from my seat in the back of the ambulance, holding me tightly against his body. "Can you give us a moment?" he said to the EMT.

"Sure," the man said. "She seems to be breathing okay, but if there's any pain, let me know immediately."

Shannon held me as I convulsed. "This is a temporary setback," he said in my ear. "You have insurance, remember? And I'm pretty good with a hammer. The important thing is that you're okay. The rest of it, we can do again."

Calm seeped from him into my body. He was right. I loved my antiques, but they were only things. Even those in my apartment, the ones that connected me with the past, weren't more important than my life—or anyone else's life.

I sagged against him, and he held me for a long moment before pushing me back slightly to search my face, making sure I was okay.

I smiled at him, lifting my chin slightly as I had in the old days when we'd been at each other's throats. "Maybe this is the universe's way of making sure I take time off for a honeymoon with a certain stubborn detective I know."

His lips twitched. "Maybe. But I'd understand if you want to postpone."

"We're not waiting." My tone dared him to object.

He was smart enough not to. "Okay." He paused a moment before adding, "I think they've about put it out. And it hasn't spread. Good thing they sent two trucks."

I dared look, and he was right. Huge billows of smoke, illuminated by the streetlights, still poured from the broken display windows, the door, and what had once been my roof. But flames only burned in the front middle section of my store where most of my furniture had been displayed. The Herb Shoppe and jazz store would have to deal with odor from the smoke, but their contents were otherwise safe.

I stepped back from Shannon. "I want to know what happened. My store didn't just spontaneously erupt into flames."

I thought of the car that had followed me. Was it related? If it was, I was going to find out.

Chapter 17

The morning sun was peeking above the clouds before the fire department had an answer for us.

"Deliberately set," said the fire inspector, who had shown up after the fire was out and the two fire trucks were rolling up their hoses. "We've identified three points of origin— probably three containers of gasoline with rags in them."

Shannon stared at the man. "Someone deliberately set the fire?"

"The display window was broken, so that's probably how they got in."

"But the window's alarmed," I protested, remembering the crash I'd heard, the one that had briefly awoken me before the fire alarms. Not a dream, after all.

The fire inspector shrugged his big shoulders. "Electricity's been cut to the whole section of stores here. And if there's any doubt"—he lifted a flattish rock about the size of his gloved hand—"they left a message. Probably what they broke the window with."

I could barely make out white lettering on the rock that said *Butt out.*

Shannon whipped out an oversized evidence bag. "I'll be taking that," he said, showing his badge. "I'm a detective with the Central Precinct."

The investigator tipped back his hard hat to look more intently at Shannon. "Yeah, I thought I recognized you. Homicide, right? The arson team from your district is already here. They might have better luck at tracking those responsible. A witness has already come forward to say they saw some kids running from the area."

Shannon visibly bit back a response. Taking a calming breath, he nodded. "Thanks for letting me know. I'll pass it on to them, but I believe this may be connected to a murder case Miss Rain here is consulting on. Could be in retaliation. I want to make sure I get a stab at the rock before it disappears into an evidence locker."

The investigator slipped the rock carefully into the bag. "I'll let them know you've got it. It was hot enough when we first found it that any fingerprints are probably gone, but they might be able to compare it with the MO from other cases." He smiled at me. "Or maybe you can find something on it."

He left us staring after him. "Guess someone told him about me," I said. Not surprising, since he was connected with the Central Precinct.

Shannon turned his back to the other officers and opened the bag. Once, I would have had to beg him to let me touch evidence that hadn't been thoroughly examined; now he was as anxious for me to test it for imprints as I was.

I held my hand above the bag. Not even a faint tingle registered. "It was really hot in there, so any imprints are likely gone." Even so, I let my knuckle touch the surface. "Nothing. Sorry."

"It was a long shot." He shut the bag and tucked it under his arm.

"I need to get inside," I said, staring over at my store. "I need to see if there's anything to save." It had all happened so fast, and yet during my escape, it had felt like slow motion.

"Let me talk to them. We need to make sure it's safe first. Meanwhile, you'd better call Jake and Tawnia."

"I already texted Jake. He'll come when he wakes up and checks his phone." I peered at the time on my own phone. Five in the morning. Only four hours since I'd called the fire department. "I'll give Tawnia another half hour to sleep. She wakes up early enough with Destiny."

Shannon leaned forward and kissed my lips. "Do you really want to wait?" he murmured against my skin. "She'll want to know sooner than later, and you know how she gets when she's mad."

"You're right." Once more, I felt a rush of gratitude that I'd escaped the fire. Shannon and I still had more time together. I still had time to annoy my sister and play with Destiny.

A crowd was gathering now, and traffic backed up as people drove by and noticed the burnt building and police cars still out front. As Shannon strode away, I wished I had my keys so I could get into Jake's shop to check out possible damage there. If the smell was bad, he'd probably have to throw away a lot of inventory. I was sure the adjoining doors hadn't helped that.

Jake appeared as I was texting my sister. His dark face was pinched with worry, and his locs had more escaping hairs than normal. He enveloped me in a bear hug that threatened to bring tears again.

"You look like you came straight from your bed," I said.

"I did." His voice was thick from disuse. Or maybe worry.

"I stopped by your place and brought the clothes you asked for. Did you know that your drawers are almost empty? All I found was a pair of holey jeans and a couple of shirts."

I clung to him. "I was inside, sleeping. I almost didn't get out."

An angry growl sounded in his throat. "I knew we both should have put in back doors to the alley. The connecting doors aren't enough."

"I know that now," I said, drawing back and rolling my eyes.

"I'm not mad at you. It's me. Come on. Let's get inside." With an arm around my shoulders, he pulled me past the caution tape someone had put up along the sidewalk in front of both our stores.

The interior of the Herb Shoppe appeared undamaged, except for peeling and blackening on the wall next to my shop. Our connecting glass doors were miraculously intact, though the soot was so thick on my side that we couldn't see through.

"I'm really sorry about this," I murmured as he punched his alarm code into the panel behind the counter that was located near the door. There seemed to be something odd about him doing that, but I couldn't pinpoint what.

"It's not your fault."

"Does it smell terrible in here?" I couldn't tell if the stench of smoke was coming from his shop or from me.

"Not as much as I thought it would. If my fire alarms ever went off, they've stopped." He handed me a reusable grocery bag with my clothes inside. "Why don't you go change? I'll turn my air filters on high so they'll clear the air faster. Remember the time we burned that pizza in your oven?"

I remembered. I'd been so impressed that I'd bought one

of his portable filters for my apartment and another for my store. There were often a lot of strange smells associated with antiques. Usually baking soda did the trick on individual items, but the air filter kept the shop fresh smelling. Now that filter was likely a hunk of scorched metal.

"You won't be able to use the filter," I told him. "Power's out. I think they're working on it now."

Grinning, he leaned over to punch buttons on the two-foot-high filter behind the desk. "Good thing Winter installed that backup generator."

Winter had worried about the refrigerated items, I remembered. That hadn't been a priority in my store. "Right. That's why you had to punch in the alarm code." My brain felt as soggy as the parts of my sweats that refused to dry.

I went into his bathroom, locked the door, and took my time cleaning up, even washing my hair in the sink with the herbal hand soap and using half a roll of paper towels to clean my body. I didn't want to add to the smell in his store. He'd included a bra and underwear with the holey jeans, both of which had seen better days, but which made me feel human again. I plopped my old sweats into a plastic garbage bag from his supply cabinet, knotting it tightly, which I then put into the cloth bag before emerging.

The air filter hummed on its highest setting near our connecting doors, opposite the cash registers, where Jake was printing up a stack of papers. "You'll need to call your insurance right away," he said. "I'm printing an inventory list. Good thing you've kept it up to date."

With everything on our joint database so we could ring up in either shop, there hadn't been much choice. Each inventory item had a value assigned as well, not necessarily what

I paid, but what it would cost me to replace the item. My goal was always to make thirty percent more for the antiques than replacement cost. Large ticket items, or items I sold on consignment, were usually a smaller percent increase but gave me more profit overall.

I supposed someday soon, I'd feel grateful I didn't have to make up a list from the wreckage, but that day wasn't today. I sank down on the stool behind his counter with a faint sigh.

Jake gave me a sympathetic glance. "I'll make you some herbal tea. Something with ginger in it will wake you up without a caffeine rush. You'll need to sleep when you can. Feel free to use the couch in my office." He left without waiting for a reply.

Being in the Herb Shoppe was comforting, like in the old days when Winter had been alive. I'd worked here all my teenage years, and that was how I'd come to buy the shop next door. The shop that was now in ruins.

Kids had been seen running from the area, which meant the fire could be related to the vandalism at Franklin High School. I'd have to fill Shannon in on that case, so whoever got the case could follow up on the lead. If it had been kids from Franklin or Lincoln who torched my store, they probably hadn't known I was inside.

Something niggled at my brain. I had to comb through my thoughts to find what it was. Robby Hartman had said forty thousand dollars wasn't enough to risk going to prison for murder, so how much did the person responsible for burning my shop have on the line? The vandalism at the school had done a hundred thousand dollars' worth of damage. Was hiding the identity of who did that worth risking burning down not one but six retail shops?

I didn't think so. But teenagers often didn't think like experienced adults.

A pit of dread opened in my stomach, but I didn't let it stay. Even though my store's computer was destroyed, all my customer and business files, including those I didn't share with Jake, were on a cloud server somewhere, which meant I could get to them through Jake's system. Time to get to work. I logged on, found my insurance documents, and called the agent directly. A machine answered, directing me to a twenty-four-hour number. I ignored that and left a message.

"I need someone out here as soon as possible," I said, giving my name. After ten years, I knew the agent well enough to know she'd come herself or send someone.

I was double-checking Jake's printouts to make sure my insurance inventory included my display cases and my air filter when Tawnia burst through the door, looking rattled.

"Oh, you poor thing." She ran to me and held me tight. "I saw Shannon. He went inside your shop with a couple of officers. It looks bad."

"Yeah." I hadn't told her in my text that I'd been inside when the fire had started. Seeing her now, I knew I couldn't tell her. Not now. "Where's Destiny?"

"With Bret. He's staying home today. He'll come down later when she needs to nurse, but I have frozen milk in the freezer he can use and that baby food I can never get her to eat." She fingered the printed pages. "What's this?"

"My insurance forms," I said. "And an inventory list."

"Good. That'll save a lot of time with the insurance."

It had been Jake's doing. He'd pushed for more automation, and now I was grateful. "I need to get over there," I said.

She nodded. "But before you start calling a demolition

crew, remember, every bit we save and can do ourselves means more money for the repairs and reconstruction. There's a lot we can do. I also think we should call Cody."

"Cody?"

"Of course." She grabbed my hand. "He's built a ton of houses—or had them built. He knows people in the business. We need to get you up and running again as soon as possible." She searched my face. "At least, if that's what you want."

I'd known the question was coming. Maybe I'd been thinking it myself. I could cut and run. I could use the insurance money to pay off the mortgage and start reading imprints full time, or I could retire to Shannon's acre and grow herbs. Of course, that would be more like hiding out.

I started laughing. "Of course, I'm rebuilding. I love antiques. I love my customers. I love my employees. You can call Cody."

Tawnia laughed with me. "I'm so glad to hear you say it because I already called the girls, and Cody too." She released me and started typing on Jake's computer. "We'll need to email your customers, and don't you have a list of all the people you've helped with imprints? I'm sure some of them will be in for a little demolition."

Before I could respond, Jake set down two cups of tea that he'd made in the kitchenette at the back of his store. "I knew you'd show up any moment," he said to Tawnia. "Hope you like ginger."

She made a face. "Neither of us do." But she picked up the tea and began sipping. "Oh, this is actually good."

Shannon opened the outside door to the Herb Shoppe and peeked in. "I've got the all-clear for you to go in, except into the far back where the ceiling is still intact. They're afraid it will fall."

The entire ceiling was gone? I'd seen some of it go, but that was worse than I'd expected. Tawnia and Jake trailed behind me as I left with Shannon.

It didn't take long to ascertain the extent of the damage. Everything in the middle of the store, where apparently most of the accelerant had been left, was gone. Even the cabinets near the middle were melted or sooty refuse. The sides of the store were a little better off, but all the merchandise was scorched and blackened. Only the clocks on the side next to Jake's store were still intact, along with the case of vintage Fisher-Price toys. The clocks would cost more to clean than the reimbursement money, unless I did it myself, and I wouldn't have the time. I could try with the Fisher-Price that had been somewhat protected by the fancy, heavy-duty case, but I doubted it would be worth the work, and the deep cleaning could destroy the items.

Which meant the store was nearly a total loss.

Who was responsible? The thought had reverberated in my head ever since the firefighter had pulled me from the flames, but now other thoughts were making their way into my tired brain. Not new thoughts, but I was connecting them in a new way.

First, burning down the shop to get me off the case was a big risk.

Second, the Futura smart glasses were worth a billion dollars.

Third, a new black Jag was very expensive.

Fourth, Titus Grey had been proud to tell me that the tech behind Futura was something no one else had.

And fifth, Peter Griffin locked the microchip production file with a new password shortly before his death.

The only logical conclusion was that the production file was worth murdering for, and I just happened to be caught in the middle.

"We might be able to save the safe and the appliances in the back room," Shannon said, his arm around my shoulder. "If you can get rid of the smell."

"Once we get the store all cleaned out, it shouldn't be too hard to rebuild." Tawnia reached over to squeeze my hand. "Thera's always complaining about wanting the checkout by the door, and Jazzy wants more window space. And you can still have a counter near the back. Or, better yet, a worktable. That would give you more room in the back for other stuff."

"Right, because putting in a back door is going to cost you some of the space there," Jake said. "It's the only way to give you access to the alley, since it leads out to the other block instead of to our block. And you know what? You could make the new ceiling higher." One of the first things Jake had done in the Herb Shoppe was to remove the three-foot storage space between the ceiling and the roof so he could make his shop appear larger. I'd been trying to find the funds to remodel my ceiling ever since.

I looked up at the morning sky through the ruined ceiling. The large blue expanse seemed promising rather than indifferent to our deliberation.

"Well?" Tawnia asked tentatively. She looked ready to cry, an expression I knew too well from my own face.

I smiled. "I guess it's time for a complete redesign."

They all seemed to breathe a collective sigh of relief. "I'm okay, you guys," I added. "Change like this . . . it's okay." Or at least I was going to make the best of it. "You know what? I'm just glad I didn't finish all the cleaning last night."

Tawnia stared at me a full ten seconds before snorting loudly. We all burst into laughter.

"Come on," Jake said. "Let's go finish our tea. And it looks like Thera and Jazzy are here."

Sure enough, the "girls," as Tawnia had called them earlier, despite the fact that Thera was in her sixties, were peeking in through the broken door.

Back at Jake's, Shannon took off to check in at the police bureau while the rest of Autumn's Antiques and the Herb Shoppe employees gathered and talked about plans for rebuilding.

My mind, however, was on the Futura case. I excused myself and went to Jake's office to call Elliot. "Look," I said, once I'd explained about the fire. "The police think it might be kids who did this, but they haven't found any suspects yet, and the timing is suspicious."

"Could be the Franklin kids. Or whoever did the vandalism."

"I thought the same thing at first, but that's a huge upscale from damaging football equipment. If I hadn't been here, the whole row of buildings probably would have burned. That means millions of dollars. Even if the school vandals were trying to scare me, throwing that rock through the window would have been enough. But cutting off the electricity so they could get in with containers of gasoline? That took more forethought."

"You think it's related to Futura then."

"Peter Griffin locked up that final production file for a reason. I'm thinking that if a company didn't have to go through all the years of development, but someone handed them the files instead. . ."

"That's got to be it," Elliot said, his excitement spilling through the connection. "Someone is trying to sell the tech behind Futura. It has to be one of the sons."

"Not necessarily. It could be anyone who has access to all the production files—or normally did."

"You still figure the partner didn't do it?"

"I don't think he's involved. But I need to get back into the Griffin house. I think someone in Peter's family knows more than they're telling, even if they don't know what they know."

"The funeral's tomorrow morning. According to the paper, there's a gathering for family and close friends afterward at the Griffin residence."

"That's it, then. I'm planning to go to the funeral, and if we don't have answers by then or I can't find them, I'll tag along to the house. Meanwhile, you need to find a link between one of our suspects and a company or person willing to pay big bucks for the technology."

"I can check recent filings for patents and trademarks," he said. "And I'm going personally to the Jag dealers today." Which meant he'd wrestled his anxiety into submission for at least those visits.

"Good. Call me when you can."

"Okay." He hesitated. "And Autumn?"

"Yeah?"

"I'm really sorry about your store."

"Thanks."

"Let me know when you need help. I'll come."

"You can do that?" I had to ask.

"Maybe. I'd need to know what to expect." He didn't sound upset, just nervous.

Too nervous to have him onsite. "I'll need new display cabinets," I said. "If you hear of anyone selling some second-hand, it would be a big help."

He chuckled. "I'm on it."

"But only after the case."

"Right."

Chapter 18

At some point, I closed my eyes on Jake's couch to rest a minute, and when I opened them, I knew immediately that time had passed. A lot of time. My eyes were still gritty with lack of sleep, or maybe smoke irritation, but I felt better. I uncurled and stretched, then coughed a bit. My throat was dry rather than hurting.

I wandered out into the Herb Shoppe, which seemed busier than normal for a Wednesday morning—no, it was well after noon now—but the traffic was still unusual, even with this BOGO sale going on. I made myself a cup of tea as I considered how I'd clear out the interior of my store. Maybe Cody could give me some advice.

Thera, Jazzy, and Jake's sister, Randa, were working at the counter. "I hope you got some sleep," Thera called to me. "Tawnia peeked in on you and made us promise not to wake you."

All the customers turned to stare at me in sympathy. Many I recognized from my years in this location. I nodded a greeting to them.

"Where is Tawnia?" I asked.

"With Cody." Jazzy abandoned her register. "I'll show you." To my surprise, the customer she was helping nodded amiably.

Outside, things had changed drastically. A huge truck was parked at the curb, and a line of people were coming in and out of my store. Or what used to be my store. The entire front wall was gone, and a good third of the shop was cleaned out. Shannon was inside with Cody, Jake, and Tawnia's husband, Bret, all four wearing face masks and covered in soot. They weren't the only ones. A couple whose daughter I'd rescued from a cult was also there, along with Tawnia's neighbors, who were related to the mobster I owed a favor to. A half-dozen of my regular customers, a few total strangers, and an entire biker club—one of whom I'd saved from a serial killer—were also working hard. They were laughing and cleaning and carrying garbage out to Paige and Matthew, who were inside the huge truck, helping to lift things inside.

Tawnia appeared at my elbow carrying a sleeping Destiny next to her chest in a baby carrier. "Bret brought Destiny to nurse, and my neighbor Sophia will take her home in a bit. They're about ready to turn things over to the next shift."

"Next shift?" I asked lamely.

"Yep. Cody called in a contractor he knows to give a bid, and he's directing the demolition. It'll save thousands of dollars. We have a backhoe coming soon."

"I thought we needed to wait for my insurance agent."

"Oh, she's come and gone. She said not to worry, that you're fully covered. She also told me not to bother saving anything unless it costs less to fix than replace—but you already knew that. They do depreciate things, but since you've bought everything second-hand anyway, that won't affect you as much as it does some people. She'll be getting you an initial check soon so you can pay your mortgage and other essentials. She also told me—off the record, mind you—that after you submit the claim, the insurance company will try to close the case as quickly as possible, but you shouldn't sign anything to that effect for several months in case you discover new items you forgot to tell them about."

"Good to know," I said. "Thanks."

She grinned. "You'd better talk to Cody first. He has questions for you about the rebuild, and so will the contractor—who isn't officially on the job yet. He's here only as a friend of Cody's."

"If Cody approves of him, he's probably the best I can get," I allowed.

"That's what I figure. By the way, Cody asked me what you were going to do with your apartment, and I said you didn't know. I think he might be interested in buying it, if that makes it any easier than selling to a stranger."

"I'm not going to sell him a place he doesn't need. He knows he's always welcome to stay with one of us when he comes to town."

"Well, if you sell your apartment, it'll be a little more difficult for him to stay there, right?" She gave me a light slap on the arm. "Just think about it."

"Okay." But if I decided to sell the apartment, I wasn't going to dump my problem off on Cody.

I hurried into the blackened remains of my store, nodding at people and thanking them for being here. Some stopped and hugged me, so I was almost as black as everyone else when I finally reached Cody. Shannon passed me carrying one end of a partially melted cabinet. His face was smudged with soot, and his hair was streaked dark.

"I thought you went to work," I said.

He shrugged. "I worked until one," he said, his voice muffled by the mask. "They owe me a few hours. I'll have to leave soon." He winked and moved on.

"We're making good progress," Cody told me. "And we'll make more once the backhoe gets here for the big stuff. The side and back walls are good, so once we rip them down to the underlayers and check for damage, the rebuilding can begin. The key is getting out everything that's been burned and washing down what we don't take out. The chemicals will kill any remaining smell."

"I really appreciate your help," I told him.

He shrugged. "It's not me. It's Stanley over there. He's the best when it comes to this sort of thing, believe me. You want to meet him?"

"In a bit. I need a moment to take it all in."

"You don't have to hire him if you don't want to," Cody said. "But he'll save you thirty percent easy above the others, particularly because of this clean-up and because he'll let us do sweat equity." He scratched at the beginnings of a beard. "But I've been thinking. What this place really needs is another floor. Stanley thinks so too. He says it's zoned for it. And this location makes any addition worth far more than the extra materials and work. You'll be able to sell for a lot more down the road."

I frowned. "I don't need another entire floor. Sure, extra storage would be nice, but it doesn't pay to keep too much around that isn't selling."

"I'm not talking about a sales floor." He waved his hand as if to toss away the very thought. "Your sister told me you're concerned about having space for the antiques in your apartment, and I've been thinking about it. Stanley says this strip of land is zoned for both residential and commercial, one of the few places that are these days. That's why some of your neighbors have apartments above their shops. With all the money we'll save, you can build an apartment upstairs, and you can move your antiques there, and stuff from your parents too. Leastwise, the ones you want to keep. You'll also have plenty of room for storage. Then you can extend the shop into the back room and finally have a bathroom for customer use instead of sending them over to Jake's. You can even make the new back door an entrance for people who come from the other block." He cut off, as if suddenly having run out of words.

I folded my arms stubbornly across my chest. The whole idea was ridiculous. A fire had just taken everything I'd worked for, and wasting insurance money that I needed to restock didn't make sense.

"And do what with my apartment?" I countered. "Sell it to you, I suppose? So you can rent it out? Is that what Stanley says I should do?" If Cody thought he could swoop in and save me, he didn't know me at all.

He blinked and then snorted loudly. "Oh, right, Tawnia was going on about some sort of nonsense. Of course not. Sure, you could sell the apartment and pay down your mortgage here. But it's a main floor unit, and that's big with visitors and retirees. The best thing to do is to use some of your cheaper antiques and make up a nice place to rent it out for short periods of time. Ever hear of Airbnb? A location this close to the Hawthorne district would get you several thousand a month. Then you use that to help pay your mortgage here at the store."

I stared at him, unable to think of anything to say. Renting out my parents' apartment instead of selling it? A sudden rush of emotion filled my chest as I thought of all the strangers my parents had dragged home over the years. I'd usually ended up sleeping in my parents' bed with them on those nights, probably to keep me safe, though I hadn't realized it at the time. Having their home used and loved by others would be . . . perfect. I could even help people out for a night or two without charge as they had, though I wouldn't say as much to Cody. His business sense wouldn't appreciate that plan.

"Think on it," he said gruffly. "Don't matter none to me. I already found a place to buy for when I'm in town, but I can buy yours too if you really want to give up that sweet deal. Except I'd be a liar if I told you it was good for your future." He turned and headed for my counter, which was burned and blackened on the closest side.

"Come open the safe," he called over his shoulder. "I want to see if it's worth saving. By the way, I'd like to have this counter—or pieces of it—for one of my art projects, if you don't mind. With a little bit of shaping, it'll be perfect for my new Dante's Inferno representation."

"You can have it." That was when I remembered my gun, which was still in the safe.

"Doesn't look like it went off," Cody said, as we examined it.

"Yeah." I'd have to ask Shannon to check it out. For now, I'd put it in the Herb Shoppe with my phone and rings while I helped with the demolition.

Minutes later, I donned borrowed gloves and a mask and became consumed by the work like everyone else. My blue jeans were black in no time—and my T-shirt, hair, and feet as well. The truck went away, and another took its place.

Shannon and other volunteers had to leave, but new faces

arrived, mostly customers and people I'd helped with imprints. Their hard work was inspiring. When I stopped to grab a bottled water from a table Tawnia had set up outside with refreshments, I ran into two more faces who surprised me.

I removed my mask. "Pax, Opal, what are you two doing here?" The teens were covered in soot and enjoying pizza at the moment. They had obviously been helping to clear the store, though I hadn't run into them before now.

Pax grinned at me. "We brought the stuff you asked for."

"How did you know about the paint?" Opal asked, looking around to be sure she wasn't heard. "I guess this means my brother did it, didn't he? My dad is going to be so mad."

I was glad she understood that she couldn't protect Otto. "I don't know yet. But if he's involved, it's better for him to take responsibility now."

Opal chewed on her lip. "Otto plays pranks like he did with the pointers, but he's not usually so stupid."

That made me wonder. "Were the cans full or empty?"

The kids looked at each other. "Full, I think," Pax said.

"What color did Otto do the pointers?"

"Blue," Opal said.

"That all might be good news then." For Otto, I meant. It didn't help the case I'd been building against him in my mind, but I wouldn't really know the whole truth until I read his imprints. "Where is the stuff?"

"Your sister put it under the counter inside that store." Pax thumbed at the Herb Shoppe.

"She is your sister, right?" Opal added, glancing over at Tawnia, who was talking to a woman I didn't recognize. "She looks just like you, except for the hair."

"She's my sister," I said, grinning. "My much older sister.

She was born just before midnight, and I was born twenty-seven minutes later the next day." They laughed as I knew they would. "Thanks for helping out."

"It's fun," Pax said. "And I owe you for helping me."

"Well, I still appreciate it." He was a good kid, that was clear.

Now that I'd stopped moving, I felt dead on my feet. "Opal, do you know where your brother was last night?" While I was almost certain Futura was somehow involved in the destruction of my store, there was always the chance that a dumb kid had gotten himself in even deeper.

She nodded. "We went to my grandmother's for dinner. Then he was home most of the day today. That's why it took me so long to get everything, but he finally went out about three, and then I met up with Pax. You weren't answering your phone, so we came here. We were worried you'd already be closed."

"I left my phone inside the Herb Shoppe." I looked down at myself. "I'd better get cleaned up before I look at what you brought. Is it okay if I bring the stuff back to you later tonight?"

Opal hesitated, then nodded. "I can tell my father I learned about your store and came to help, and maybe you could stop by to say thanks."

"Or I might need to talk to him about your brother," I said gently.

She nodded. "I still don't believe Otto did this, but if he did, he needs help."

The two kids went back to work, but fifteen minutes later, the burly contractor, Stanley, who was every bit as professional and experienced as Cody had promised, called a stop to the work, with the invitation to take up again at nine the next morning. It was a good thing because I didn't think I could take another step.

I had Tawnia go into the Herb Shoppe for Opal's sack and my own belongings. She tried to convince me to go home with her, but I told her my bathtub was a lot closer than hers, even if it meant I had to do laundry.

Thanking everyone, I spread a couple of the garbage bags Jake was handing out on my seat and drove home. Before parking, though, I did another loop around the block, looking for a black Jag to make sure I wasn't being followed. No sign of it or anyone else suspicious.

Going inside my apartment felt different today, and not only because I was filthy, but because I was seeing it with different eyes. It was a good location with covered parking, close to the Hawthorne District, but not close enough that we heard any noise from the bars or clubs. There was even a little park down the street.

Inside, I could see no evidence that Shannon had cleaned up here, so he must have gone out to his place. While I washed clothes, I showered, then filled the bath with the hottest water I could stand before lying down to soak. I dozed a little, and my body felt less sore when I was finished. Wearing my only clean T-shirt and a pair of dirty shorts, I put the clothes to dry and threw in another load.

The bag Opal had brought me was by the door, and once I had things under control, it called to me even more than my bed. It was time to learn the truth. Inside the bag, I found pens, a pack of cards, a football ring, a woven bracelet, a comb, a notebook full of doodles, and the two cans of paint.

I started with the paint because that was the obvious link, but all I saw was a teen's hand holding the paint cans as he shoved them into the drawer, and before that a glimpse of a cash register when the paint was purchased. Most of the other items had nice imprints, but they told me nothing about the paint or the night in question.

Then I touched the notebook, and I understood everything.

Chapter 19

I didn't call ahead as I probably should have, but Principal Tillmon was home all the same. He answered the door himself and smiled when he saw me. "Does this mean what I think it does?"

"Yes. I know who is responsible for the vandalism, or at least one of the boys. I think he'll tell you who the others are that are also involved, though I can narrow that down for you." I had the black and white paint with me, but the rest of the objects Opal had brought me were in the car. The paint was the strongest evidence I had if you couldn't read imprints.

"Let's go into my office." He glanced behind him, as if checking to see if any of his family was there. I wondered how many other children he and his wife had, and how the next few minutes would go.

I followed him inside. He sat on the couch in his office, and I sat on the other end, though I didn't plan to be there long. It was a nice room, comfortable and homey, with an oak desk and bookcases full of books.

I pulled the paint from my bag and set it on his desk.

"What's this?" he asked.

"How well do you know Otto Anderson?"

He nodded. "Fairly well, I'd say. Not only is his father a colleague and friend of mine, but our sons are friends."

"Was he here on that Thursday night before the vandalism was discovered?"

"Yes." He started shaking his head. "Oh, no. It can't be Otto. He's a great joker, but he wouldn't do this. And the boys were here all night."

"You're right. Otto didn't do it. Remember the pointers I told you Pax fixed? Otto knew about it, and that night he told his friends. That's why the ringleader decided to use black and white paint."

"He wanted to frame Pax?" Tillmon's brow creased. "Wait, are you saying some of the boys planned this here at my house?"

"I'm saying that's where the idea was born. The next day at least one of the boys went around buying paint—probably at different stores. I'm betting he was careful to wipe off his fingerprints so they wouldn't be found later by the police. Then he took four of his friends, all football players from Lincoln High School, over to Franklin. Otto was one of the boys, but when he learned about the plan to vandalize the equipment room, he took the paint he'd been given and cut out." That was what had been on the notebook, memories of his leaving and the boy who gave him the paint.

Baird Tillmon nodded. "He's a good kid at heart. But how did the Lincoln boys get the keys? Or did they break in?"

This was the hard part. "Not all the boys were from Lincoln. And I believe he used your keys."

Tillmon's face drained of color. "My keys? But . . ." Understanding dawned. "No," he murmured, but it was decidedly less emphatic than it had been when defending Otto. "Why would my son do this?"

"Because Pax was taking up playing time on the field, and because Opal likes Pax."

Tillmon stared away from me in the direction of the window, though the blinds were pulled and only faint rays from the setting sun filtered through.

"You may have to bring Otto in on this to find out who the other boys are. He might not have helped, but he knew what they intended. He could have stopped it. Or some of it." The irony that two school officials' sons were involved didn't escape me.

"It's not Otto's fault. It's mine. I shouldn't have forced the coach to put Memphis on the team. I just thought . . . he wanted to play so much." He sighed and stood. "Thank you, Miss Rain. I'll look forward to getting your bill. I will, of course, cover it myself."

I came to my feet. "The other boys should also take responsibility. Better now than in ten years when they'd have to go to jail."

He met my gaze. "I won't cover this up, if that's what you're asking. My son and the other boys will take full responsibility. You have my word."

"Then that's enough." When he didn't respond, I added, "I can see myself out."

He nodded absently, his face lost in thought.

I paused at the door. "I have an idea of how we can help the boys raise money to replace or repair the equipment. I'll be in touch in a few days. If that's okay."

"I'd appreciate that." He heaved a sigh that carried the

weight of the world. "There's nothing worse than the disappointment a child can bring, you know? The real trick is to keep loving them afterward."

I smiled. "If you're already thinking that far ahead, Memphis is a lucky kid."

"Maybe," he said with a grunt, "but first, I'm going to kill him."

I was hopeful Tillmon and his son would make it through.

Next, I drove to Opal's house and left the sack with her brother's belongings, minus the paint, at the base of her mailbox, and texted her about it.

Your brother didn't do it. But he knew about it. And there are three other Lincoln football players and one from Franklin who I suspect won't be playing this year. Thanks for your help.

Back at home, I found Shannon waiting for me—with food that wasn't pasta. It was the perfect ending to a really rotten day.

I went to change into a comfortable pair of lounge pants and to wash my feet in the tub. I turned to see Shannon in the open doorway, staring down at me. "It's so odd that your feet weren't burned."

I studied them as I blotted the water off with the towel. Only my usual thick skin and calluses were apparent. No burns. "It is weird," I said. "I mean, I could feel the heat on my face, but I felt enveloped in cold. I thought it was the water dripping from the blanket."

"Your feet are pretty tough. Maybe the water was enough."

"I don't think so." I explained about the odd sensation of cold that had been following me around—or had I been following it? Well, for sure, I hadn't followed anything to my store.

"This has to be another aspect of your ability," Shannon said. "And if it helped you get out of that fire, I'm all for it."

He extended a hand, and I let him pull me up from the edge of the tub and into his arms. He kissed me deeply, tasting warm and slightly minty. For a moment, all was right with the world. That was the way he always made me feel—as if the world could fall apart, and as long as I could touch him, everything would be okay. Even back in the old days when he doubted me and I'd purposely taunted him, that connection had been there. I'd trusted him to be around when I needed him.

Taking my hand, he led me to my Victorian sofa, where he'd laid out the food on the coffee table. He handed me a Smokey's pot pie, and the heady aroma made my mouth water.

"Just so you know, I'm not giving up this apartment," I said, snuggling up to him on the couch. "I'm thinking about renting it out."

"That might be a good idea. I know you aren't excited about letting it go. This place has a lot of memories."

So maybe I'd given him less credit than I should have. I'd never been good at hiding my feelings, and he was a detective, after all.

"By the way," he said. "I called my parents and told them about the fire. I asked them to postpone their visit until the wedding. I know they wanted to get to know you before we tie the knot, but the last thing you need is to meet their expectations while dealing with all this. And they will have expectations, even if they aren't excessive."

Relief poured through me. "Thanks. That takes a lot of pressure off. I've been wondering how I was going to fit it all in, especially when we still haven't finished with the Griffin case."

He laughed and gave me a long kiss that almost—almost—made me forget how hungry I was. "It's not as if I'd ever change my mind, even if my parents didn't love you." The tone of his voice sent shivers through my body.

"Me either."

We kissed a little more until my stomach growled loudly enough for him to hear. Then silence ruled as we concentrated on our food.

"Hey," Shannon said after a bit, "do you think adding another floor to your shop is a good idea? Cody and the contractor seem to think it wouldn't add all that much cost, especially if they left it bare bones, and we finish it on the weekends."

"You know how to put up drywall?"

"Oh, I've figured out a thing or two since inheriting my grandpa's house, but I'm really depending on you to show me the ropes." He laughed. "But maybe we can get the wall to look a little better than the one in your back room. Those seams were rough."

I laughed. "I might have skimped a little. It's not as if any customers saw it."

I was sleepy by the time we finished eating, and my occasional cough made Shannon look away from the cop show he was making fun of. "You sure you're okay?"

"I think I need a little chamomile tea," I said, rising. "You keep watching. I'll be right back."

The water was almost boiling on the stove when Elliot called. "Bingo," he said. Before I could laugh at that, he rushed on. "You aren't going to believe this. I did a patent search and found one filed by Viewpoint, a local company for a product called Smart Eyes that sounds very similar to Futura. They have a supposedly new, state-of-the-art microchip that has never been used before."

"A lot of companies are building smart glasses," I said. "That doesn't mean they're any good."

"Yeah, but I compared this to the Futura listing, and it sounds suspiciously alike. Oh, it's been carefully written to seem different so they could get a patent, but here's the clincher: Guess who worked for them three years ago?"

"Who?" It could be anyone.

"Niklas Griffin. I found a picture from a Viewpoint Christmas party on his Facebook page."

"Anyone else we know in the picture with him?"

"No. But Niklas's connection with Viewpoint could be the reason Peter Griffin locked the microchip file."

"You think Niklas planned to sell the production files to Viewpoint? But Peter was going to give his son a job—and the imprint I read was after he locked the file. Besides, what good would it do to have the specs if Futura has an earlier patent?"

"Viewpoint has strong ties to China and Japan, so even if Futura won a suit here, once their secret files are out there, it might be too expensive to fight in those countries. And if Viewpoint can undercut Futura's sales price because they didn't have to invest thirty million in the creative process—"

"Then Futura won't be able to compete or sustain a long lawsuit."

"All that would certainly be worth burning down your store."

Silence fell between us as we both considered the implications. "Niklas Griffin has to be our primary suspect now," I said after a few moments.

"Peter could have been trying to keep him close."

"Any leads on the tadalafil prescription?"

"So far, I've tracked the company and paid someone there to release the prescription interview. The man who talked to the doctor is made up to look like Peter Griffin, but he isn't anyone on our suspect list. I think he might be a hired actor. I'm having my programs check for matches on local actors' sites."

"What about a money trail?"

"Our easiest bet for that is the car, and I should know who bought that sometime tomorrow. But now that we know what we're looking for, we'll have to find a way to examine all of the family's expenditures of late. We don't know who else might be involved."

"Call me when you get something. For now, I'm going to have some tea." Hanging up, I put the loose tea in a couple of infusers and put them and the boiling water in the cups.

Shannon looked up as I reentered my living room and handed him a cup. "I take it that was Elliot I heard you talking to?" he asked.

I told him about Viewpoint and Niklas's connection with the company. "I'm going to ask him about it tomorrow at the funeral."

"I think Peter Griffin's laptop may be key," Shannon said. "That might be one of the few devices that can access their network without going through the company computers and setting off alarms."

"Maybe you and Quincy can get a warrant for Niklas's place." I scooted closer to him, pulling the afghan Summer had made when I was a young child around me. Her imprints on the crocheted threads surrounded me with her love. It was what I needed today.

Shannon nodded. "Good idea, though I don't know that we have enough proof to convince a judge to let us look for the laptop."

"I think you're underestimating your gift of persuasion," I said. "Because whoever is trying to steal Futura, they were willing to murder Peter and burn down my store. We need to make sure we catch him before he does something worse."

Chapter 20

Thursday morning after running through my taekwondo forms, I dressed all in black for Peter Griffin's funeral, except for the black crocheted shawl that was edged with fake, white ostrich feathers. I'd been planning to meet Shannon there, but he and Quincy had managed to convince a judge to give them a warrant to search Niklas Griffin's apartment, so I was on my own until they finished the search and met me at the funeral home.

I wasn't wearing my gun because I wasn't at all sure it still worked after the heat of the fire. Shannon had agreed we needed to have it tested so it wouldn't blow up in my face. But I was confident I wouldn't need it at the services. Besides, my hands were my real weapon—at least that's what my taekwondo instructor always told me. I believed him; Shannon didn't. We agreed to disagree.

Part of me felt I should be at my store, cleaning up the mess, but my shop was in the capable hands of my sister and Cody, who would be supervising the removal until I arrived. The contractor was also bringing in a few of his own men to test the remaining structure and demolish what was needed.

The other part of me was grateful not to be there. Every time I'd lugged out one of my antique treasures, my heart hurt. I knew it could all be replaced, and I was happy to be alive to do it, but that didn't mean I stopped wishing it hadn't happened.

Throwing a few essentials into a matching black bag, I added a handful of chamomile chews that had been doing a good job of helping me stay calm since the fire. Popping another one into my mouth, I headed out of my apartment.

To my surprise, I found Jazzy outside the lobby doors, her blue hair in tight pigtails and a box balanced on her hips as she struggled to put a key in the lock. With her was Claire Philpot, the fifty-something attorney who had taken Jazzy in. She wore a gray suit, as if on her way to work, her dark hair swept up on top of her head, revealing her long, graceful neck. She also carried a box.

"Oh," Claire said as I opened the glass door for them. "We thought you'd be gone already." Her perfectly accented, light brown eyes wandered down my black dress. "You don't look like you're going to your shop."

I shook my head. "I'm on a case. I'm going to a funeral."

"Oh, yes. You're helping Paige."

I sometimes forgot that the two women had been friends long before I'd rescued Jazzy and facilitated her placement with Claire, and before I'd found Claire's missing husband and helped him come out of hiding from a vindictive former client. "Yes. I think we're getting close to discovering who's responsible."

"That's great," Claire said.

"Anyway, we brought you some stuff." Jazzy grinned broadly. "Jake told us just to bring it here. He gave us keys. I hope you don't mind."

Half my building and most of my friends had keys, so I didn't mind, not really. Or I wouldn't normally. Now, quite suddenly, I worried about the antiques I kept in the apartment.

"Of course, I don't mind," I made myself say, because I never wanted to be more attached to things than people. "But what is all this?"

Jazzy grinned. "It's your first batch of new antiques. New antiques sounds weird, but you know what I mean. At the rate we're going at the store, we'll need them soon. Claire sent out an email yesterday to all her fellow attorneys and clients, saying she'd owe them a favor if they donated antiques to the cause."

My gaze went to Claire, who nodded gently at my shocked expression. "Of course, we don't know how many things here are actually antiques. Most of it I'm sure was sitting in their attics for years, though. Some of my associates come from old families, so we might get lucky."

Jazzy pushed past me. "We have more boxes in the car. I figure as soon as you price everything, I can start selling some of it online. I already canceled all our current sales and auctions, seeing that everything's up in smoke—literally." She gave me a wry grimace. "Claire helped me work things out with eBay for the ones that were bid on already. And you don't even have to pay my hours until you're back in business. Plus, Jake said Thera can work at his place full time until you need her again."

"My insurance covers working capital, including wages," I said. "And I should have enough to buy more antiques."

"Well, now you have more. And these are better because they're free." Jazzy laughed and hurried up the three stairs to my apartment on the main floor.

That was when I remembered the Chippendale armchairs, now a charred mess at the landfill. "Oh, Claire," I said with a moan I couldn't hold back. "Those lovely chairs you gave me to sell weren't covered yet by my insurance. I have to file the expensive things separately for approval. Of course, I'll pay you what they were worth." That would cut out thousands of dollars from my insurance money, but it was the right thing to do.

"I don't want anything from you." She shifted her burden so she could touch one of my hands. "I gave you that stuff because Jazzy wanted to clean out the attic, and I wanted it all gone. I knew the chairs were valuable, but it was a thank-you for all you've done for me. Not just for saving my husband from that mobster, but for bringing me Jazzy. She's changed our lives, and that's something I have every day." She tilted her head toward the box she carried. "And this stuff is from people who can well afford it, and who would have demanded favors from me anyway. Jazzy needs work while you're rebuilding. Someday, she'll be ready to go out on her own, or maybe even become your partner, but for now, she needs you to help her learn what to charge and where to find things."

I felt a little better knowing she was also acting for Jazzy, but gratitude made a weepy lump in my throat. "Thank you," I managed. "It means a lot."

She smiled her elegant smile. "What goes around, comes around. I'll make sure everything's locked up when we're finished."

"Thanks." How she knew I needed to hear that my remaining antiques were protected, I didn't know, but I was grateful.

"Oh," she said as I started away, "you might want to read the fine print in your policy. Usually there is a timeframe for having to report new inventory, even if they need proof. And I'll be glad to be a witness. It won't hurt to ask."

"I will." I hurried toward my car. The exchange had only taken a few minutes, and I'd still make it to the funeral on time, but now I'd go knowing tonight I had antiques to price for Jazzy to sell, even without the store.

I arrived outside the Riverview Abbey Funeral Home with twenty minutes to spare. Titus Grey was outside wearing a fitted black suit, a black tie, and a dark shirt that was a mix of navy and black. He was deep in an intense conversation with Robby Hartford, who was also dressed in black, though his suit was baggy and out-of-date. Robby's gestures were wide and pleading as he bent his tall frame over Titus, whose shorter frame was rigid.

As I approached, I heard Titus say, "I already told you, I haven't decided. We'll talk about this later. I don't want Brigit to overhear. Or Stevan either. They've been through enough."

"You haven't told Stevan?"

"No. But he'll have to know. He's a partner now. And it's only fair."

Robby nodded, his hawkish nose seeming more prominent in profile. "I always intended to pay it back. I swear."

Titus's jaw tensed in what looked like a painful clench, and his hand moved in a chopping motion. "Later. But you need to be ready to help us understand why."

With a grunt, Robby lurched away, never even glancing in my direction as he followed a group of mourners into the funeral home.

"Hi, Titus," I said.

His face relaxed as he focused briefly on my face before

dropping his gaze. "I didn't expect to see you here," he said, awkwardly studying the ground. "Do you have any news?"

"I'm hoping to be able to tell you something today. Unfortunately, I need to ask the family more questions."

He swallowed hard. "Can't it wait?"

"I don't think so. I believe someone is after your company secrets. Someone from the inside."

He looked straight at me, shock making his awkwardness vanish. "You're talking about the locked file. No one can get to it from work. After your visit on Tuesday, I made sure only Stevan and I have access now to the area of the server where we store all our production files."

"What about Peter's laptop?"

"Well yeah, that could get to them, but it should be at his house, right?"

"It's missing." I let that sink in a minute before adding, "Have you ever heard of Viewpoint?"

He snorted. "Yeah. They sell cheap knockoffs of a lot of different electronic products. They were one of the companies I went to when I was looking for funding, though I wasn't aware of their reputation then."

"Did they not want Futura?"

He rubbed a finger over his left eye. "Oh, they were interested, but they wanted to buy Futura outright, and I wouldn't get a final say on anything. Plus, I didn't have a lot of confidence in their ability to raise the funds I knew we were going to need. They're worth millions, but they wouldn't have been able to raise near what Peter did." His eyes narrowed. "Why, what do they have to do with this?"

I was tempted to tell him about Niklas's connection, but

he might inadvertently alert Niklas before I had the chance of talking to him. If Shannon managed to find the laptop at Niklas's apartment, secrecy wouldn't be so important. But for now, secrecy was in our favor.

"I can tell you they filed a patent two years ago for a product called Smart Eyes that looks suspiciously like Futura."

He snorted. "Let them try. There's no way. Unless . . ." He paled. "That's why you're worried about the locked file. You think someone's trying to give Futura to Viewpoint."

"Yes. That's why I want to be sure no one else has access, not even Peter's wife and older son."

"I don't think they have access." He closed his eyes. "If someone is trying to steal those files, they've probably given Viewpoint all the other production files we've finished and sent to our factories. That means I need to get into the microchip file as quickly as possible so I can transfer it out of the database. But I've tried all of Peter's usual passwords, and so has Stevan."

"Maybe Brigit has an idea. I know the police asked her about passwords already, but she might know of a catchphrase he used."

Titus gestured up the walk. "Let's go ask her. There's still time before the service."

"About Robby," I said as we moved forward. "You should know that the reason he took the money was because of his wife. She became addicted to prescription painkillers. She's in a rehabilitation center for drug abuse. He needed money to pay for that, and also a sitter for his daughters."

He stopped moving. "What? Why wouldn't he tell me that? I know his wife, and she's a lovely person. Very supportive of him and our work, and so good with her girls. I can't imagine that she . . . oh, no, of course he wouldn't want to betray her to me or anyone. I'd feel the same. It's a stigma that would hang over her forever."

"Well, not in my book," I said, "but I can imagine it feels that way to them. I wonder what's going to happen to his girls. I mean, once you report him."

Titus sighed. "He's been there from the beginning, right along with Peter. I would never have thought this of him. I wish he would have come to us."

We started walking again toward the entrance. The place was less ostentatious than I expected, but a smiling employee stood by the door welcoming everyone and directing them toward the funeral home's chapel.

The chapel itself was quickly becoming packed, and I wondered why they hadn't decided to use a larger church house instead. Maybe Peter Griffin hadn't been all that religious, or maybe his family hadn't expected so many people to attend.

We found Brigit in a nearby room with Stevan, apparently waiting for the crowd to settle before being ushered in by the funeral home personnel. Both were dressed in full black, and Brigit wore a shawl similar to mine but without the feathers. A half dozen other somberly dressed people, extended relatives most likely, stood across the room next to a shiny, elaborate casket that was currently closed. Niklas was not among them, which worried me, but it was better for the conversation we were about to have.

Brigit came to us, her eyes skimming over me, apparently not connecting me with the woman who had visited her house three days ago with the police. But her younger son, who stayed by her side, studied me for a moment before nodding in recognition. I wondered if Titus had filled him in on my dual role for the police and their company.

"Oh, good, Titus, you're back," Brigit said, stepping slowly closer to him, looking frail and lost. She was made up today, and the makeup added to her haunting beauty. "You will sit with the family, won't you?" Without waiting for a response, her hand went up to adjust his tie. "I knew this would look good on you; I just never thought you'd be wearing it to Peter's funeral."

Titus closed his hand over hers momentarily as it lowered from his tie. "Me either." His expression was shuttered, which made sense knowing how he felt about her. At least the mystery of his clothing was solved. Brigit had excellent taste, and I could well imagine her offering to help him shop. I wondered how Peter had felt about it, or if it had been his idea to impress the investors.

I shivered, becoming aware of an odd coldness that pushed at my back and seemed to want me to step forward. I recognized the coldness immediately, like an annoying buzz I couldn't get rid of.

"Look," I said, pulling the conversation to where I needed it to go. "I'm sorry to ask right now, but we need to know if there is any kind of phrase that Peter might have used as a password. Something that was special to him."

Brigit shook her head, a line of puzzlement on her face. "They already asked me that. Stevan would know better, though." She shifted her gaze to her son. He'd shaved today, and his hair was oddly slicked back as if he'd used too much gel.

"I've tried everything," Stevan said, frowning. "We're going to have to hack into it."

Titus held up a hand. "If we do that, I want to hire someone outside the company for the job."

"You think someone at Futura will do something to the

file?" Stevan sounded almost offended. "Dad and I vetted all the employees ourselves."

Titus shot a nervous glance at Brigit. "After what happened to your father, we can't be sure."

"Is this about that other drug they found in Peter's body?" Tears welled in Brigit's eyes. "Niklas told me this morning the police are saying it was murder and not an accident. But who would want to hurt Peter?" Her voice was on the shrill side, and the rest of the family near the coffin looked our way. Both Titus and Stevan reached out to soothe her.

"Mrs. Griffin," I said gently, taking the opening, "were you ever aware of your husband taking tadalafil? The police found a prescription bottle for the medicine in your outside trash." I was going to answer to the police for giving them the information if Quincy hadn't already confronted her.

"What?" Brigit blinked her eyes in an exaggerated shock that under other circumstances might have been comical. "M-my trash? That's ridiculous. Peter didn't take anything but his heart medicine."

"You didn't get the pills for him?"

"No, of course not! I don't know anything about another drug. Or why he'd need it." She turned to her son. "I think I need my medicine, after all."

Stevan's green eyes turned to me with a look of sheer anger. He might be the younger, milder brother, but there was no sign of that now.

Titus took Brigit's hand and put it on his arm, covering it with his other one as if he really were some long-dead, old-fashioned movie star. "Can you hold off a little bit? Pastor Tim has a beautiful sermon prepared, and you'll want to hear the service. I'll be right here with you. So will Stevan. Ms. Rain is finished asking questions."

"Yes, she's definitely finished." Stevan's hard voice referred to more than my questions.

Feeling guilty, I dug into my purse and brought out a small handful of calming chamomile chews. "These should help," I said, thrusting them at Titus. "Without dulling her senses." To Brigit, I added, "I'm really sorry. I'm going to find out who did this. I promise." I didn't think she had anything to do with purposefully drugging her husband, but I couldn't say the same for either of her sons. I hoped I wouldn't have to end up telling her that one of them was responsible for her husband's death.

I started for the door, but Brigit's voice stopped me. "Thank you for trying to help us. I wish . . . I wish I could help more."

Having lost both my parents and more recently watched my world burn around me, I knew how she felt. "It gets easier," I said softly. It was only then that I noticed the cold was gone, and I was actually a little too warm.

Warm? I remembered what Cody had said about warmth. Maybe there was more here than even I could see. "Brigit?" I said as she started to turn away. "In my investigation, I found . . . you should know that Peter loved you. He really did."

"Thank you." Her color as she moved away was better.

My next stop was Niklas, and I didn't have to go far to find him. He was in the hallway, talking with some of the Futura employees I recognized from my interviews—all women, of course. He wore black slacks and a sports jacket instead of a regular suit, and his black shirt was open to show the top of his bare chest.

I strode up to Niklas, who was obviously enjoying the attention. "Excuse me," I said, "can I talk with you privately?"

He nodded and extracted himself from the women. "Hey, I remember you from my mom's house."

Was he a cold-blooded killer? I couldn't see any sign of it in his blue eyes or the expression on his handsome face. "Look," I said. "Are you aware of any passwords that your father might have used?"

His snort was so loud that it drew the attention of the people still filtering into the chapel. But when he spoke again, his voice was low. "I don't think you understand how it was between me and my father. I'd talk and he'd laugh and tell me why I was wrong. He hated the choices I made and never hesitated to tell me so. His work was always more important than me and my mother and even my brother. His opinions were worth more than all of ours together. We all knew that." Bitterness dripped from his tone, reminding me of the words he'd whispered to his mother in the hospital about Peter Griffin never hurting anyone again.

"But you were going to work for him."

"Yeah. And I'm still hoping that happens. I need to be at Futura for my brother and my mother." Was it only words, or was he awaiting a huge payoff before jetting away to some tropical island?

"Do you know anything about a bottle of prescription tadalafil found in your mother's garbage?" Now that I was already in trouble for spilling that information, I might as well judge his reaction as well.

"What are you talking about?" he said, moving closer and lowering his voice. "Isn't that the drug they say helped killed my dad? Along with the bumbling cardiologist?"

The cold was back, pushing at me. "Did you know about the pills?" I restated. "Did you hire anyone to get them for him?"

"Of course not. Why are you even asking that?"

I thought about the pictures I had on my phone, of him and Arthur together. Should I ask him about it? *No,* I decided. I wanted to talk to Arthur first. If he'd been silenced, I wanted to know why before I confronted Niklas.

"I'm trying to find out who may have had access to the pills."

Niklas blew out an impatient breath. "If they were at the house, we all had access. But for the record," he said, "if I was going to kill someone, it would be with a gun and not with cowardly poison." He glared at me.

Was that a threat? I lifted my chin. "You had an argument a few weeks ago with your father. What was it about?"

"Not that it is any of your business, but I needed money. I asked him for a job."

"And did he laugh at you?" If Peter had thrown his words back at him, that might have been what set him off.

"At first, but later he came around."

"Why was that?"

He shrugged. "He just did."

"And when did he make you the job offer?"

"Last Friday."

"Did he know you once worked for Viewpoint, his competitor?"

"You mean, did he know that I was in the call center there?" Niklas said, his shapely mouth twisted in a mocking smile. "Yeah, and he didn't blame me for leaving, either. Now, if that's all, I need to find my mother before the service begins."

I'd planned to ask a lot more questions, but none of it had

come out right so far. A little break to regroup might work in my favor. At least I knew he wouldn't be going anywhere until after the service.

"That's all for now," I said. "Thanks." I offered my hand with the hope of reading the rest of the imprint on his ring, but he ignored me and strode away.

I hadn't exactly expected him to break down and confess, but it was frustrating to have so little to go on. I was beginning to suspect that if I'd gone with Shannon and Quincy, I might have uncovered more than here at the funeral.

I pulled my shawl tighter around me and moved to the chapel's double doorway. There were only a few seats left, scattered throughout the crowd. Even as I stopped to consider if I should find a seat or go outside and start reading imprints from car door handles, someone from the funeral home stood at the pulpit and asked everyone present to move in so that there would be seats available at the ends of each pew. People began shifting.

The cold seemed to grow worse, and I turned to see if I was standing under an air vent. I wasn't, but a short distance away, I spied Arthur Dean, the weak-chinned programmer from Futura, talking to Niklas, who hadn't made it very far toward the room where his mother waited.

Niklas's voice was tense, but whatever Arthur said made him relax. Niklas gestured toward the chapel—and me, since I happened to be standing in front of the doors.

Arthur smiled at seeing me. "Are there any seats left?" he asking as he approached, looking attractive in his dark gray suit and striped tie.

"A few. But can I talk to you for a minute?" I pulled out my phone and with cold-stiffened fingers found one of the pictures of Arthur and Niklas together. I showed it to him without explanation.

"You got me," he said, stepping back and holding up his hands with a grin. "Did Niklas give you that?"

"In a manner of speaking. I thought you didn't know him."

"I didn't exactly say that I didn't know him." He fell silent as a person passed us, heading into the chapel. "Look at it from my point-of-view. It's not very wise to admit you were once friends with the black sheep of the family who currently writes your paycheck." He shrugged. "Besides, that was a very long time ago."

I needed more than that. "I know Niklas was hoping you didn't say anything to his father about something in his past. Was he blackmailing you?"

Arthur stared at me for a long moment before dropping his gaze. "No."

I didn't believe him. He was hiding something. "Because if he was," I added, "we need to know why."

His eyes met mine again. "You think Nik killed his father?"

"I'm not saying that. I want to know what Niklas didn't want you to tell his father."

He shook his head. "It's not like that. Just some partying we did back then. He was going to start a new leaf. He didn't want his father to know about it, and I really didn't either." He snorted. "Though, frankly, I wouldn't be surprised if Niklas wanted the old man out of the way. In fact, now that I'm thinking about it, Peter changed the password to the microchip file on Friday after Niklas was there. At least that's what the timestamp said when I was trying to get in for Titus." He blew out a breath and shrugged. "Well, I guess it's

Titus's problem now. But no way do I want to be connected with Nik. I'm holding out for a permanent job once Futura is launched."

Before I could respond, an employee of the funeral home emerged from the chapel. "If you'd like to go in now, the service is beginning," the man said. Music coming from the organ at the front of the room punctuated his suggestion.

"I might have more questions later," I told Arthur.

"Sure, anytime."

Arthur and I took seats in opposite rows near the back of the room. I checked my phone for messages since I'd turned off notifications for the funeral. There was one from Elliot.

A new black Jag was purchased last week by Arthur Dean, that programmer at Futura.

My gaze flew across the aisle to Arthur, who was also checking his phone. I wish I'd known about the Jag two minutes ago. No way could he have afforded a new car with the wage he earned at Futura, so did that mean the car was a bribe? Or did it go deeper than that? And if the car was his, why would Arthur Dean be following me?

There were, of course, numerous reasons. He could be working for someone. He could be trying to scare me off. Or maybe he'd wanted a date.

A man in a black suit walked to the pulpit. "If the audience will please stand," he intoned in what I thought was an eerie voice.

Everyone stood as the pallbearers, Niklas and Stevan in the front, entered the room and slowly carried the casket up to a stand in the front, next to an easel holding a large picture of Peter Griffin. The family followed the casket, Brigit clinging to Titus's arm and to a woman I didn't know. All of them kept their heads slightly bowed, their faces forward, not looking at the guests. By contrast, everyone in the crowd paid scrupulous attention to Brigit as she settled in the front row between her sons.

Everyone except me. I was staring at the gilt banner that draped the side of the coffin facing the audience. In large letters, it read, *Until we meet in Venice.*

A sigh escaped my lips before I could control it. Venice had been on Peter's mind, especially after buying the tickets for his wife, and I knew immediately that I'd found the password or a version of it.

And so had everyone else in the room.

As the service commenced, I angled my phone slightly away from the woman sitting next to me and texted Shannon.

I think I know the password. Did you find the laptop?

No, his response came back almost immediately. *If Niklas has it, it's not here.*

Okay, I'll get to Titus as soon as the service is over. Maybe he can stop at the office and move the file before going to the Griffin home.

You're sure Titus isn't the one we should be hiding them from?

I was mostly sure, but I could never forget that I always experienced imprints through the eyes of the imprinter, who may or may not feel guilty for anything they'd done. I'd talk to him and Stevan together. After that, it was their problem.

Stevan Griffin was at the pulpit now, talking about how much he'd admired his father. "He could be tough," he said, a hint of pain in the words, "but if you convinced him of something, he'd get behind it one hundred percent. Everything I know about business, he taught me. He also passed on his addiction to cinnamon Coke, not only to me but to practically everyone at Futura."

At that, light laughter came from the crowd. I glanced at Brigit and Niklas. She was listening, her face moist with tears. Niklas's jaw was clenched. He was staring, not at his brother but at the casket.

Or was he staring at the words on the casket?

The lady next to me was fanning her face with the program while I was freezing, as I had been since coming to the funeral home. Was my ability trying to tell me something? With the cold was the growing urge to move.

I checked my phone and saw that Elliot had texted again. *Get this. Arthur Dean also worked for Viewpoint. As a programmer. He quit two years ago, but that information isn't in the personnel files from Futura. He's definitely hiding something. Maybe he's a part of it.*

I looked at Arthur, only to see that he was no longer sitting where he had been. A woman was there instead, so maybe he'd been kind enough to offer her his seat. A quick glance showed me he wasn't in the back of the room.

I rose, ignoring the dirty looks from the woman next to me and the usher by the door. I hurried out of the chapel and sprinted from the funeral home past a small group of latecomers.

Outside, no one was in sight, but seconds later, a black Jag roared from the parking lot. I caught a glimpse of Arthur's face as it turned onto the main road.

Chapter 21

I ran to my car, and for once it started on the first try. I pulled out in the direction the Jag had been heading, gunning the motor. The Jag was so much faster, but surely he wouldn't go too far over the speed limit.

There he was, up ahead. I slowed slightly so he wouldn't notice me.

I pushed Shannon's icon on my phone, put it on speaker, and clipped it into the holder.

"Hey, Autumn," Shannon said when he answered. "We're on our way to the funeral. We'll go with you to the house."

"It's Arthur Dean," I said. "He just left the funeral. I think he might have the laptop. Elliot uncovered that he used to work for Viewpoint as a programmer. He quit two years ago when he started at Futura."

"Where is he now?"

"In his car. I'm following him."

"You're what?" The words were so loud I was glad the phone wasn't at my ear.

"You heard me. He either figured out the password like

I did, or he got suspicious when I showed him a picture of him and Niklas. Either way, you don't skip out on your boss's funeral, not when his son and widow now own most of the shares and your job future depends on them. He's going to run, and if he gets the file before we do, it's over."

"Okay." Shannon's voice was calmer now. "Tell us where you are."

"I have my location on, so follow my phone with your app. And since there's two of you, call Elliot and ask if he has any information on where Arthur might go to get the laptop. Maybe we can get someone there before him."

"He could already have it in the car. Give me his license plate number."

"I can't. It's a new car. There's a paper in the tinted window I can't read. Elliot can give you a description. He's got a drawing. It's one of Tawnia's."

"Okay, stay on the line. I'll use Quincy's phone."

I was glad when a low mumbling told me he was connected with Elliot because we were running into traffic now, and I needed to concentrate. A car pulled between me and the Jag. I didn't mind because if Arthur had followed me the other day, he knew what my car looked like.

I thought back to the Futura parking lot. Some of the employees had left when I did. I hadn't noticed Arthur or the car, but he could have followed me to Franklin High School and then to my store.

After a few more turns, I could tell he was heading toward the freeway—and fast. Had he noticed me?

"Come on, car," I muttered, jamming my foot harder on the pedal. It gave a warning cough.

Shannon came back on the line. "Elliot says he already checked, and the address Arthur Dean gave Futura is bogus. Elliot can't find any property records either. You can't lose him."

"Great. Maybe your office should lend me a car for all my high-speed chases. This one's dying."

"Stay on him. I've contacted the precinct; they're running a check and sending backup. We're almost at your location."

"He's turning off the freeway." Three cars were between me and the Jag now.

"Good. You should be able to stay with him now."

I followed the Jag through the streets of Portland. I didn't recognize this part of town. It was a commerce area, but none of the ones I was familiar with. Soon the stores gave way to a quiet residential neighborhood similar to Tawnia's—newer starter homes and townhouses designed for couples with a child or two. A few children were playing in their yards, and others were on bicycles. A mother pushed a stroller on a very white sidewalk.

"I've got you in sight," Shannon said.

I checked my review mirror. Sure enough, he was behind me in his unmarked Mustang. I eased my car over to the side, thinking he'd speed past me, put on his lights, and pull the Jag over, but at the same time, the Jag pulled into the double parking space of a twin town home. Arthur Dean emerged from the vehicle and shut the door before hurrying up the driveway.

Shannon pulled over behind me. "We'll get him inside the house," he said, still over the phone. "Less likely that someone will be hurt."

I eyed the two children sitting on the porch across the street. They weren't more than five or six years old. Arthur was no longer in sight, so I climbed out of the car and went to meet Shannon and Quincy.

Quincy nodded at me with a grin. "Good job staying with him. That's some car he's got." To Shannon, he added, "I'll take the back. You take the front."

"Aw. You get all the fun," Shannon joked. "They almost always go out the back."

"Hurry," I said. "Arthur may not be armed, but I don't know how long it will take him to figure out the password."

"If he doesn't open up, we don't have a warrant," Quincy said.

"This qualifies as hot pursuit," Shannon countered. "We're going in."

I gave him a big smile. I was definitely rubbing off on him.

Pulling out their guns, the men rushed up the double driveway. I realized I hadn't seen which of the two townhouses Arthur had entered, but Shannon went to the door on the right. The black Jag was parked on the right side of the joined driveway, so it made sense. He knocked while Quincy continued on around the house.

No one answered. I imagined Arthur in his bedroom, typing in versions of the password: untilv3nus, tilwemeetinvenUS, or s33UinV3nus. It could be one of dozens of combinations, and finding the right one would take time—unless he'd rigged some sort of program to help him.

Shannon removed a baton from his belt and broke the glass next to the door. Seconds later, he had it unlocked and disappeared inside.

I decided to sit in my car in case Arthur had a gun. In fact, I should tell those children to go back inside their house. I was halfway across their lawn when a muffled scream came from Arthur's townhome. Whirling, I saw a large lump of dark gray sprawled under an open, second-story window, whose screen was still partially attached. Even as I watched, the lump rose and became Arthur Dean. He clutched a thin black laptop to his chest. He hurried toward his Jag, limping as if something was broken.

In seconds, he'd be in his car. Backup hadn't arrived, and who knew how long Shannon and Quincy would be in the house. My car would never keep up once Arthur knew he was being followed. I had to beat him to the Jag.

He saw me coming and paused in the front of his car, raising the laptop like a weapon. "Get out of the way," he demanded. Sweat slid down his forehead.

"So you and Niklas can sell Futura to Viewpoint? I don't think so. How much did they pay you?"

"I don't know what you're talking about." He came toward me, his face twisted in anger. "Move!" He lashed out with the computer. I stepped back as he lunged toward the car door. He tried to open it, but I kicked it shut. The metal felt warm against the sole of my bare foot.

He swung the laptop at me again, laughing as I pulled my head back. "I don't think they're paying you enough to get in my way. But for twenty mil, I *will* hurt you. You should have learned that already after what I did to your quaint little shop."

"Yeah, but you forgot you're just a programmer." I faked a punch, then kicked out at his hurt leg.

He screamed and collapsed to one knee. I hit him hard, grabbing the laptop before it slammed into the ground as he fell back.

Grabbing it was a mistake.

The police were in the house. I had to get away. The one million deposit wouldn't help if I was caught now. Especially not if they knew I'd killed Peter so I'd have time to get the last file.

What had tipped Peter off? It had to be Niklas. I should have cut him in on the deal when he'd shown up at Futura and saw me there. But as soon as I got the rest of the money, I'd make him pay for ratting on me.

I shut and locked my office door, shoving the desk against it. It would take them time to break in, and by then I'd be gone. The new Jag was waiting.

For the moments of that imprint, I was paralyzed, having to relive those frightened moments when I knew I—no, Arthur— either had to get out or be hauled to prison.

Finally, it ended. The imprint was followed by earlier ones from Arthur as he tried numerous combinations to get into the laptop after Titus had called a halt to the hacking at work. The imprints were irritating but not paralyzing.

A fist slammed into my jaw, sending stars shooting across my vision. I loosened my body and let it throw me back— into the Jag. I bounced off it, blocking another blow with the laptop. Regaining my balance, I slammed it into Arthur's face. He grunted in pain, but he screamed louder when the laptop flew from my fingers and crashed to the ground, hitting on the spine and popping open. A few broken pieces scattered over the cement.

"No!" He lunged at the laptop, but I kicked it away, flipping it up several feet in the air to come down hard on the screen.

Try hacking that, jerk, I thought.

He came at me, fists pumping. One hit my left shoulder. It hurt, but there wasn't much strength behind it—not like the lucky blow he'd landed on my jaw. Sidestepping, I saw an opening and sent a roundhouse kick to his gut. Arthur curled forward. I finished by slamming my joined hands on his head like a hammer. He crumpled to the ground on his side.

I rolled him onto his back and put my foot on his throat. "I win," I said, my chest heaving. "And for the record, you hit like a programmer." Mentally, I apologized to any programmers out there who were good at martial arts.

He struggled and tried to speak, but I pushed down harder on his throat. He was lucky I wasn't wearing shoes.

Seconds later, Shannon was at my side, flipping Arthur over and snapping on handcuffs. "You okay?" he asked me gruffly.

"Yeah." My jaw hurt, but I wasn't telling him that.

Cheering made me look around, and I saw the children across the street now standing on the sidewalk, jumping up and down with their fists in the air.

"He started the fire at my store," I told Shannon. The words made my heart numb.

"You can't prove anything," Arthur growled. "This is police brutality. I want to press charges."

"I'm pretty sure these new Jags have state-of-the-art GPS systems that will help us trace your steps," Shannon said to him. "And we'll find where you bought the three containers of gas, even if you used a different car or bought them in Washington. I already have someone working on it."

In answer, Arthur snarled a curse.

Ignoring him, I squatted down by the open laptop. The screen was obviously cracked and parts of the hinge were missing. I doubted it would ever work again. I'd already left my fingerprints on it—what was one more? I touched the top of the machine and relived the terror Arthur had experienced getting out of the house, but this time I was prepared for the desperation, and it didn't capture me.

I let the imprints run backward, through days of hacking, until Saturday during Peter's operation when Arthur disguised himself as an orderly and slipped the laptop from Peter's duffel practically under Brigit's nose as she waited during his surgery.

I had to get that last file. I'd nearly spent the million-dollar deposit on the townhouse and the car. Viewpoint would only give me the other twenty million after they received the microchip specs.

Twenty-one million. That was the price of a person's life. At least it was for Arthur Dean.

Finally, I arrived at Friday, and the next imprints were Peter Griffin's.

"I bet you're wondering why I called you in here," I said, my hands resting on my closed laptop. "A few weeks ago, my son saw you here and told me you worked for Viewpoint. He said you were a spy, come to steal our tech. I didn't believe him, of course. I thought he was feeding me a line to get into my good graces."

"It's not true." Arthur leaned forward, his face sincere. "I never worked for them, and I'm fully committed to Futura. You have to know that. I've given two years of my life to this company and hope to be here a lot longer. Yes, I was friends with Niklas, but that was a different time in my life. I've changed since then. I'd never do anything to hurt his family. Especially not you. I look up to what you've built here, sir."

Such a suck-up, I thought. "The thing is," I said aloud. "After thinking about it, I decided to call in a few favors and look into it. They got back to me today. You aren't on Viewpoint's employee roster, past or present, but nevertheless, eyewitnesses verify that you were a programmer there at one time. And I've completed a checkup of our system and discovered that someone has downloaded production files without permission. Now that we're finished with the last tweaks on the microchip specs, I've locked the file until I get to the bottom of this. Don't come in on Monday. If you're cleared, I'll let you know."

"If someone's stealing anything, it's Nik!" Arthur sputtered indignantly. "I'm sorry to say this, but he hates you and always has. Remember that party you crashed at Nik's apartment, the one when you called the police? Well, I was there that night. When I bailed him out at the police station, he told me we should come to work here and steal Futura secrets to get back at you. Other people heard him, if you need proof. I was the one who talked him out of it. I admire what you're doing here so much. I never thought he'd come back to that idea."

Arthur's story was probably true. Two years ago, I'd still been trying to make Niklas behave. I hadn't understood that he'd have to learn life's lessons the hard way and come back on his own terms. No wonder Niklas had been so worried about telling me about Arthur. He hadn't ended up telling me all of it, but he'd told me enough to protect Futura, and I was proud of him. I'd done right to offer him a job. Under that playboy guise, he had my instincts. Stevan would need to rely on him when I retired from the company.

"Niklas will be working here soon," I told Arthur. "He won't need to steal from himself."

Something gleamed in Arthur's eyes—something that told me he was the one spying for Viewpoint. I wanted to call the police, but it could wait until after I drove myself to the doctor for my emergency appointment. The pain in my back was increasing. Lousy time to happen, but everything would all be right soon.

The next imprint was on the keyboard of the laptop—Peter, putting in the new password, which was exactly what had been on the banner, but with the e's changed to number signs or the letter three, and one l changed to a bracket: unti]w#m33tiN-v#nic3. It was also the password to get into his laptop. No one would be accessing the file from this device, but Titus could now get to the file from Futura.

I pulled away, having seen enough. "You knew Peter would trace the file downloads to you," I said to Arthur, who sat glaring at us miserably from the cement driveway. "When you heard he was in the hospital, you went to get his computer so you could download the rest of the files. You got it, but you couldn't hack in, so you killed him for more time. I wonder if twenty-one million dollars was worth the risk of going to prison for the rest of your life?"

"I don't have anything to say," Arthur retorted.

"Niklas isn't in on it," I told Shannon and Quincy as I rose to my feet. "He saw Arthur at Futura and warned Peter."

"What about the secret he didn't want Arthur to tell?" Shannon asked.

"That it was Niklas who gave Arthur the idea in the first place one night when Niklas was angry at his father." I paused, looking at Arthur again. "What I don't know," I mused, "is how you drugged Peter."

He glared up at me, his mouth pursed tight, making his jaw even more pointed.

Quincy motioned to the Jag. "I don't see another car, so he probably traded in his old one when he bought this. Maybe you can find some imprints." His wink, I decided, wasn't flirtatious so much as it was a habit. "He obviously loves the car."

"Right." I opened the door, ignoring the spattering of imprints there—mostly greed and excitement. I settled into the leather seat. The car smelled new and rich. I bet it didn't have trouble starting.

"Watch him," Shannon said to Quincy, moving closer to the open car door. The wail of sirens filled the air, so I knew we didn't have a lot of time before our backup arrived. The Jag would likely go into evidence.

I put my knuckle on the steering wheel at the three o'clock position. The most recent imprint was Arthur's excitement that what was on the banner would get him access to the laptop so he could finish hacking the microchip file—he hadn't guessed that the passwords were the same. He'd heard Peter mention Venice a time or two in the past month, and he was positive it would work. Non-tech guys always liked to use passwords they could remember.

The next imprints were from earlier as he followed me from Futura to the high school and then to my store, where he had the idea of starting a fire to throw me off the case. He'd suspected if I kept digging, I'd find out about his connection to Viewpoint or even to the actor he'd hired to buy two prescriptions of tadalafil. He wouldn't use the Jag to transport the gas, of course, in case it was spotted.

Even worse were his thoughts as he drove to the hospital on Sunday night with a box of tadalafil-doctored chocolates and crushed nitroglycerine to put in a fresh cinnamon Coke for Peter Griffin.

I pulled my hands back when I'd seen enough. Without speaking, Shannon helped me out of the car—and it was a good thing because I was shaking.

"He hired an actor to get the tadalafil," I said. "And inside his house, you should be able to find a pill crusher and the rest of a box of chocolates he used to cut out the bottoms and put in his own mixture. He used stevia to mask the flavor. The nitroglycerin, he put in a soft drink. But he knew Peter would recognize him, so his plan was to dress up as a hospital worker and ask one of the nurses to deliver the drink and the chocolates, saying they were from his wife. The nurses knew about his love for cinnamon Coke."

Arthur stared at me, fear showing in his eyes. "You can't know any of that."

"Oh, but she does." Shannon gave him a scary smile. "And the sooner you confess, the better it'll go for you."

"No!" Arthur said. "I didn't do anything." Everyone ignored him.

"That's why the nitroglycerine showed up in the three o'clock blood tests, but not that much of the tadalafil." Quincy waved at a police car that was pulling up at the curb, signaling for the officers to cut the siren. "Griffin drank the Coke, and later finished off the chocolates, probably hoping the sugar would give him energy since he was feeling so weak after the nitroglycerin."

"Where'd you get the nitroglycerin?" Shannon asked Arthur. "We'll know as soon as we find the bottle, so you might as well tell us."

So far, it appeared Arthur had been acting alone. That was good for the Griffin family, but it was a lot for one person to carry out, even a greedy person who'd been planning for two years to steal a fortune.

"I want an attorney," Arthur protested as uniformed officers reached us.

Shannon motioned for the officers to take Arthur. "Book him for the murder of Peter Griffin. I'm sure Futura and the Griffin family will get to the espionage charges later."

Arthur let the officers drag him to his feet. They'd gone only a few yards when he stopped and said over his shoulder, "Okay, okay, I did have help."

I held my breath. At this point, he could accuse anyone, and it might be true.

"Viewpoint paid me to work at Futura so that I could get

the files for Titus's smart glasses," Arthur went on in a rush. "It was why they hired Niklas for support and why I became his friend. And the nitroglycerin belonged to the CEO of Viewpoint. When I told him Peter was in the hospital, and that I had the laptop, but not the password, he had the idea for both the drugs. I didn't know they would kill Peter. I thought they would keep him in the hospital and give me a few more days. Maybe I could even go into work and hack into the files from there if he hadn't told anyone what he suspected about me. It almost worked." He glared at me. "Until she showed up and told Titus not to let me finish."

"I can tell you're heartbroken that Peter Griffin died," Shannon said dryly.

Maybe Arthur hadn't intended for Peter to die, but Shannon was right that he also didn't show any remorse.

"I guess twenty-one million is enough to make Peter's death an added benefit," Quincy remarked. "Take him away, boys." Arthur strained against the officers, but they dragged him to the car.

Quincy smiled at Shannon. "I think Viewpoint is located in my precinct. Want to ride along?"

"No." Shannon pulled his keys from his pocket and tossed them over. "Why don't you go with Paige? She deserves to get in on this after what they almost did to Matthew. You can tell her the good news. I'll wait here for a warrant and the forensics team."

"Okay. I'll give her the car to get back to you when we're finished." Quincy switched his attention to me. "Thanks for your help. Paige and I both owe you a favor."

I thought of how Paige and Matthew had been at my store most of the day yesterday after his release from the precinct.

"No, you don't. Futura will get the bill. Rumor on the street has it that they're going to be able to afford it."

"And so they will." With another flirty wink, he laughed as he sauntered toward Shannon's Mustang.

"You did it," Shannon said, his arms going around me.

"*We* did it."

"I'd better call the precinct and let them know what's happening." Shannon reached into his pocket for his cell phone. "There's still one thing I want to know."

"Oh?" I arched a brow, wondering what else was left.

"Are you going to let me attend your blackbelt test tomorrow or not? Tawnia, Jake, and Cody said you turned them down flat."

"There's a reason I'm paying for a private test," I said in all seriousness. "But I guess I can make an exception for the man I'm going to marry."

"Yes!" He punched his fist into the air, much the way the children had earlier.

"Although"—I pointed to the ruined laptop, still on the driveway—"I think I've already passed."

"That you have," he said, pulling me tighter. "Autumn Rain, you know what? I'm definitely in love with you."

That was good, because in two weeks and two days, we were getting married. Even if we didn't have any of it planned. Before that, however, there was something important I had to do, and it involved Pax Medina and Opal Anderson's father.

Chapter 22

A week after passing my blackbelt test, I drove to my store to pick up Cody, who was checking on the contractor. I was once again wearing my funeral attire, complete with the ostrich-feathered shawl, but we weren't going to a funeral. Cody and I had a date for a night of entertainment. Just about everyone I knew would also be there, even Shannon, who was working and would meet us there.

The shop had been cleaned and deodorized, and rebuilding had begun two days earlier when the contractor sent one of his crews over after finishing another job. I knew I was lucky that I wasn't going to be stuck in limbo for more than a few months, and I was surprised at how much they'd already accomplished. The walls on the main floor were framed, as were the stairs going up and the floor to the second story. A new door had been installed between my place and Jake's.

Cody came from talking with one of the workers to meet me inside the shop near the opening that would be my new door. To my utter shock, he was wearing a suit—an old and out-of-date, sapphire blue suit, but a suit nonetheless. I'd never seen him in anything but jeans or sweats, and most of those had holes in them.

"Nice suit," I said.

"You like it? Because I'm wearing it for your wedding next week."

I laughed. "It's perfect."

"I thought so too." He gestured to the shop. "They'll have the glass and doors and all the upstairs framing finished by next week," he said. "I'm glad you decided to go with the second floor."

"Thanks to you."

He shrugged. "It was an obvious call."

"You ready to go?"

He nodded. "But first, I want to give you something." He reached into his pocket. "Look, I know you said all you wanted help with for the wedding was one of those canopy rentals, but as I was going through my mother's things to bring up to you girls, I found this." He held out a box. "Tawnia told me your mother's necklace was ruined, so we thought you might like this. My mother wore it on her wedding day. The imprints are good. My parents were happy for the five years they were married. Mom never really wore it after Dad died."

My hands trembled as I accepted the box. I loved antiques, but those connected with my own family meant a thousand times more. And while I had a lot from my adoptive family, I didn't have anything from my biological side.

I flipped open the lid to see two connected strands of freshwater pearls, with a larger teardrop-shaped pearl in the middle. There were matching teardrop earrings and a bracelet. The set was small, and not very expensive by today's standards, but I loved it immediately.

"Thank you," I said, tears pooling in my eyes. "I would be honored to wear them." I removed a glove and touched the surface, finding an enormous sensation of love. There were also two vivid scenes of Cody's father and mother on the day they'd married, and another when he'd given her the pearls during their engagement. I could see their faces in the mirror as he put them on for her.

It was priceless.

"I know," Cody said gruffly. "I'm glad you get to see her like that." He meant before life had taken her husband and her ability had driven her insane.

I was glad too.

We walked out of the shop together, leaving the workmen to finish their day. Jake met us outside. He was also dressed up, but in slacks and a casual brown blazer that matched his skin.

"I thought you were meeting us at the school," I said.

"I'm on my way to pick up Melinda, but when Cody told me you were picking him up here, I wanted to stop and give you this." He handed me an envelope.

I opened it to see full payment for what he still owed on the Herb Shoppe. I stared at the check. "But you couldn't get a loan."

"That was two years ago. I was able to now." His gaze dipped in embarrassment. "We both know I should have tried again a long time ago. It's better terms for me too."

"You found a lender . . ." My gaze snapped to Cody, who looked uneasy. I knew exactly who Jake was talking about.

"Don't be mad," Cody began.

I leaned forward and kissed his cheek. "I'm not mad. For my necklace and what you're doing to help the football team tonight, you get a pass." Besides, if Cody was carrying Jake's loan, no doubt he was also profiting nicely.

Cody's sigh of relief was almost comical. "Good." He dusted off imaginary dirt from his gloved hands. "Now we'd better hurry or we're going to be late."

For someone who wasn't really my father, he was doing a good job of making me feel as if I still had a parent. I was smart enough not to look too deeply at the moment.

When we arrived at Franklin High School, the auditorium was packed. I wasn't worried about seating, though, because the first two rows were reserved for the sponsors of the high school football team fundraiser, which meant us. We'd billed the event as best dress, and everyone present looked great. My sister, sans baby today, sat in the second row. She wore a navy lace dress, and Bret sported a navy suit. Thera wore her favorite sky-blue dress, and even Jazzy, sitting with her foster parents, was wearing a frilly black top that was almost long enough to be called a dress.

Cody took the remaining seat in the second row, so I went to the open seats in the first, next to Titus Grey and Brigit Griffin, who were both still wearing black and looked like they'd stepped from the pages of a magazine. Titus stood up to meet me, joined by Niklas and Stevan Griffin, who were seated on their mother's other side. Brigit seemed to be deep in conversation with Jazzy's foster mother, Claire, seated behind her.

"I never got a chance to thank you," Titus said, shaking my black-gloved hand.

"The five thousand dollars you paid us for solving the case, and the money you donated tonight for this fundraiser, is thanks enough," I returned with a smile. Elliot and I had split the money, along with the five hundred Principal Tillmon had given us, and which, to Elliot's disgust, I'd insisted we donate back toward the equipment fundraiser.

Stevan shook his head, raising his hand with his thumb and forefinger an inch apart. "We were this close to losing everything."

"I was glad to help. I heard on the news that the CEO of Viewpoint was also arrested?"

"Yeah," Titus said with a solemn shake of his head. "The nitroglycerin traced back to him, and they found evidence of the espionage as well. They had all our previous files and had begun production with them. He's looking at accessory to murder and corporate espionage charges. Arthur, too, of course." He sighed. "I can't believe he was stealing our files right out from under our noses."

The hospital administration had felt the same way after footage from the nurses' desk and a nurse's testimony had corroborated my findings of how Arthur had given Peter the drugs. Matthew had been immediately reinstated.

"I should have told you what I suspected about Arthur," Niklas said. "But when I mentioned it to my father that day at Futura, he blew up and told me he'd vetted everyone. He didn't need me poking my nose where it didn't belong. My father was never wrong, so I thought I had to be. Even that Friday before he died, he said everything was fine. I had no idea he'd discovered something was actually going on."

Stevan shrugged. "That's the way Dad was. He didn't like to worry people if he had things under control. I'm sure he would have told us when he had proof about the files."

"Yeah, maybe." Niklas's expression was sorrowful. "I know

Arthur and Viewpoint targeted me, and that they didn't get the idea of stealing Futura from me like I thought, but I can't help thinking that if I hadn't brought it up, Dad would still be alive."

"It's *not* your fault," Stevan said firmly, placing his arm on his brother's shoulder. "I know you'd never do anything to hurt Dad." He hesitated and added more quietly, "Or me. Whatever happened in the past, we always had each other's back. The way I think of it, if you hadn't told Dad your suspicion about Arthur, we would have lost the company, and that would have destroyed Dad. He'd want to save the company so we could have his legacy to remember him by. You came back just in time."

A glint of relief showed in Niklas's eyes. "Takes a scoundrel to recognize one, I guess. I won't let you down."

"I know," Stevan said.

"I take it the publicity hasn't hurt your sales?" I asked.

Stevan looked away from his brother, his smile growing wide. "Fortunately, every bit of media coverage has been positive toward our company, and that's given our presales a tremendous boost. We have a waiting list now to fill orders. I guess if something is good enough to be stolen, everyone wants it."

"What about Robby Hartford?" I had to know. It was the one thing that still bothered me about the case. So far there'd been no arrest and nothing on the news.

Stevan's smiled faded a bit, but his tone was upbeat. "We're keeping him. With more oversight and reports, of course. We've also told him that after the launch, Futura will cover his wife's expenses, including counseling, which they're both going to need."

"That's a good call. People in desperate situations often don't think straight." I was glad to know the man wouldn't be losing custody of his children.

Cyrus Anderson, head of the school district, chose that moment to walk onto the stage, and we found our seats. I'd asked him to be the announcer for the fundraising event because of his job and influence, but more importantly for Opal and Pax, though Cyrus didn't yet know of their relationship.

I leaned over and whispered to Titus. "The trip to Venice—will Brigit still be going?" I'd been hoping she would, but with both her sons wrapped up in the launch, it wasn't likely, unless she had a friend to go with her.

"How did you—?" He shook his head. "No, don't tell me. But, yes, she's going. She's taking a friend from her sewing circle."

"I thought you might go with her."

He darted a glance toward her, his eyes softening. "Maybe someday. I think Peter would like that."

I thought so too. I hadn't felt that strange cold since capturing Arthur, so maybe, if Peter had been haunting me, he'd gone on his way. His family would all have to do the same.

The musical numbers began, presented by talented students, people in the community, and a few professionals from around the state. Shannon, Paige, and Matthew finally arrived when Pax Medina was on the stage, shortly before the intermission.

Shannon took my hand and kissed it. "Sorry I'm so late."

"It's okay," I said. "Listen. It's Pax."

Despite the large crowd, everyone paid rapt attention as Pax expertly played the rapid-fire notes of Chopin's Étude Op. 10 No. 4. I'd heard him play during the practice and had been impressed enough to learn the name of the piece, but tonight his performance was even more amazing. When he finished, everyone in the audience rose to their feet and clamored their applause. I was glad I'd scheduled him to play another number at the end.

"Believe it or not, that's one of Franklin High School's football players," Cyrus Anderson said when the applause died down enough so he could be heard. He put his hand on Pax's shoulder. "I'm told that's one of the toughest classical pieces to play. Good job, son. And I understand we'll be hearing from you again later." He chuckled and added to the crowd, "After he rests those fingers a bit."

Pax nodded. "Yes, sir."

Cyrus looked back at the audience. "We'll pause now for a ten-minute intermission. Please visit the concession stand manned by members of the football team from Lincoln High School. Remember, this is to help repair or replace the equipment that was recently vandalized. Thank you so much for your support."

It had been Cody's idea to make the Lincoln High School football players who had been part of the vandalism work off some of their debt. Their parents were all here tonight as well, and the families had been assigned to buy or sell a certain number of tickets at ten dollars apiece. They'd also be helping with repairs.

Meanwhile, Pax had gone from primary vandal suspect to the star of tonight's show, exactly as I'd intended. Opal rushed up onto the stage to talk to Pax and her father. Cyrus Anderson didn't know Pax was the boy he'd bawled her out about, but he was aware of the boy's talent now. Maybe he'd even help him.

A week later, Shannon and I stood in the same field where my parents had exchanged vows all those years ago. Everyone I loved was present. Tawnia stood next to me in a bright yellow dress, with Destiny in baby pink on her hip. Paige wore fuchsia, Jazzy was in orange, Thera in blue, Randa in green, and Shannon's mother in wine. Each woman held a bouquet of gerberas that matched her dress.

Shannon had asked Cody to be his best man, and he stood next to Shannon in his ancient, rumpled, sapphire blue suit, looking as proud as any father. Next to Cody were Jake, Tawnia's husband Bret, and Shannon's father, also dressed in that marvelous sapphire color.

Longtime customers, neighbors, Tawnia's adoptive parents, officers from Shannon's work, and a few people I'd helped by reading imprints were also present. I knew them all better now from their help at the shop, and having them at the wedding meant a lot to both of us.

Tawnia had recreated a flower-covered arch like the one my parents had used, and we stood in front of it on a low dais, hands linked. I wore Summer's slightly yellowed dress, and Shannon had donned a crisp black suit. On my right ring finger, I felt the love of my mother, and the pearls from my grandmother radiated even more love.

As the pastor from Tawnia's church asked me if I would take Shannon to be my husband, I nodded and managed a nervous, "Yes." Then I waited for Shannon's response. As the pastor asked him the question, I whispered so only he could hear, "You can still say no."

Grinning, he mouthed, "Not a chance." And then, a little too loudly, he said, "I do. Absolutely!" A ripple of laughter spread through the crowd.

As Shannon kissed me to seal the deal, he whispered, "I love you, Autumn Rain. And I promise"—he choked up then, and we stood, cheeks pressed together as he fought to continue—"I promise to spend the rest of my life making you happy."

"I promise too," I whispered, tears beading on my lashes.

Thankfully, before we made utter fools of ourselves, Tawnia announced dinner, already set out beneath two canopies. Music filled the clearing as everyone gravitated to the food, catered by Smokey's. As we ate, there were toasts and frequent bouts of laughter, especially when Jake mentioned my newfound love of Google Maps.

When we cut the triple-layer cake, Shannon and I ended up with white icing and chocolate cake all over our faces just like my parents had at their wedding.

We went to Tawnia's trailer to clean up. "We have to stay for the bonfire and the dancing," I said, dabbing at his suit where the cake had fallen, "but let's take off as soon as possible."

Shannon nodded, but I could tell he wasn't all there. "Look," he said, his voice a little strained. "Last night, my parents gave me this." He pulled an envelope from his jacket pocket and passed it to me. Inside was an elaborately printed coupon for a free week stay at their bed and breakfast in Florida.

"When's this for?" I asked.

Surely his parents couldn't mean for us to go to their bed and breakfast on our honeymoon. In the two days they'd been in town, Tawnia had put them to work, and they'd been incredibly helpful. I liked them both more than I'd hoped, but a honeymoon with in-laws wasn't exactly part of any bride's dream.

"Well, they know I have two weeks off, so they're asking if we can come for the second week. They'll pay airfare, food, and give us their best, most remote room, all for a wedding gift." He made a face. "I would have told them no immediately, but . . ." He paused, his forehead furrowed. "My mom was acting really strange."

I had noticed that she'd seemed anxious since her arrival, but I'd thought it was because her son was marrying someone she didn't really know. I'd made a point to avoid reading any of her imprints to allow her some privacy.

"Did you ask what was wrong?" I couldn't imagine him not pressing for more information. He was curious to a fault, and pushy when he wanted to be. Almost as pushy as I was.

"Yeah. That was what was so strange. She clammed right up, and usually I can't get her to stop talking. She wouldn't let my dad talk, either. She gave him a stare, and he immediately decided it was time for bed. I think something happened in Florida, and she wants me there to look into it."

Having spent only part of two days with his parents, I didn't have much insight. "Your dad's a former officer. If there's a problem, I'm sure he's got it handled."

Shannon shook his head. "My dad never liked police work. He put in his time and got out the minute he could. Plus, I got the feeling it was him she was worried about." He frowned, rubbing his hand across his hair and messing it up just the way I liked it. "I'm not sure what to do. I mean, this is our time, and I'm really looking forward to it."

I considered the idea. Two weeks in a remote cabin with no cell service sounded wonderful after my last few cases, but if Shannon's parents really needed him, we should be there. They were my family now too.

"Their bed and breakfast is near the ocean, isn't it?" I asked.

"Yeah. The beaches in Jacksonville are great this time of

year." He grinned. "If it weren't for them owning the bed and breakfast, I might have wanted to take you there instead of the cabin. They normally charge two hundred a night."

"It could be fun to walk along the beach, especially on a free vacation." I wasn't exactly calculating what we'd save on the cabin rental fees, but ten years of scraping by in the shop had taught me to be frugal. "I'll have to buy a new swimsuit." The stay would also give me a chance to get to know his parents better.

Shannon's slow smile burned its way into my heart. "I promise I'll make it up to you."

"You won't need to. I'm sure it'll be fun. If we hate it, we can always leave."

"You just say the word." He pulled me close and kissed me, tasting like cake and frosting . . . and the future.

Much later, we went to join the dancers who were already lighting the bonfire. The sun was almost gone, and stars began to scatter across the sky. I felt warm, and I didn't know if it was the fire or something more.

As we danced, my mind wandered to sandy white beaches, moonlit walks on the beach, and a new mystery to solve.

TEYLA BRANTON has worked in publishing for over twenty years. She loves writing women's fiction and traveling, and she hopes to write and travel a lot more. As a mother of seven, it's not easy to find time to write, but the semi-ordered chaos gives her a constant source of writing material. She's been known to wear pajamas all day when working on a deadline, and is often distracted enough to burn dinner. (Okay, pretty much 90% of the time.) A sign on her office door reads: Danger. Enter at Your Own Risk. Writer at Work.

Under the name Teyla Branton, she writes urban fantasy, paranormal romance, and science fiction. She also writes romance, romantic suspense, and women's fiction under the name Rachel Branton. For more information or to sign up to hear about new releases, please visit www.TeylaBranton.com.

Made in the USA
Las Vegas, NV
18 October 2021

32613916R00174